W9-ANI-529

DEAR
FAMILY

Previous novels by Camilla Bittle

The Boy in the Pool
A Change of Plea
A Sunday World

ASBURY PARK PUBLIC LIBRARY
ASBURY PARK, NEW JERSEY

DEAR FAMILY

Camilla Bittle

St. Martin's Press
New York

DEAR FAMILY. Copyright © 1991 by Camilla Bittle. All rights reserved. Printed in the United States of America. No part of this book may be used or reproduced in any manner whatsoever without written permission except in the case of brief quotations embodied in critical articles or reviews. For information, address St. Martin's Press, 175 Fifth Avenue, New York, N.Y. 10010.

Design by Glen M. Edelstein

Library of Congress Cataloging-in-Publication Data

Bittle, Camilla.
        Dear family / Camilla Bittle.
                p.   cm.
        ISBN 0-312-05847-0
        I.   Title.
    PS3552.I7739D4   1991
    813'.54—dc20   90-27895
                                                 CIP

First edition: August 1991

10   9   8   7   6   5   4   3   2   1

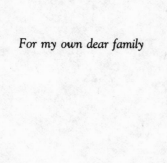

For my own dear family

I wrote *Dear Family* because I lived it. I grew up in just such a house, I went to just such a school, I had just such a family, two grandmothers, and parents who felt very much as Dorothy and Ed did. I fell in love with just such a person and visited him all over the country, and we were married in Monroe, Louisiana.

There was no research, except for the fact that I wasn't sure of a good milker's production. I loved writing it. I can remember going to Boston as a child and down to the market section and eating at Durgin Park. I graduated from grade school in a town hall with a class of about six.

Of course there are lots of people and lots of events that didn't exist except in my imagination. That's the beauty of fiction. You can change what actually was, make it happier or sadder, bestow talent, create the character who will endure sorrow with grace, and so on.

—Camilla Bittle

PART ONE

In the desperate days of the Depression there was one constant that most people could count on—family. This was true of the Beanes, who had endured in the past and would certainly do the same now. Their ancestors had survived an early crossing of the Atlantic and established themselves in a hamlet that later became the village of Hopkinton, Massachusetts. Beanes had proliferated and dispersed, driven before the bitter winds of fortune like the winged seeds of the maple trees from which they had taken shade and shelter and sap, so that eventually small clusters of the family set up communities of their own, and within these groups they had individually endured the Revolution, the Civil War, assorted natural calamities and the plagues of poverty, hunger, cold and sickness.

The branch we are concerned with is the family of Ezra Beane, formerly pastor of the First Congregational Church in Millbrook, now deceased, leaving his widow, his son Edward and his daughter Evelyn. More specifically, Ed's family.

Edward Beane's family lived in a large frame house in the city of Holyoke, Massachusetts, where Ed worked for a tap and die

I

company. They had lived in the same house since 1922, when they were married at Dorothy's home in Havenhill. In 1935, the second year of Mr. Roosevelt's New Deal, Ed's salary was twenty-five dollars a week, and this was enough to pay the rent, the premium on his five-thousand-dollar life insurance policy and most of the other things Dorothy felt were necessary to the family's existence. They did not have a car, but Ruthie and Virgil walked to school. Ed took the bus to work. Martin's Grocery delivered. The School Street Congregational Church was around the corner and trips to visit relatives were few and accomplished by train.

Granny Beane, which is what she was called to distinguish her from Dorothy's mother, who was Grandmother Howard, lived with them, occupying the large front bedroom into which had been crammed all the fine old furniture that remained from the Beane estate. Granny Beane (born a Poole), having known better times, was inclined to fret, something they all accepted placidly. Even Ruthie, who was almost thirteen, had adopted the soothing tone of her parents and would say, "Poor Granny, you're upset. You'll feel better tomorrow."

"Humph," muttered her grandmother, "I'll be dead tomorrow. You just wait."

Of course she wasn't. Wearing a flowered wrapper, a hair net, and gray felt slippers, she came carefully down the narrow back stairs and into the kitchen at the usual 7 A.M. following, completely indifferent to her survival and ready for the cup of coffee that her daughter-in-law poured from a blue and white enamel pot on the kerosene stove and placed before her.

By seven her son, Edward, had left for the tap and die, taking his lunch in a black tin lunch box, to be eaten at his bench when the noon whistle screamed. Still at the table sat Ruthie and Virgil, eating Ralston and drinking hot cocoa. It was a cold morning with frost all over the grass and Dorothy said wistfully that it made her think about Halloween at home.

Home to Dorothy was the farm in Havenhill and the reference to Halloween conjured up visions of cornstalk wigwams, open fields where frost sparkled over the dull remains of last summer's vines, gold and scarlet leaves in blazing bouquets among the evergreen of distant hills, memories of her own childhood that became a crazy quilt of color and a potpourri of smells. In the bountiful beauty of Havenhill she could see pumpkins scattered across the fields, cows trotting out of barns into muddy barnyards, their warm breath rising in white spirals and their empty bags slapping between their spindly legs. By noon the warmth of Indian summer would spread across the pastures that crackled now with fall, and the aroma of wild grapes and ripening apples would combine in a heady winy fragrance.

Dorothy thought of all this with some longing, although not enough to diminish her satisfaction with life itself. Her large square kitchen with its kerosene stove, its black soapstone sink, its new kitchen cabinet—a large white piece of furniture that had drawers and shelves behind doors and a flour bin that held twenty pounds of flour and dispensed it through a sieve when a crank was turned—was something that she had wanted for a long time. Besides that, all she had to do was look around her kitchen and be thankful because there sat her children, eating good food, and there sat her mother-in-law, blessed with good health, although her hearing and eyesight were less acute than in the past. And Ed had a job. So many didn't, she thought sadly.

Granny Beane sat with her coffee, turning the toast just as it began to burn. She liked it that way. Ruthie and Virgil ate their hot cereal and discussed the problem of saving box tops. If he had three Ralston box tops and a dollar, Virgil could send for a Tom Mix six-shooter. Since the dollar was an impossibility, he was faced with having to save thirty-six box tops. It seemed hopeless, but Ruthie (who had outgrown Tom Mix) said she would ask her best friend, Mary Catherine, if Virgil could have the Callahans' Ralston tops. Clearly Virgil saw a glimmer of hope, and squinting at the milk bottle, he took careful aim.

Dorothy sat at her kitchen cabinet with the white enamel tray pulled out, making sandwiches that she wrapped in smoothed-out bread paper. She washed and polished two apples and poured milk into two small thermos bottles.

"Hurry up, children," she said, "you'll be late for school."

3

Virgil and Ruthie thundered up the back stairs and jostled each other in an attempt to reach the bathroom first. Ruthie won and slammed the door, leaving Virgil outside to growl and kick softly at the bottom of the door with the toe of his boot.

"Stop kicking, Virgil," shouted Ruthie through the door. "You're eleven and that's too old to kick."

In a little while they were both back in the kitchen, pulling on caps and jackets, taking up lunch boxes and pounding down the back steps and cutting across the garden to Summer Street and from there along Summer to the Jefferson Park School.

When they had gone Dorothy poured herself a second cup of coffee and sat down with a sigh. She had a bushel of green tomatoes in the cellar and planned to make pickle that morning. The wash was in the set tubs soaking, and the sun, burning off the frost, promised a good drying day. It was Thursday, the first Thursday of the month, October third to be exact, and this meant her literary society was to meet in the afternoon. She wondered whether to offer to take her mother-in-law. She always asked and Granny Beane always declined except at Christmas, when the literary society abandoned its purpose, which was to pursue the study of literature, in favor of Christmas readings, Christmas music and Christmas cookies. Nevertheless Dorothy said, "Now, Mother Beane, wouldn't you like to go to literary with me this afternoon? We're reading *Bleak House*."

"Oh, dear," said Granny Beane, "I suppose I ought to."

Dorothy, who might have taken offence (after all, it would be no particular pleasure to assist Edward's mother down the front steps and along Elm to the trolley and thence across town to Doris Matthew's, where the October meeting was to take place), responded pleasantly, "Nonsense, it's nothing you ought to do, but you might enjoy it. Doris makes lovely sponge cake."

"Well," said Mrs. Beane, "I would if I could hear, but I can't so there's no use in it."

"That makes it hard, I know," said Dorothy.

"It's the clatter," said her mother-in-law. "All those women talking. It makes a terrible roaring in my ears."

4

She put another slice of bread in the toaster, and as smoke began to curl up from the sides she flipped it over with satisfaction. The brown streaks would crunch deliciously under a smearing of marmalade and butter.

"Well," said Dorothy, "I can't just sit here. I have all those green tomatoes down cellar and you know how Ed likes green tomato pickle."

"I suppose I ought to help," said Granny Beane, who had absolutely nothing else to do and had made gallons of pickles during her lifetime and knew more about the process than anyone else. Dorothy was aware of this and accustomed to Mrs. Beane's tone of injured complaint.

"That would be grand," said Dorothy. "Yours are always the best."

"Humph," said old Mrs. Beane, getting up from her chair with more alacrity than she'd shown all morning and going upstairs to dress.

While the morning passed rapidly at 36 Elm Street, Ed Beane stood at his bench filing new fittings for the ball-bearing molds. He was a good machinist and he would have been a good engineer if he had had the chance to go to college. He used to think about it bitterly, but that was before things got so bad. Now he was glad to have a job, and sometimes he wondered how long it would last because the tap and die business in 1935 wasn't what it had been. Sewing machines manufactured in 1935 were no different from sewing machines manufactured in 1929, that's what it all came down to. New models meant retooling, and retooling cost money. Ed didn't dwell on it during the day, although he couldn't say the same for the middle of the night. He was thankful to have a job. Half the crews had been cut, and he supposed they'd get down to him one of these days, although with ball bearings there was always the chance he'd be kept on—they were as basic as nuts and bolts.

At that moment his foreman, who was also half owner in the

shop, came up behind him and put a hand on his shoulder. "You do a good job, Ed. I'm going to hate to lose you."

Mr. Carter's face was gray and drawn, and if his expression counted for much it would have lessened the pain as he wielded the ax, but it didn't help Ed particularly and he went right on filing until he had smoothed the rough edge he was working on right down to satin. He'd never thought that Mr. Carter would be the one to lay him off. He'd imagined a piece of paper in his pay envelope. Come to think of it, he wasn't exactly sure how the others got their bad news. Men he had worked with for years simply didn't show up one day. They might have been swept away in a flood or dropped dead while shaving.

He turned, nodding stoically, and said, "Well, Mr. Carter, I'll miss my place, but I know how things are. I could see it coming."

"One of these days, Ed . . ."—Mr. Carter pounded his clenched fist against the palm of his hand—"one of these days things will look up and we'll call you back."

"Yes, sir."

"You can pick up your pay," said Mr. Carter. "There's a week extra. To tide you over."

"Thanks," said Ed.

When he reached home with his lunch box and his pay envelope he was greeted by the sharp vinegar odor of green tomato pickles. The washing moved in dazzling whiteness on the clothesline, and the Callahans' yellow cat lay stretched out in the sun on the back steps. Since he usually reached home at the end of the day when the wash was in and folded and the predominant aromas from the kitchen were dinner smells, and the shadows of late afternoon rendered the back steps dark and chilly, he felt as though he had emerged from a dungeon into the brilliance of life. On the one hand he was terrified that he was out of work, and yet, on the other, there was an exhilaration as his liberation became apparent just in the bright spread of white sheets on the clothesline. As a little breeze rustled among them, they became

6

the white sails of a ship that was somehow, mysteriously, destined to carry him on to a new life.

Dorothy and Granny Beane sat at the kitchen table, eating pot roast sandwiches. In a cereal bowl between them the new pickle steamed and as he entered, his mother, who had taken some onto her plate to taste, said, "I don't know what's wrong with it, but it doesn't quite suit, Dorothy."

Dorothy, whose back was to the door, tasted it then and was about to make the usual reassuring sounds she always made when confronted by her mother-in-law's anticipated expression of disappointment, when she noted a look of surprise on Granny Beane's face and, turning, saw Ed in the doorway.

If he had not been carrying his lunch box she would have known instantly that one of the children had been hurt, or worse, but the lunch box told her they had now crossed the line from employed to unemployed, and having already imagined every horror connected thereto it was possible for her to smile and say, "Just in time for lunch."

Ed put his lunch box on the table and washed his hands at the kitchen sink.

His mother said plaintively, "Taking off, I see. Can't say as I approve. Your father never took a day in his life. You won't get ahead, Son, if—"

"Now, Mother," said Dorothy sternly, "I'm sure there's a good reason. Sit down, Ed, and try your mother's pickle."

Ed spread out his lunch and poured coffee from his thermos bottle into his thermos cup, proclaimed the pickle excellent and said casually, "Looks like I'm out of a job, Ma."

Granny Beane's thin veined hand flew to her mouth but failed to stop her exclamation of dismay. "Oh, son," she cried, "what will you do?"

"He'll find another job," said Dorothy, although she knew that nobody, these days, was finding work anywhere. She reached furtively under the table and squeezed Ed's knee, and he said easily, "Now, Mother, don't you worry."

Worry was already a cold knot of terror in his stomach, but Ed ate his sandwiches and hard-boiled egg and his mother's

7

pickle and then he went outside and walked slowly around the house three times, looking for those weak spots in the foundation that he had meant to take care of before winter.

Inside the house Dorothy and Mrs. Beane cleaned up the kitchen and Dorothy said firmly, "Now, Mother Beane, I want you to come to literary with me and I won't take no for an answer."

There were no machinist jobs in Holyoke or Springfield or anywhere and there wasn't much use looking elsewhere because there wasn't any money for bus fare or moving the family. Ed went around to the hospital and the thread factory and applied for night watchman or anything else they needed. In fact he went from one such establishment to another, schools, churches, office buildings, stores, and most places wouldn't even take his name. Men looked at him and shook their heads before he even said, "I'm Ed Beane, and . . ."

He started out in the morning and came back at lunchtime and went off again for all afternoon, but there wasn't much use in it. One week he picked up two days' work at the McGhee Coal Company, shoveling coal into bags, twenty pounds of coal to a bag. People were buying it that way because they couldn't call up and order a ton of coal the way they used to. Houses with coal ranges in the kitchen were better off than those with furnaces in the cellar. He wished the black iron monster Dorothy used to cook on was still there instead of the kerosene stove. There was no lasting warmth in kerosene.

Ed came back from McGhee's covered with coal dust. He looked black, like a Negro Granny Beane said, with his big white eyes staring out at them, and Ruthie and Virgil thought it was funny, but Dorothy said, "Colored people are not funny, children. They're just like us only their skin is dark," then she went upstairs and ran a tub and carried Ed's clothes down to the back entry and wondered what was going to happen next.

After supper, when Mother Beane had gone up to her room to read until nine, her bedtime, and Ruthie and Virgil had finished the dishes and played a game of Parcheesi and had baths and were in bed, Ed and Dorothy sat down at the kitchen table with paper and pencil and refigured their assets. It didn't take long. They had seventy-five dollars in the bank. Ed had his life insurance, they could borrow up to fifty dollars on that. They could get along without ordering kerosene for a while, but winter was coming and they needed coal. They'd already taken the phone out and the children never left a room without hearing "Turn off the lights." The canning closet was full of jars of tomatoes and beans and peaches and there were dozens of jars of pickles and jelly, but they owed Martin's Grocery twenty-three dollars and were out of coffee and low on flour. The rent was due in another week and Dorothy said, "We could sell my silver, Ed." It was the silver her parents had given her when she married. "I heard there was a place downtown where they buy silver," she continued, but Ed said, abruptly and harshly, "No."

"What do I care about things," said Dorothy in a careless voice. She actually cared greatly, and Ed, his jaw tense, rammed his hands, twisted into hard knots of frustration, into his pockets. "No," he repeated, and he thought *Sell it all and then what?* There weren't any jobs. This was something he had known, but as long as he was working he knew it the way a healthy man knows about death—something that happens to somebody else.

"Something will turn up," he said.

In her room upstairs Mrs. Beane was reading the Bible. She knew perfectly well that Ed had been laid off and that there weren't any jobs in Holyoke for him or anyone else. It helped to read the Bible; all the old sustaining passages that she knew by heart leaped out at her, and it seemed as if things would have to be all right. She looked around the room at Beane and Poole furniture, her rosewood plant stand and walnut dresser, all the things her mother had had left from the house full of things she'd owned before her husband, Granny Beane's father, had gone off to fight the war down in Virginia in 1862. He'd left his wife with five children and a barrel each of flour, sugar, salt pork and apples, and three years later he'd come back a cripple. Little by little the furniture disappeared, but the children grew up and worked and married and in the end her mother had lived on in the old Poole place in Westfield and died there ten years after her husband had been taken out and put under a GAR marker in the cemetery. It had been easiest for her, Granny Beane reflected, because she had been the baby of the family and couldn't remember how it was before the war. She remembered her father in his chair, wearing a black suit and a stiff collar, sitting with a rug over his knees, rocking and talking about the boys they'd left behind down in Vur-ginnee. Her mother, doing other folks' mending for cash money, would lift her eyes now and then and bite off the thread and make knots in it by rubbing her fingers together, but she never said much. Granny Beane had loved to sit on her father's lap and listen to his tales, but it didn't take her long after marrying Mr. Beane, who was a fine and pleasant gentleman with no head at all for figures, to appreciate what her mother had endured. Four barrels didn't last long—then or now.

But Ed—now Ed was different. He was a good man and a hard worker. He had goals and purpose, she was sure of that, but Ed didn't have causes, like his grandfather. Ed wouldn't have gone off and left Dorothy and the children with four barrels of sugar, salt meat and so on, for the sake of a cause. The Bible was written for good men like Ed who, through no fault of their own, fell on hard times, and as she read, Mrs. Beane tore little scraps of paper from the edge of an old *Collier's* magazine and left them between the pages of the Bible as markers. When the time was right she'd read those passages to Ed. It would help him.

The week before Thanksgiving Dorothy had a letter from her mother. Dorothy had written that Ed was out of work, but things were all right because they had savings and Ed was out looking every day, to which Mrs. Howard replied that she was sure Ed would find work, but meanwhile, Mr. Godwin was going to drive her down to Holyoke for Thanksgiving and she was bringing the turkey. Vera would come too.

Vera was Dorothy's cousin, a nervous pale woman of thirty-seven whose fiancé had been killed at Château-Thierry in 1918. When Dorothy married Ed and moved to Holyoke, Vera gave up her job in Boston and went to live with her Aunt Alice on the farm in Havenhill. Others in the family said it was a sacrifice for Vera to do that, but it wasn't. Vera worked for a bank, behind bars, like a monkey in a cage, and Vera loved the country. She sometimes went for long walks at dawn and at dusk and kept a record of the birds she observed in the thickets and fields around Havenhill. She even liked to fish, and in the spring Homer Godwin, handyman in residence, dug worms in the garden, and she put on a straw hat to keep the sun off her face and tramped across the fields to the river to fish. Inasmuch as Vera was a slight, retiring person, this seemed both brave and interesting to those who knew of it.

In 1930, when she had been with her Aunt Alice for eight years, Vera adopted a cocker spaniel that was snuffling along the road with no collar or other identification, and kept it in the woodshed until her aunt overcame her prejudice about dogs in the house. Now the three of them, Vera, Mrs. Howard and Angus, the dog, lived a pleasant orderly life within the few rooms they occupied in the sprawling square farmhouse on the hill.

The house was called Havenhill by Dorothy's family, and distant cousins elsewhere, because it was situated in the town of Havenhill and no Howard had taken the trouble or imagination to give it any other name—like Roundtop or The Maples. It had not been a working farm even in her father's day. His business was timber and he traveled in Maine and Vermont searching out new forests to cut and turn into pulp, leaving the homeplace, with its two hundred acres of black dirt that had supported generations of Howards, to take care of itself. What remained of the farm was managed by Homer Godwin, who was nearing sixty and had, with his employer's blessing, allowed the land to grow up in brush and berry bushes. The fields lay dormant except for a kitchen garden and Mrs. Howard's flowers, which grew in profusion along the front of the stone wall by the lane and in orderly rows beyond the birches on the south lawn. Mr. Godwin kept a flock of chickens, chopped enough wood for open fires, tended the furnace and the hot water heater, put on storm windows and screens, mowed the lawn, raked leaves and drove Mrs. Howard's old Packard car. He lived in a room over the garage, which had been in the golden days of the eighteen nineties the carriage house, over a collection of old sleighs and farm machinery, now rusted and useless.

Mrs. Howard hadn't visited them in Holyoke since she broke her hip three years ago, which made Dorothy view Thanksgiving with some alarm. Her mother, with a turkey and Vera, was due at noon and would not spend the night, she had written. Surely this meant something.

Homer would eat in the kitchen, Dorothy said, although Granny Beane said it wasn't Christian. Nevertheless, he ate in the kitchen at Havenhill and it seemed to Dorothy her mother was due some consideration after a drive of forty miles.

The rest of the family gathered in the dining room and after dinner, when Ed's mother excused herself to retire for a nap, Mrs. Howard said pointedly to Vera that she would like to talk with Ed and Dorothy. Vera jumped up and said to Ruthie and Virgil, "Let's go for a walk. I always like to go for a walk after a big dinner, don't you?"

They didn't, but Ed nodded at the door and so they pulled on their coats and disappeared down the front steps and into the raw cold of the gray afternoon.

Dorothy had known her mother would want to have her say. It was obvious she wouldn't have come all this way with a roast turkey without being sensitive to their desperate situation, and sure enough, once the table was cleared and the children off with Vera, and Granny Beane hobbling up the front stairs complaining that she had eaten too much, Mrs. Howard said, "Now then, Dorothy, I want to talk to you."

"I'll just go out back and visit with Homer," Ed said.

"No," said his mother-in-law, "I mean you too, Edward. This concerns both of you."

The three of them sat down in the living room, and as the afternoon was dark, with snow clouds thick in the west, Dorothy turned on a lamp regardless of the reckless expenditure of electricity. She did not want her mother to realize the extent of their poverty, although things were fast approaching the hopeless stage, so what did it matter?

"How's Vera?" she asked for the third time, although she had seen for herself that Vera was perfectly well.

"Never mind Vera," said her mother, "I've come about you. What are you going to do?"

"Oh," said Dorothy, "Ed's looking for work. He's bound to find something soon."

"Of course," said Mrs. Howard kindly, smiling at Ed and stopping momentarily the almost visible shrinking of his body as his spirit withered.

"However, let's be sensible," she said. "Until he does it seems foolish to me for you to go on paying rent here. And then there's coal and electricity."

"That's true," said Dorothy, "but of course we try to be careful."

"Well," said her mother, "there's the house, just sitting there. There are four bedrooms in the west wing all closed since your father died, and Homer's not much use, never has been. The orchard's going down. It seemed to me that Edward, while he's waiting for something better to turn up, might try his hand at that."

There wasn't any point in saying they couldn't, or wouldn't, but Ed, who didn't like being referred to in the third person, said, "There's my mother, you know."

"Of course," said Mrs. Howard, and although she always found Mrs. Beane very tiresome she continued, "I meant for her to come. And the furniture. There's room in the attic." She paused and regarded them with an expression of benign authority. "Well, what do you say?"

Dorothy felt like crying with gratitude and relief, and this forced her to hold back. (After all, she had always known her parents hadn't wanted her to marry Ed, and that rankled.) She said, "That would be very nice, Mother."

But Ed, who felt as though he'd just been dragged back from the rim of a bottomless black abyss, stood up and crossed the room and took his mother-in-law's two hands in his and said, "Bless you, Mother Howard."

"Well, well," she said, "that's settled then. Hire a truck if you've got any money . . . have you?"

"Yes," said Dorothy.

"And come along before another month's rent is due."

"What about Vera?" asked Dorothy.

"Vera will be tickled pink," said her mother.

Vera was not tickled pink; she could see their pleasant days disappearing in a cyclone of stamping feet, wet raincoats and hearty meals. All the same she had a pot roast with carrots and onions and browned potatoes ready when they arrived.

They came in a truck driven by Mick Callahan and borrowed from Mick's brother Kevin, who owned the lumber company. Ed and Virgil rode up in the cab with Mick, and the rest of them, Dorothy, Ruthie and Granny Beane, took the train. They had all spent the night at the Callahans' because by the time the truck was loaded it was pitch black and too late to travel.

After supper, which was one of Edith's famous boiled dinners, the women did dishes and then went into the living room to talk. Edith Callahan sat with her darning basket in her lap and Dorothy, who had packed her mending and her knitting and everything else that gave meaning to her life, said, "Let me do some of that, Edith. I feel so fidgety it would help."

Mick was better off than a lot of people because he was a maintenance man at St. Timothy's, which was supported by the Roman Catholic Diocese and destined for continued assistance as long as there were good Catholics in New England, which meant in perpetuity. In the School Street Congregational

Church, where the Beanes attended, the minister had taken a cut a year ago and another more recently. The furnace ran only on Sundays and the missions in China and India would soon feel the tiny ripple produced by these pinched circumstances. Inasmuch as three grains of rice in those desperate areas made a difference, Holyoke's imposed frugality would become a tidal wave of misfortune overseas. That's how it was.

Edith said, "Oh, Dorothy, how I'll miss you. There's no one on the street I can talk to, not the way we talk."

"I know," said Dorothy, thinking she would have only her mother and Vera, whose interests couldn't be very much like her own. She didn't even think of Granny Beane.

"I wish . . . ," said Dorothy, and paused. What was the use in wishing? She meant to say she wished the Callahans would come up to Havenhill to visit, but they wouldn't, and even if they did it would be awkward. She was sure her mother thought very little of Catholics. "I wish we didn't have to go," she finished.

"It won't be forever," said Edith.

Upstairs in Mary Catherine's room Ruthie was looking at Mary Catherine's movie star scrapbook. There were pictures of Janet Gaynor, Jean Harlow, Clark Gable, Wallace Beery and Jackie Cooper. It was funny to think that she and Jackie Cooper were the same age.

Mary Catherine opened her top bureau drawer and took out a little box in which, wrapped in tissue paper, was a small enamel cross hanging on a black ribbon. Her aunt Mary had given it to her for her birthday and she liked it, but her grandmother had given her a gold one for confirmation and she didn't need two. When she asked her mother if she could give the enamel one to Ruthie, Edith had said, "If you want to, but she might not want it."

"Why not?" asked Mary Catherine.

"Protestants don't light candles the way we do, or wear crosses."

With Ruthie sitting there on her crocheted bedspread looking at her scrapbook, Mary Catherine felt suddenly shy; nevertheless it seemed important to do something. Ruthie was her best friend. So she took out the little cross and dangled it in front of Ruthie's face.

When Ruthie's attention was lured away from a glittering Jean Harlow, she saw the small white cross with its tracing of tiny green leaves and roses and she put out her hand to touch it and said, "Oh, Mary Catherine, how beautiful."

"I want you to have it, Ruthie."

Ruthie gasped. "Me? To keep?"

Mary Catherine nodded. "You're my best friend. I don't want you to ever forget me."

"I wouldn't do that."

"Put it on," said Mary Catherine.

When it was in its place on Ruthie's chest Mary Catherine said, "My mother said you might not want it because of its being a cross and all. You know. Catholic."

"Well, I do want it," said Ruthie. "We believe in the cross too, if you see what I mean. I'll treasure it," she said grandly, putting her hand around it and holding it tightly. "Always," she said.

"And you won't forget me?"

"Never," said Ruthie. "I'll write to you and maybe you can come up to see us in Havenhill."

Dorothy didn't see the cross until they were getting ready for bed in her mother's house the next night and then she said, "Where did you get that, Ruthie?"

"Mary Catherine gave it to me. It's a cross."

"I can see that," said Dorothy, looking at it closely, and suddenly tears filled her eyes and she turned away quickly.

"Mary Catherine said you might not let me wear it because it's Catholic. Can I wear it anyway? Can I?"

"May I," said Dorothy automatically, struggling to control herself. "Yes, of course you can wear it."

"I told her you wouldn't care."

"But I do care," said Dorothy quickly, thinking of Edith, who was always there when the children were sick. "It shows how much Mary Catherine cares about you, and a cross isn't just for Catholics. Christ died for all of us, you know."

"I'll never forget Mary Catherine," said Ruthie.

"I hope you won't," said Dorothy, but she knew better. The vivid memory of Mary Catherine would recede, fading to a hazy pastel of remembered fondness, becoming probably one of Ruthie's pink memories, a rosy glowing essence entitled "Dear Friend," soon to be replaced by someone in the Havenhill Grade School, she supposed.

"Go to sleep, dear," said Dorothy, and turned out the light.

The rooms they occupied in the west wing were identical in size and shape and had been added to the house in 1878 for third-generation Howards—a large family produced in the peak years of Howard prosperity. In those days Howard paper products were known around the country. Now they had dwindled to one plant in Lowell, where toilet tissue was manufactured. Mrs. Howard fortunately retained only token shares in the business, having sold out in 1921 when Dorothy's father died. Howard Products was all but extinguished in the crash, but no matter— her mother was comfortably secure in utilities and government bonds. Sometimes Dorothy wondered if her mother was rich, and, if so, why she had been brought up to feel poor. Perhaps, she thought, it was her mother's meager girlhood on a farm in Maine that accounted for the surface parsimony in her mother's manner. What did it matter? They were there, and for the first time in days she felt really warm. At the moment, heartfelt gratitude replaced all bitter feelings of the past.

Through the years Mrs. Howard had softened in her attitude toward Ed. It wasn't his fault that he had to go to work after his father's death, and she supposed he would have made a competent engineer. It was true she hadn't seen much of her grandchildren, but they seemed bright and attractive, and insofar as her character, which was dedicated to hard work, discipline and self-denial, would allow, she welcomed the opportunity for learning to know them better. She saw to it that the rooms were fresh and heated for their arrival. Vera had a good dinner ready and Mr. Godwin hired two local boys to help unload the truck.

"Everything up to the attic," commanded Mrs. Howard, waving them on with her cane. "There's space cleared out over the east end."

"I thought we could use our own linens, Mother," said Dorothy.

"I have a closet full," replied her mother. "Leave yours in the boxes, Dorothy, there's no need to get them all mixed in together."

Clearly Mrs. Howard was looking ahead to the time when all of the Beanes' possessions would be trundled back down the attic stairs and taken to their next home. Havenhill was a port in a storm, not a permanent roosting place, her tone made that clear.

"Well," spoke up Granny Beane, "I will have my Poole rocker. I always sit in my Poole chair. There's plenty of room and I mean to have it."

The two old women, both in black, both white haired, both stout, confronted each other in the front entrance of the Howard house through whose portals passed the remnants of a happy life in Holyoke. Granny Beane could see the Poole rocker coming off the truck and up the flagstone path and she wrung her hands and fluttered in misery.

"I will have it," she peeped, and Grandmother Howard thought furiously, *How dare she?*

All the same, Mrs Howard had been bred with English blood and baptized with stubborn New England conviction. The former cried out for emotional control and the other demanded one speak one's beliefs no matter what. As the war between the two raged inside of her, the English side of her nature took precedence, and she turned to the boy and said abruptly, "Very well. Take that chair to the room at the head of the stairs and set it down by the front window."

18

It was after six, the usual hour for supper, before the truck was unloaded, and by then Vera was fluttering around in agony. Things would get cold.

"Nonsense," said her aunt, pot roast didn't get cold. "Set it back, Vera," she said, "and bring me my pocketbook. I'll need to pay these boys."

She opened her black bag and rummaged around for her change purse. They had been working almost two hours, wrestling trunks and bureaus and boxes of china up two flights of stairs to the attic. Luckily for all of them, the beds and living room furniture of the Holyoke house went, or rather stayed, with the house. The boys stood quietly, waiting, and she knew that if she gave them fifty cents apiece it would be enough. Still, she admired a man who was willing to work, and she drew out two dollar bills.

"Now then, boys," said Mrs. Howard, "here's your pay. You've done a good job."

During this Ed was speaking urgently to Dorothy. "Mick ought to stay for supper," he said. "We've got to ask him to stay, Dorothy."

"I'll ask mother," she replied in an undertone, thinking how terrible it would be to embarrass Mick. Suppose her mother refused or told him to eat in the kitchen, and it came home to her quite forcefully what it was going to mean to them all to live under her mother's roof. It was going to be impossibly hard— always to have to ask, like a child, and her face was drawn with conflicting emotions as she waited her turn while her mother paid the boys.

Ed, observing his wife's dismay, cursed silently. He saw his friend waiting with cap in hand, ready to depart and at that moment Vera came through the door and said to no one in particular, "Oh dear, aren't we ready yet?"

Ed turned to her with a smile that was wholly disarming, and he said firmly, "Just set another place at the table for our friend, Vera."

Vera didn't hesitate. It's true that as she slipped through the back hall to the butler's pantry for linen and silver she thought, with a strange small thudding of her heart, *What will Aunt Alice say?* Nevertheless she put in another place.

In the front hall Mick, twisting his cap in his hands, said, "Now, Ed, I ought to just get along home."

"Not without dinner," said Ed. "Come along upstairs and we'll have a quick wash."

Mrs. Howard saw instantly that her dining table was to receive not only one unsuitably dressed man, but two, as well as two rumpled children, poor Dorothy who looked exhausted, and Mrs. Beane, a creature from whom she had already experienced insubordination. Mrs. Howard was old and wise enough to know that gratitude was not always forthcoming from those who ought to offer it, if not wholeheartedly, at least as fair payment for assistance proffered, and she took a deep breath. It was *her* house. She decided who ate at her table and who ate in the kitchen with Ruby. The idea that Edward, her son-in-law, would presume to make policy, not after a month in a gradual, if mistaken, assumption of privilege, but now, was preposterous. But—as she looked at Dorothy, her own daughter, sweet, gentle and hopeful, confidently expecting the best of everyone and every situation—something tender moved unexpectedly in Mrs. Howard's corseted bosom. As Ed and Mick descended the stairs she said grandly, "Shall we all go in to dinner now?"

Mrs. Howard, who had a talent for anticipating potentially unpleasant confrontations, had ordered Ruby to carve in the kitchen. She wasn't prepared yet to surrender the carving knife to her son-in-law, and so the meal was handed round on platters and in bowls. First, however, when they were all seated, Mrs. Howard gave thanks for the safe arrival of her daughter's brood and expressed appropriate gratitude for the bounty they were about to receive. As she raised her eyes she saw Mr. Callahan cross himself, and she thought grimly, *Well, just in time. I might have known. Catholic.*

They were all tired and hungry, but as she ate, Dorothy paused to note the soft glow of lights through the lower part of the house. She could see into the parlor and across the entrance hall to the sitting room. When Ruby pushed through the swinging door, Dorothy glimpsed the glass-fronted china cupboards in the pantry and then the lighted kitchen beyond. Her mother was careful, often to the point of frugality, but she kept the lights on. How wonderful, Dorothy thought, stifling an impulse to sob. She was so tired. She smiled at Virgil and Ruthie who were eating even their carrots, and trying, although they drooped with fatigue, to behave properly.

Mick ate silently, except to say to his hostess that he was near starved and had never tasted better. And Ed, sensitive to his mother-in-law's ordinary standards, said heartily, "This is a wonderful welcome, Mother Howard."

"Thank you, Edward," she replied.

Granny Beane picked silently at her plate and wished she could have a cup of tea. Not later, but now. If she had been at home she would have asked for it. She hadn't hesitated to do battle for her Poole chair, but she wasn't up to another confrontation. The move, at her age, was terribly unsettling. Things had started out so brightly for Ed. In Millbrook, where his father was minister of First Church, they had lived simply but well. Ed was accepted at MIT and went into the mills only during the summer to earn tuition money. What a misfortune it was that her husband died suddenly—pneumonia was like that—and then Ed gave up MIT for her sake and for Evelyn. The last time they'd heard from Evelyn was three months ago from California. Evelyn was sure she was going to be a movie star, but from all they could tell she earned a living of sorts waiting on table. To think Ed had sacrificed his chances for Evelyn's sake. Mrs. Beane sighed as the familiar scenario of her past life passed before her eyes, and at that moment, Vera, who was seated beside her and had been observing her lack of appetite, leaned over and said softly, "Wouldn't you like a cup of tea, Mrs. Beane?"

With those few words Vera endeared herself to the old lady forever. To Granny, Vera's offer was evidence that someone cared. Someone who would understand if she were to say—if only Evelyn had married well, she was such a pretty girl, or if, at least, she had become a movie star . . . She looked up quickly and saw Vera, really saw her for the first time, and thin, pale, nervous Vera became a Madonna to Mrs. Beane, who said gratefully, "Oh, thank you. Yes."

After dinner Mick drove off in the truck and Dorothy and Vera cleared the table. Granny Beane said good night and dragged her tired old body slowly up the wide staircase, pausing at the landing where, through a tall uncurtained window she caught a glimpse of the moon.

Down below, Ed approached Dorothy and said quietly, "What do you want me to do?"

"Get the children to bed," she said.

Ruthie and Virgil were in the sitting room looking at a stereoscope. "Look at this funny old thing," said Virgil, and Mrs. Howard, who sat in her favorite chair with the *Atlantic* monthly opened in her lap, said tartly, "It is called a stereoscope. There are photographs in the box, Virgil. Put a photograph into the slot and hold it to the light. You may be surprised at what you see."

What they saw was the Paris of 1904. The Tower of London. A gondola in Venice and a view of the Alps. To someone acquainted with Tom Mix in the Saturday serials, the pictures looked funny, faded, antique and unreal, but Ruthie poked Virgil threateningly and said, "They are very interesting, Grandmother."

At that moment Ed came into the room. "Say good night to your grandmother, children. It's bedtime."

It was only seven-thirty and bedtime was an hour away, but they were tired and besides, they were ready to escape the stiff surroundings of their grandmother's domain.

"Good night," said Ruthie, bending to put a quick kiss on her grandmother's cheek. "Thank you for dinner."

"Good night, Ruth," said Mrs. Howard. "I hope you will sleep well."

Virgil had given up kissing female relatives and stood watching Ruth and wondering if he would have to kiss his grandmother too. His relief was enormous when she took his hand, shook it firmly and said, "Good night, Virgil. I will see you in the morning."

When they were safely up the stairs they saw that Mrs. Beane's door was open and there she sat with the Bible in her lap, snoozing and rocking in the Poole rocker. It was so familiar a sight they both wanted to cry but Virgil, being a boy, couldn't and Ruthie didn't think she should even feel like it. What was there to cry about?

They went in and hugged Granny and said, "Good night, Granny," and she, spluttering as she waked up, began to fuss comfortably that they ought to settle down and why wouldn't they sit still and listen to the scriptures? "We will," they said, edging out of the room and then they pelted down the hall, each trying to get to the bathroom first.

In the kitchen below, Dorothy was wiping dishes and the sound of Virgil and Ruthie thumping overhead distressed her. She was thankful their rooms were above the back of the house. It was upsetting even to imagine her mother's reactions to running overhead.

Ruby washed, using two enamel pans, one for soapy water and the other for rinse, and Dorothy dried while Vera put away. Things hadn't changed much, except that now it seemed more like Vera's home than her own, and Ruby had replaced Mrs. Ware, who was now living in Wakefield with her daughter.

Ruby, a somewhat sullen woman of forty, worked doggedly on, making her way through six extra place settings. She was used to cooking for two ladies and Mr. Godwin, who, being help, didn't count. She had not bargained for a whole family, and if times weren't so bad, she told her husband, she'd quit. Ruby's husband, Jack, did odd jobs in Havenhill. He was good with horses, but not many folks had horses no more, he said. The New York summer people who used to keep saddle horses were lucky if they were able to hang on to their summer places. It was a changing world since the Depression, but one of these days, he said, his tone indicating that riches were just around the corner. Meanwhile he told Ruby to tuck in her pride. They needed the money.

"That was a delicious meal, Ruby," said Dorothy, "and a lovely dessert."

"Ayah," said Ruby.

"What shall I do in the morning, Vera? I'd be glad to get breakfast."

"I always do it," said Vera. "I don't mind."

"But I ought to," said Dorothy desperately. "There are five of us. I want to help." What she meant was that she didn't want to be idle, and she didn't want to feel like a guest in her own home. It wasn't right. Vera was only a cousin.

"Don't you pack lunches?" asked Vera. "And there's the wash and the house." She paused. "But I could use help at breakfast. Can't we do it together?"

When the kitchen was straight Ruby put on her hat and coat and pulled on her rubbers and went off down the road to the crossing where Jack would be waiting. Before the Depression he drove a Ford car, but gas cost money and now he hitched Nel to the buggy and met Ruby at the corner every night at eight. She could have walked home, it was only a mile and a half, but seeing as his business was off, he said, he was glad to fetch her home.

Vera turned out the lights, and she and Dorothy went into the sitting room, where Mrs. Howard was reading an article in the *Atlantic*. Vera took up her knitting, she was making a red sweater for the church Christmas fair, and Dorothy sat down and waited. What more might be expected of her, she wondered, feeling obliged to display a willingness to be sociable, but as Vera's needles clicked and her mother continued reading, she rose. She was very tired.

Upstairs Ruthie and Virgil were already in bed, waiting for her to listen to their prayers. Bright moonlight streamed down over the bleak countryside beyond the warm walls of the house. In the morning they would go to school, the same school she had gone to when she was their age, she told them. After the Jefferson Park School in Holyoke, Sunnyside would seem like a funny old-fashioned school, with eight grades in one room and a well in the yard. Unless the school board had prevailed on the selectmen to put in flush toilets and running water, they would also find two outhouses at Sunnyside, one for girls, one for boys.

"School tomorrow," she said, kissing Ruthie. "Go right to sleep."

In Virgil's room she sat down on the edge of the bed and said, "Go ahead, Virgil, I'm listening."

He began the familiar mumble of "Our Father," ending with his God blesses, and that night he blessed all the Callahans individually, his grandmothers, his family, Vera, the lady in the kitchen, Mr. Godwin, and—

Dorothy said, "That's enough, Virgil." She leaned down and kissed him. "Oh, I'm sorry," she said, "I forgot."

But Virgil said he didn't mind. Not on this first night.

He didn't say that he felt strange, but he did. In Holyoke they could hear the trolley at the end of the street where Elm intersected School. Here there was only silence, a deep solid silence that pressed against the house as though to hold it steady as it sailed sedately through the dark night toward dawn. Occasionally little gusts of wind stirred the treetops, making their bare branches rattle. In the distance a dog barked, but mostly the stillness reigned unbroken.

Dorothy turned out the lamp beside Virgil's bed and went along down the hall to Granny's room. She found Granny in her flannel gown, a heavy hair net, like a fishnet, over her white hair. She moved slowly and restlessly about the room in the half dark, for she had carefully extinguished all the lights except her bed table lamp.

"I hope you'll sleep well," said Dorothy.

"I don't expect to," said Mrs. Beane. "I'm too old for all this change. If it weren't for the children I'd not have come."

What would she have done, wondered Dorothy in despair, gone out to Hollywood to be with Evelyn? She sighed and murmured appropriately. They all felt upset, she said.

"Well," replied Granny Beane, "your mother's a good woman, Dorothy. Not everybody would take in a whole family and I'll not hold her stiff neck against her."

25

"She means well."

"I daresay," commented her mother-in-law.

"Would you like a tray in the morning, Mother Beane?" asked Dorothy, thinking that it would simplify things, but Mrs. Beane said, "Certainly not!"

Down the hall Ed was already in his pajamas and the bed was turned back. He moved restlessly, with a sort of subdued excitement, around the room. The move was affecting him in a way unanticipated by them both. What was actually defeat—coming home penniless to Dorothy's mother—had become in some inexplicable way a liberation. Driving along beside Howard fields, past a tangled expanse that had once been Howard orchards and up the long lane to the house, Ed had felt the stirring interest of a property owner. What was Dorothy's was his and vice versa. If he could open those fields, restore those orchards, clear and cultivate and make productive a property that had been allowed to go wild, becoming a jungle of weeds and underbrush, then their coming to Havenhill would represent a beginning. He had never wanted to be a machinist anyway. He had wanted to be an engineer.

He watched as Dorothy undressed, moving silently in and out of the closet, modestly disrobing so that she seemed to slip from one attire to another without actually ever appearing naked. The process fascinated him.

For a while she sat at the dressing table and brushed her hair. When she unwound the bun at the back of her head a wealth of brown hair streamed over her shoulders, and as she brushed she shook it back, a little lift of her head accompanying this so that she too, suddenly, seemed more free of constraint.

Putting down the brush she said, "Do you think we could put Virgil and Ruthie together in one room and make ourselves a sitting room, Ed?"

"I don't see why not."

"If we had a place where we could be a family," she mused,

"just by ourselves. They aren't really too old. Not yet. It would make all the difference."

"Come to bed, Dorothy," he said.

She slid in beside him and turned out the light, and as she stretched out wearily she felt his legs around her and his hand on her breast.

"No, Ed," she said firmly.

"Yes, Dorothy."

"No," she said, pulling away. She couldn't. Not in her mother's house. Not in the house where her virginity had been so guarded. Not with Vera downstairs.

Ed sighed. It would take time after all, he thought, and he kissed her carefully and rolled over.

Breakfast at Havenhill was a dining room meal, at seven, and everyone was expected to appear. Dorothy, who remembered, made sure the night before that her mother still followed this routine and at six-fifteen she went down the hall tapping on doors and calling, "Time to wake up." Then she went into the bathroom and locked the door for the only privacy she could hope to have all day.

When she descended to the kitchen Mr. Godwin was already at the table drinking coffee. He had been up since five, when he started the hot water fire, a small coal burner in the cellar, and took out the ashes and shoveled coal into the furnace. When he say Dorothy he half rose and said, "Morning, Mrs. Beane. Fine morning."

"Good morning, Mr. Godwin," she replied. It was going to be a good morning.

Vera was at the stove stirring oatmeal. She had already filled a dish with grape jelly, and she smiled at Dorothy, who stood in the middle of the room turning this way and that, as though unable to think what to do.

"There's ham in the ice box and apples in the pantry," said Vera.

It was going to be a beautiful day. There was a thin tracing of frost on the lower part of the kitchen windows through which the sun shone radiantly. Here it was the second of December and still no snow, Vera remarked to no one in particular. Since Mr. Godwin would do the shoveling of that snow when it came, as it surely would, he muttered that no snow suited him fine. He said out loud, "You'll want the car, Mrs. Beane."

"Thank you," said Dorothy, "but I thought we'd walk." She had always walked to school.

"You'll have to go by the road," said Vera. "The south fields are all grown up, and they've run a new fence along the Berry Bay line, so you can't cut through. Let Homer drive you this morning."

Dorothy made sandwiches and wrapped them in wax paper. There were no bread wrappers in the drawer because her mother wouldn't buy store bread. When she finished the lunches she began to make toast, and when she had buttered eight slices and put them on the table it was seven o'clock, the children were in their places, Mrs. Howard said grace and the ritual of breakfast began.

There were two pots on the table, a brown crackle pot of tea, and a china pot of coffee. Mrs. Howard drank tea because she thought coffee was a stimulant and tea, always offered in times of crisis, was, by virtue of its reputation, soothing. Why she should need to be soothed was something she hadn't thought about recently. As she sat, watching her grandchildren eating applesauce and cereal, she heard Virgil whisper to Ruth, and she said, "It's not polite to whisper, Virgil."

Dorothy looked up quickly. Was she going to have to listen to her mother discipline her children? "Grandmother's right, Virgil," she said, "you shouldn't whisper at the table."

"All I said was that I wished it was Ralston."

"And why is that?" asked Grandmother Howard.

"I save the box tops," said Virgil. "When I get enough I can send for a Tom Mix six-shooter."

"I see," said his grandmother.

"He already has nineteen," said Ruth. "All he needs is thirty-six."

"Eat up," said Ed, "it's getting late."

He actually had no idea what time it was, but he was impatient to be off. Sitting at the table, as if at dinner, was an unnatural act for a working man in the morning, and the fact of his idleness was slow to take hold. He was ready to be out, ready to take a look at that orchard, ready to tramp the fields and walk the lines. Coming in the day before he had spotted a stand of fir trees in the distance. From the truck they had looked like a village of Christmas trees, and as he thought about it he had begun to wonder if there would be any way to cut a load and haul it down to Boston. He'd have to find a truck somewhere, but it was worth a try and it would make them a Christmas.

At eight o'clock Homer backed the Packard out of the barn and came around to the front of the house. Driving Mrs. Howard's black Packard was the one thing Homer Godwin liked to do. To turn the key in the ignition of the big black car elevated him from handyman to chauffeur. He would have worn a driver's cap if he had one.

Children were congregating in the yard at Sunnyside, and Virgil looked hopefully at a group of boys kicking a ball. Ruthie smiled shyly at three girls who huddled and whispered outside the door. Both of them would have preferred to stay in the yard, but Dorothy hustled them up the steps into the entry.

Miss Norris stood at the blackboard writing the words— *Monday, December 2, 1935.* She turned and smiled and put down the chalk. "You must be the Beanes," she said. "Your grandmother wrote me a note and said you were coming."

The schoolroom with its smell of chalk and floor oil seemed unchanged to Dorothy and she was touched to think that her mother had written to announce their arrival. The American flag drooped on a varnished pole in the corner and the map of the United States hung from a roller between the windows just as it always had. Looking around she felt a pang of sadness.

Life had been so blindingly bright when she'd been in this school. Great expectations had colored all her thoughts so that she had not hoped for all the rich fulfillment of life, but expected it. Now all the things she cared about, the things that gave shape and meaning to her life, were gone—a home of her own, her literary society, the women of the church, Edith Callahan and the others. She stood with folded hands while Miss Norris showed the children their desks, asked them what grades they were in, and told Virgil he could ring the bell if he liked.

When the Packard moved away, past the flagpole and out the drive, she saw the door burst open and heard a wild clanging that expressed Virgil's personality exactly, and feeling somewhat cheered she settled back and took a deep breath. *Shame on you, Dorothy Beane*, she thought, *you have everything in the world to be thankful for*.

One of the last things Ed discovered that morning was an old truck up on blocks at the back of the barn. It was gray with dust and hens had roosted in the hay that lay matted and powdery in the flatbed of it. It was the last thing in the world he had expected to find.

"Well, look at this," he said. "What's this doing here?"

Homer had put up with Ed's comments all morning and had taken most of them as personal affronts. What did he think it was doing there? Homer mumbled irritably, "Tried to sell it but couldn't get a thing for it."

"I don't wonder," said Ed, "left here to ruin like it is. Does she run?"

"Did."

Under the hood a tangle of pipes and cylinders that any machinist would have understood looked all right to Ed. He'd know soon enough when he got into it. His fingers began to itch with excitement, and when he went upstairs to wash for lunch he said to Dorothy, "Did you know there was a truck out there in the barn? If I can get it running I could cut a load of trees and haul them down to Boston. It would make us a Christmas, Dorothy.''

"Change your shirt, Ed," she said, "that's a work shirt."

"It's clean," he said, wetting his hair and brushing it back.

"Hurry up," she said, "we'll be late."

"Did you hear what I said, Dorothy?"

"I heard you and I think you're crazy. Nobody cuts trees, except for firewood. She wouldn't let you cut trees to sell, Ed. Timber's different, but trees. Well, she wouldn't."

"They're growing wild," he said, "if they don't get thinned out half of them'll be stunted and no good to anybody."

They took their places once more, pulled napkins out of rings, submitted to Mrs. Howard's supplication to the Almighty, although it was unnecessary to ask for the grace to accept with gratitude what was about to be provided. Dorothy and Ed were profoundly grateful.

What was provided happened to be beef hash, beets and cabbage salad. There was a dish of piccalilli, a plate of bread, a covered dish of butter, and Vera had baked an Apple Betty for dessert, which she served with whipped cream. There was no need for Vera to make whipped cream, thought Mrs. Howard, a cornstarch sauce would have done as well. She would have to speak to Vera. Ed's hands were grimy. She knew they were clean because he'd gone upstairs to wash, but there was a line of black around his nails. *Machinist's hands,* she thought. They had always assumed Dorothy would marry a professional man.

Granny Beane ate sparingly. She had never liked beets and Ruby's piccalilli lacked something. She'd spent the morning darning the children's stockings. Ruthie's long cotton stockings were so full of holes they wouldn't have been good enough for the Morgan Memorial box and she thought *If I was back in Millbrook where I could charge things, I'd* . . . Since it had been years since she had been able to charge anything, Granny ended up by thinking, *Poor Ed,* and as soon as lunch was over she struggled up the stairs to her bedroom and shut the door. She rested from one to three and everybody knew it.

Mrs. Howard did not rest. She read and wrote letters until two, when she retired to her bedroom to change into an afternoon dress. Before she reappeared at three-thirty, when Vera rolled in the tea cart, she might have reclined in her rocker or even stretched out on the bed for a few minutes, but she did not take a nap. Children napped. She rose from the table and sailed sedately into the sitting room and sat down at her desk while Vera and Dorothy cleared the table.

Dorothy watched anxiously as Ed followed her mother into the sitting room. She knew there was no chance of their being evicted, but life could become unpleasant, and she prayed that Ed would just leave things alone. He didn't know her mother the way she did, and she turned her back and followed Vera into the kitchen.

Mrs. Howard looked up from her account book. "Yes, Edward, what is it?"

"I want to talk about those trees in the north wood lot," he said, suddenly feeling less certain of everything. "They're pretty thick in there, it would be a good thing to thin them out, and I could truck a load down to Boston and get a fair price, I think. Enough to pay for putting the truck in shape with some left over for Christmas."

Mrs. Howard was used to Homer's slow ramblings about ordering coal and getting in firewood, but Ed's proposition took her by surprise, and her first reaction was negative.

"I don't want that stand of firs touched and the truck's been up on blocks for longer than I can remember," she said sharply. "I doubt you'd get as far as Clinton, let alone Boston."

"I know engines," said Ed, "and the tires look sound. All I need is money for gas and parts."

"And where do you think you'll get that?"

"From you," said Ed, his tone as crisp as hers, but he was the beggar and he knew it and he said, "if you could let me have that I'd get it back to you, and have a little left over for Christmas too."

Christmas, she thought, she had forgotten Christmas, but she said stubbornly, "Once you cut a tree it's gone."

"I know that," Ed said, and added bitterly, "you let go of a lot of things and they're gone."

"Yes," she said, and the inner battle she was experiencing, as her will to command was challenged by her desire to love, threatened to take her breath away . . . . But she had heard him and was quick enough to catch the tone of anger and defeat in Ed's voice. Whatever it was she wanted to win in this tug of war wasn't as sweet as she had thought it might be, and, surprised at herself, she heard her voice gasp out, "I'll let you have twenty dollars and mind you don't cut them all from the same place."

Ed had the truck running in eight days, and on Thursday he and Homer cut trees, lashing them to the bed of the truck, working against time while Homer muttered that he didn't know anybody rich enough to pay a dollar a tree and if folks had that kind of money in Boston maybe they'd best all move down there.

People had money all right, Ed thought. All you had to do was go where it was and that's what he was going to do. Sitting at the table that night he said, "I'm off to the big city tomorrow. What do you think of that?"

Virgil thought he ought to go too. Ruthie thought she ought to go if Virgil went. Dorothy thought it was ridiculous because it was a school day, and besides that Boston was a long way from Havenhill and it might snow. Vera sat silently, imagining the Boston where she had lived before the war, seeing it in the glow of a promising past that shone like the gold of the State House dome. Granny worried out loud that the truck would break down, and muttered "the idea" several times.

"Maybe next year," said Ed to Virgil.

And then Mrs. Howard, who was still troubled by her capitulation—hadn't she always felt a reverence for the woods that surrounded and protected her property?—said that girls belonged at home, but it might be a good experience for Virgil.

Her reasoning, although unexpressed, was that Virgil might as well, from the beginning, see the futility of basing life's decisions on hopes rather than common sense. Life was hard and grew more so with the passage of time. It would be a good thing for Virgil to set his sights on law or medicine, she thought. Let him have a taste of ill-conceived adventure, which was, she thought sadly, what this venture amounted to.

"We'll decide that, Mother," said Dorothy.

At four when the alarm rang it sounded like a fire bell. Darkness pressed at the windows, like the middle of the night, and Dorothy pulled on her robe and stumbled down the back stairs to the kitchen to make hot cereal and coffee. She put four eggs on to boil and then she sliced bread for sandwiches. Despite the familiar motions in a kitchen that smelled comfortably of coffee, she felt uneasy. For one thing, she wished Virgil weren't going. Her mother had no business interfering. What the children did or didn't do was up to her and Ed, and she moved around the kitchen in glum silence.

"It's dark as pitch," she said to Ed, as though it were his fault. She poured his coffee with a little splash and dished his oatmeal carelessly, slopping it on the side of the bowl.

"Now, Dorothy," he said, "it's not as bad as all that. Let Virgil have his fun."

"Fun," she cried. "Suppose the truck breaks down and you freeze to death. Besides that, it's a school day."

They heard Virgil on the stairs. His face glowed with excitement and he began to eat his oatmeal as though he liked it, which he didn't.

"I'd feel better if it were light," said Dorothy. "You can't even tell what kind of a day it's going to be."

"It's going to be a great day," said Ed.

"You've got enough lunch to last you all through, if you're running late."

"We'll be home for supper," said Ed. "It's only seventy miles, Dorothy."

"Seventy miles," she said anxiously, as if each mile were a threat, and she turned to Virgil. "Wear your arctics," she said, "it might snow and if it doesn't they'll keep your feet warm."

It was still dark when they left, going through the door to be swallowed up in the blackness outside, and then the headlights of the truck came on, shooting light from the front of the barn straight down the lane, making two tunnels, like two probing eyes, that she watched until they disappeared from sight. Then she put the dishes in the sink, turned out the light and crept up the stairs and down the cold hall to her bed.

On the state road the truck moved along fast enough. There wasn't another thing on the road. As they drove up the lane, heavy frost on the fields glittered in the blaze of the headlights and later, when daylight began to come, starting with a thin pink line along the tops of the hills and changing to a pale glow that revealed the stubbled fields and pastures of Massachusetts, they could see more clearly the blanket of frost that rendered the scene bare as bone and shimmering as crystal. In the farmhouses they passed there were lights in the back and now and then a bulb threw a ring of brightness over a barn door.

The noise of the motor and the jouncing of the truck made conversation impossible. For all his excitement Virgil was getting sleepy and, after a while, lulled by the monotonous roar, he fell asleep. It was after ten when Ed shook his shoulder.

"Wake up, Son. We're here. You don't want to miss anything. Just take a look over there."

Virgil sat up, rubbed his eyes and looked as directed. What he saw was a street jammed with pushcarts. Pushcarts that were piled with fruit and vegetables. Some had chestnuts roasting over charcoal burners, others were heaped with Christmas greens. The scene swam before his eyes, pyramids of shining apples and oranges. Mountains of grapefruit. Celery stalk brigades. Companies of squash. Baskets of onions and potatoes. Sacks of nuts. As they walked slowly up the street they smelled coffee roasting and down steep basement steps they glimpsed storage rooms where sides of beef hung over clean sawdust, and cheeses as big as tractor wheels reposed on ponderous wooden tables.

"You're in the Market, Son," said Ed. "There's no way to pull our truck in here so we'd best set up right where we're parked."

They stood the trees up in a ring around a streetlight, and people, hurrying past, glanced briefly and kept going. The rose and gold of dawn had faded to become the mouse gray of an overcast day. Wind whistled up the street, tipping over their trees and blowing people's coats so that, holding on to their hats and clutching their coats to their bodies, passersby plunged along, hardly turning one way or another.

While Ed anchored his ring of trees to the lamp post, Virgil took out the sign Ruthie had made on a piece of cardboard. It said COUNTRY TREES $1.00 and he stuck it up on the windshield of the truck where people could see it.

City cold rebounded from the hard cement pavement. It was different from country cold that sank deep into the earth, surrendering in icy silence. City cold clamored for admittance, and Virgil began to stamp his feet and pound his hands together. His father had unloaded ten trees and it looked like enough. The wind would take them all if they didn't watch out. The cold came right up the street and reached under his jacket, freezing clear through to his bones.

"Crawl up there in the cab, Virgil," said Ed, "it's warmer."

Just then a woman in a red coat stopped and bought a tree. She took one of the small ones, and Ed tied a piece of twine around it to keep the branches from breaking. She paid the dollar, taking it from a roll of bills, and shouted "Merry Christmas" as she went off down the sidewalk, dragging it behind her.

Ed waved the bill triumphantly and Virgil grinned. Their first tree.

It was past noon when Ed dragged himself into the truck for lunch. Inside, out of the wind, it felt warm to Ed, but Virgil's lips were blue and his hands shook when he pulled off his mittens to unwrap a sandwich.

"Cold, Son?"

Virgil shook his head, but his teeth began to chatter and he bit into his sandwich and chewed as hard as he could to stop the rattling of his teeth and the shivering of his body.

No one had bought a tree in a long time. After the woman in the red coat there had been a man with a gray felt hat and a brown scarf. He wanted to pay fifty cents for one of the small trees, but Ed said, "No, sir, these are fresh cut trees," and the man paid his dollar, muttering as he went off down the street. After that a nurse in a black cape that flapped open showing her white uniform took one and paid for it, saying, "I can smell it." She took a deep breath, her red cheeks puffing out like apples. "I can smell the woods," she said.

After that nobody stopped. People carrying bags and baskets passed back and forth as they went along the street, but nobody stopped. Not even to look.

"You just wait, Son," said Ed, blowing on his hands. "Come the end of the day people will be going home from work and then it won't be ten minutes and all our trees will be gone."

It was almost four and the sky, as much of it as could be seen, was turning black. Snow clouds, like gray feather beds, drifted upward until the mass of them, nudging for space overhead, seemed to seethe with their burden of snow. Small flecks were whirling in the air and drifting over the truck and the trees, and by then Ed knew he'd let any of them go for fifty cents, even the tall ones. Just then a truck pulled up alongside of his and a man in a plaid mackinaw jumped out and pounded on the window beside Ed.

"Yes, sir," said Ed, jumping out, "you want a tree?"

"You got a permit to sell them trees?"

Ed didn't know anything about a permit. He'd parked in a regular parking space and his trees didn't block the street or the sidewalk.

"What permit?" he said.

"A selling permit."

"Where do you get one?"

"Down to the municipal building." The man shook his head. "They close along about now."

"Where's that?" asked Ed. He might still make it. *By God,* he thought, *I can try.* "Which way is it?" he said desperately.

"Don't see how you can make it, late as 'tis," said the man. "Best come back in the morning."

"I can't do that," said Ed. "I'm from out in Havenhill. It's over sixty miles."

"Well now, that's too bad," said the man, shaking his head and running his huge hand over his chin. "I tell you what I could do. I've got a selling permit and I could take them trees off your hands."

"How much?"

"Ten cents a tree. How many you got?"

"Forty-seven," said Ed.

"Four seventy then."

Ed shook his head. "Make it an even five dollars," said the man.

Ed thought—eight dollars, five for him and the three he already had. It wouldn't even pay back his mother-in-law. "I'd rather haul them on back and give them away," he said.

"You'll have a hard time giving them to folks as has trees in their own yard. What say I make that twenty-five cents a tree?"

"Fifty," said Ed.

The man laughed. "You must think them trees is worth something. I like helping folks out, but I can't afford to lose money doing it. What say to thirty-five cents."

Forty-seven trees at thirty-five cents. Ed figured fast and came up with fifteen dollars. That would be clearing eighteen and he had three sixty-five left from what Mrs. Howard put up to begin with. As he hesitated the man said, "I don't know. Maybe you'd just as well clear out before they come along and ask to see your permit, and I can—"

"Sold," said Ed, "thirty-five cents a tree for the lot."

When the trees were loaded, the man peeled a ten and five ones off a thick roll of bills. "Make it an even fifteen," he said, and Ed didn't know until he got home with paper and pencil he'd been cheated.

When Virgil saw what was happening he began to grin and bounced up and down on the seat. He couldn't hear the dickering, or see the money Ed took, and when Ed jerked open the door and crawled in Virgil said, "Gee, Dad, that's all of them. The whole bunch. Are we rich now?"

"No," growled Ed.

Just then a policeman, swinging his stick and walking fast to keep warm, came along the street and Ed rammed his foot on the gas pedal and flooded the engine. *Lord, Lord,* he thought, *get me out of here.*

The officer paused and stood there reading Ruthie's sign, and Ed hissed, "Take that thing down, Son." He rammed his foot down, swearing under his breath, and Virgil tore the sign away just as the officer tapped the window with his stick. He put his face up to the window and called out, "You got any more trees?"

Ed rolled the window down and stuck his head out. "Not a one," he said. "I just hauled a lot in town for a fellow with a permit."

"Permit?" said the policeman. "What kind of permit?"

"A selling permit, like you have for selling on the street."

"Can't say as I know what kind of permit you mean. Anybody can sell anything on this street. You sure you got no more trees?"

Ed nodded. His hands had begun to shake and his heart was pounding in a funny way. He let his foot come down easy on the gas and when Virgil said, "What's wrong?" Ed replied, "Nothing."

It was dark before they were through Cambridge. As they rattled along past rows and rows of lighted houses where people were having supper and sitting near warm radiators, Ed didn't say anything, and by the time they were out in the country he had decided there wasn't much use in letting on how he'd been taken in. Best just to pay Mrs. Howard what he owed her and say he'd had to let them go wholesale.

It was snowing in earnest now. The windshield wipers scraped as they flopped back and forth. The rubber on them had worn through. The road was deserted, except for a few cars in the towns they passed through. Here and there streetlights, twined with evergreen, made glowing circles of light through which snow beat furiously, like the white storms inside snow domes where miniature houses stood firm despite the gales around them. Ed felt as though he were trapped in a small globe with the Almighty shaking his world.

"How much money did we get?" asked Virgil, who wanted skates for Christmas. His need to know whether or not skates were even a remote possibility was stronger than his fear of disappointment, and he repeated, "How much?"

"Not much."

"But you sold them all."

"I did," said Ed, wondering what he ought to tell Virgil. It made a man feel small to be a fool in his son's eyes, but Virgil had frozen through the long day right alongside of him and he said in a rough voice, "I got cheated, Virgil. I don't know as I was a fool exactly, unless you're a fool to think most men are honest, but the truth is I believed a liar and it's the same as though we lost all the trees or gave them away."

"How'd it happen?" said Virgil, his voice thin as his teeth began to chatter again.

When Ed had finished he wondered if maybe he'd done a good thing. He reached out and pulled Virgil up against him, holding him tightly to stop the shaking. Virgil would never be taken in the same way, he thought, and if some good came of all this that would be something.

"Now don't tell the others," Ed said. "I'll tell your mother. We don't keep secrets between us, but no use to let the others know."

"All right, Dad," said Virgil.

40

They drove along, the windshield wipers flopping, and when they saw a lighted gas station Ed swung off the road and put on his chains. It took him twenty minutes. He didn't need gas, but he bought a gallon anyway, since he'd parked under the station lights.

"How far you going?"

"Havenhill."

"You won't get there on one gallon of gas," said the owner.

"I wasn't down to empty," said Ed.

"That'll be twenty cents."

Ed counted out two dimes. "Roads about like this?" he asked.

"Far as I know."

Virgil tugged at the ragged buffalo robe, wrapping it around his legs and pulling it up toward his chin. It didn't help much. The seat felt like cold stone under him and he wanted to get home. "How much longer?" he asked.

"Another hour," said Ed. "Close your eyes and go to sleep."

Snow had begun to pile up on the windshield, and every few miles Ed pulled up and got out and pushed the piled-up snow off the hood of the truck. He should have holed up back there at the filling station, he thought. Every time he stopped it was hard to get going again, and more and more he tried to put off stopping even though he could hardly see out the front. As he drove along, his face almost pressed to the glass in front of him, he saw something up ahead that looked like a black wall. A circle of light, like a railroad signal, moving up and down in the blackness and he thought *Oh my God. We're off the road and the train's coming.* He rammed the brake pedal and grabbed at Virgil, jerking open the door and pulling him across the seat and into the snow.

In the silence, broken only by the soft sighing of the wind, he saw that they were nowhere near a train, and shading his eyes he stumbled forward, coming up to a stalled car with its hood

41

up. A man with a flashlight was playing its beams over the motor.

Wading through the snow Ed called out, "You in trouble?" and he and Virgil, with snow blowing furiously in their faces, approached until they were close enough to see a black limousine as long as a hearse, over which a man in a black coat stood helplessly.

"You need help?" shouted Ed, and the back window of the car went down and a man's voice barked out, "Who's there, Jake?"

The man called Jake turned his light on Ed and Virgil and shouted, "Just two fellows, Mr. Bruce."

By then Mr. Bruce could see that one of the fellows was Virgil, who posed no threat, and he sang out, "Think you can help?"

"I can try," said Ed.

"Let the boy get in here with me."

Virgil ducked in beside Mr. Bruce, where it felt to him as warm as a steam-heated bathroom. His teeth chattered uncontrollably and Mr. Bruce pulled a car robe around him.

"Your dad good with engines, Sonny?"

"Yes," said Virgil.

"Well, sir, I hope he is."

Inside the car the howling wind sank to a soft moan and the thumps and scrapings from the front, where Ed, his fingers stiff with cold, worked under the light from Jake's flashlight, sounded like squirrels scuffling in an attic.

"What brings you out on a night like this?" asked Mr. Bruce, pouring liquid into a tumbler. Virgil could hear it go gurgle, gurgle. "A swallow of this wouldn't hurt you, Son. Warm your bones," said Mr. Bruce, but Virgil declined.

"So," said his host after a bit, "you and your father made a pilgrimage into the big city to sell Christmas trees. And how, might I ask, did you make out?"

"Not so good," said Virgil and he forgot that Ed had said they wouldn't tell about it. Mr. Bruce was faceless in the dark. It was no more than talking it over with himself, and Virgil's chattering teeth accompanied the story like castanets marking time in a wild dance of defeat.

By the time he'd finished Jake was back in the car trying to start the motor. It coughed and choked and finally roared and kept going. He slid back a glass window that separated the front seat from the back and said, "Ready to roll, Mr. Bruce."

Mr. Bruce opened the door to let Virgil out and he called to Ed, "What do I owe you?"

"Not a thing," said Ed. "It's Christmas."

"Well, then, let me give the boy a couple of bills for something he could use," and while he fumbled with his wallet Virgil thought, *Two dollars. Two whole dollars.*

"No need for that," said Ed, but Mr. Bruce pushed two bills into Virgil's frozen hand and said to Ed, "Better take my card and a little token of appreciation," and he thrust a bottle through the open window and would have dropped it in the snow if Ed hadn't grabbed it.

"If you ever need a friend just give me a call. It's all there on the card," and then he rolled up the window, and Ed and Virgil went back to the truck. Ed put the card in his shirt pocket, and Virgil pulled off his mitten and closed his fist around the two dollars and pulled his mitten back on, and then Ed said a prayer and turned on the ignition. The truck started right up.

For the most part Ed couldn't tell if they were on the road or not, and although he wasn't a poetic man it did occur to him that there was more than one way to get off the road. It wasn't his fault he'd been laid off any more than it was his fault there was a Depression, but as he drove along with the wind howling and snow blowing he began to see that he was indeed a fool. Not for believing a scoundrel, life was full of scoundrels, but because he had had a choice when it came to the trees and the truck and the trip, and he'd made the wrong choice the way a man can make the wrong turn.

He could feel the bottle lying between him and Virgil on the seat and it reassured him. He knew it was whisky. A man in a car like that, with a driver, wouldn't hand out bottles of soda pop. If they got stuck they wouldn't freeze to death with that on board, but if he knew Dorothy and her mother, and he did, he knew they wouldn't want it in the house, whether it saved him and Virgil or not. He'd stow it in the barn when they got in, if they got in, and then suddenly he saw that they were coming into Mumfert and he knew it wouldn't be much longer.

Dorothy saw the lights in the lane and rushed out onto the porch, hugging her sweater to her and shading her eyes as she tried to see if it was really them. She'd been frantic since dark, and now, at nine o'clock, was almost sobbing with relief. She saw the truck roll under the shed roof, and in a minute there they were, dragging their cold, stiff, aching bodies across the yard to the back porch and into the back entry and finally through to the warmth of the kitchen where Dorothy, half crying in relief, began to tug at their jackets and mittens.

It was then that Virgil pulled his clenched fist out of his mitten and saw the bills Mr. Bruce had given him. Two twenties. He stared at them and rubbed them together and wanted to scream out his surprise, but on second thought he knew that wasn't the thing to do, so he held them out to Ed and said loudly, "Here's the money, Daddy."

When Virgil saw his father's stupefied face at the sight of the two twenty-dollar bills, his latent maturity stirred. A man's need to succeed as chief and provider was so clearly pictured in his father's dazed expression that Virgil almost grasped the vulnerability of the estate he aspired to. He had the wits to say, "It's the tree money, Dad. The tree money."

Mrs. Howard had a Christmas ritual that dated from her own childhood and she observed it faithfully. This year, with the family at home, more joy accompanied her preparations than usual. Of course since Vera had been with her, over twelve years now, she had had the satisfaction of imposing her tradition on a willing subject, for Vera grasped at any straw that might give shape and substance to the barren existence she led, but Vera was not the same as family, even though they were related.

So it was that on December fifteenth Ruby was set to work

putting suet through the food chopper while Vera cut up figs and measured raisins and spices, and that dark, fragrant, heavy substance called by Mrs. Howard "my steamed pudding to be served with hard sauce" was begun.

At the same time mincemeat simmered on the stove and the Christmas baking began. Much of this was usually distributed by Mr. Godwin to shut-ins, among whom was Dr. Adams, a frail and ancient man who had once been headmaster of Willowbrook Academy, a school for the sons of the wealthy and, paradoxically, the offspring of missionaries. Dr. Adams lived in a small stone house in the center of Havenhill with his equally ancient housekeeper, a Mrs. Gibbs, who accepted the mince pie that was his particular favorite with cries of delight and her annual comment, "Bless me, now I know it's Christmas." They looked for Mrs. Howard's pie with the anticipation of children.

This year, as apples in thick juicy slices met with cinnamon and cloves, and flour sifters rained white over great yellow crockery mixing bowls, and raisins, figs, dates, prunes, dried apricots and candied peel were dispensed generously, Mrs. Howard tapped into the kitchen and said, "Well now, this year Ruth and Virgil can do the delivering."

Christmas extended beyond the kitchen and in the front of the house Mrs. Howard set out the nativity scene, a set of carved wooden figures that her father had brought from Germany in 1870 when she was a little girl. She unwrapped each piece, setting it in precisely the same spot on the mantel where, lighted by a green candle in a brass candlestick, the holy family had received both king and shepherd the year before.

Into the room came Mr. Godwin with a bushel basket of running cedar and partridge berries. Mrs. Howard trailed a runner of greenery across the back of the mantel and another around the newel post in the front hall. Then she packed red partridge berries into glass globes with glass lids and placed them here and there on tabletops in the parlor and sitting room. Since Mr. Howard's death she had rarely had a tree, but this year, because of Ruthie and Virgil, she instructed Ed to fetch one in and set it up in the large bay window in the sitting room and then she gave him five dollars and said, "Now, Edward, you go in town and buy some lights and while you're at it buy whatever ornaments you can with the change."

When the day before Christmas arrived, the house was clean and the baking done. In the pantry the turkey was dressed and the stuffing ready. Cranberry jelly and cranberry sauce had been made and were cooling in the crystal bowls from which they would be served. Mr. Godwin brought the vegetables up from the root cellar—squash and turnip and onions—and then went off in the Packard to buy oysters for supper.

The tree was trimmed and school was out. Ruthie and Virgil grew increasingly excited and raced through the house, up and down stairs, disappearing into their rooms and banging the doors because they were working on presents for the family that no one was supposed to see.

Mrs. Howard said tartly whenever they flew past her, "Softly, children, softly," but it didn't do much good and she didn't press because the truth was she liked the hustle and festivity herself.

Granny Beane, in her room with her Bible, lamented bitterly and privately that she had nothing to contribute to anyone's Christmas. At home, home being her own room in the Holyoke house, she had always managed to do something, but it had been such a hectic fall she hadn't finished any of the knitting she'd started, and she hadn't any money for presents because for five months now she hadn't had a pension check. She'd had three notices of pension due, to become available to her when the denomination was able to meet its obligations to ministers' widows, but, "in these hard times" the hoped-for redemption date was not specified. She didn't envy Dorothy's mother or begrudge her the pleasure she assumed Mrs. Howard felt in the exercise of her munificence, but it was hard to feel beholden. In Ed's house she had always read the Christmas story from St. Luke on Christmas Eve. She assumed she would not do so at Havenhill, and she sat, wrapped in her shawl, rocking, while all kinds of gaiety spilled through the house around her.

That morning, December twenty-fourth, Virgil and Ruthie bundled up and loaded an old sled (the kind of sled that had rails around it for holding in a small child or a load of wood) with boxes of Christmas things. Mrs. Howard's marmalade, made by Ruby after Mrs. Howard took scissors and cut all the peel into slivers, in pint jars, tied with red ribbon and sprigs of greenery, was lined up in a square basket and surrounded by cardboard boxes of cookies. Last of all, in a box of its own, was Dr. Adams's mince pie.

Virgil and Ruthie took their grandmother's list and started out. The sun shone brilliantly, turning the snowy fields to dazzling white. Their breath rose like smoke as they went up the lane to the road. Snowplows had pushed up drifts as tall as waves, and from the kitchen window where she stood Dorothy could see the pompoms on Virgil's blue cap and Ruthie's red one bobbing along over the tops of the drifts until the children finally disappeared as the road turned down Webster's Hill.

Dorothy gazed briefly and sadly out the window, although she had nothing much to feel sad about. Ed was unloading wood from the truck, carrying it into the barn, where he planned to rebuild the box stalls. It had been forty years since there'd been a herd at Havenhill, but Ed had to do something, she supposed, wishing he could find a job somewhere.

Beyond the barn the orchard stretched to a wood lot. Apple trees draped in snow were mounds of white from which gnarled branches waved and beckoned; they stood in white ranks, small round ghosts with knotted arms lifted capriciously in the morning sun. Come dusk they would march menacingly toward the house.

The forest along the distant property line stood in solemn silence. Tall pines, clustered oak and ash, evergreen and deciduous shoulder to shoulder, solid brown and varied green above the snow. To the other side, the south pasture lay like a vast white pond, the underbrush almost obscured by the snow, and across this sheet of white at the forest's edge Dorothy had always imagined the passage of Good King Wenceslas and his page. When, in the late afternoon, shadows began to streak the

47

snow, she could see the mighty monarch and brave page, flushed with exertion and good will, rosy cheeked and breathless, as they plunged on their errand of mercy. She sighed. It had always been one of her favorite carols.

Behind her in the kitchen Ruby muttered. Ruby was fixing vegetables for Christmas dinner. Ruby was also fixing lunch and Christmas Eve supper, doing all she could in order to have Christmas day at home with Jack. As she fussed—the squash was pithy, the onions made her cry, where was Homer and why hadn't he filled her kerosene stove—she worked rapidly, and when Vera came in from the pantry with butter in a wood bowl (Vera was making hard sauce) humming "Jolly Old St. Nicholas," Ruby snorted, "That's an old one." Her voice belied the scorn of her words and she began to chant in a toneless voice, "Johnny wants a pair of skates, sister wants a dolly . . . ."

Skates! thought Dorothy, had Ed been able to get Virgil's skates and Ruthie's muff? What was he doing hauling wood on the day before Christmas? She went to the back door and waved her apron and called, "Ed," then dancing across the yard in the cold she said crossly, "why are you doing that, Ed? I thought you were going in town."

"I did," he said, "I did, Dorothy. I've got it all out here on the truck. Soon as they're gone, I'll—"

"They left fifteen minutes ago."

Vera had done Mrs. Howard's shopping and now the old lady struggled with ribbon and paper spread out on a table in her bedroom. As she surveyed her gifts she thought that Vera was truly a good girl, not her beloved Dorothy, but a sweet, quiet, helpful girl. She had told Vera to buy Ed gloves and they cost more than she'd expected, but they were fur lined and Ed's hands were his tools. He needed gloves. For Dorothy there was a white silk shirtwaist with a ruffled collar. The blouse was extravagant and would be becoming. Dorothy needed the softness; her face rarely lost its anxious expression. Who was Tarzan, she thought as she picked up Virgil's book, and who was Nancy Drew? She supposed the children would know. It had been a long time since there had been a tree with presents under it in this house and she worked with a little smile that would have surprised her if she had happened to glance in the mirror.

Virgil and Ruthie tried to follow their grandmother's directions exactly, and managed to deliver jars of marmalade and boxes of cookies to some of the right people if not all. As doors closed after they had presented unexpected remembrances to some of Mrs. Howard's neighbors, there were surprised glances. "Mercy," said one amazed lady, "Alice Howard, well, well," and turning to her daughter remarked, "Alice Howard hasn't spoken to me in five years. What do you make of this!"

The last delivery was to Dr. Adams. Since his house was next to the post office it was easy to spot and they went confidently up the steps, lifted the brass knocker and pounded on the solid oak door. After a minute the door opened a crack and Mrs. Gibbs, a round, gray little mole of a woman, peeked out. When she saw the children and the pie plate wrapped in waxed paper and tied with a red ribbon, she knew these must be Dorothy's children, and she opened the door wide despite the blast of cold air it admitted, threw up her small paws and said, "Oh my, oh my, won't Dr. Adams be pleased. Come in, come in."

Ruthie and Virgil looked at each other doubtfully. It was late, almost noon, and time to go home, but Mrs. Gibbs waved her apron at them as though she were shooing chickens across a yard and they allowed themselves to be driven down the hall to a closed door at the back.

"Just look, Dr. Adams," she cried, "it's Dorothy Howard's children with your pie."

Dr. Adams struggled up from the fat arms of his chair, took off his glasses, rubbed his eyes, squinted, saw the pie and the children and said, "So it is. So it is. And how is your sweet mother?"

"Fine, thank you," said Ruthie.

"Well, well," he said, "come over here by the fire. Take off your things. Mrs. Gibbs will make us some hot cocoa."

"We have to go," said Ruthie.

"Car's waiting?" he asked.

"We walked," said Virgil.

"Good, good," said Dr. Adams, "walking's the thing. Keeps you fit. I used to walk as far as your grandmother's myself. My, my, I remember the oyster suppers Mrs. Howard used to serve—before your grandfather died."

"We're having oysters tonight," said Ruthie.

"Oh my," said Dr. Adams, "you don't say. It makes my mouth water just to think of it."

"You can have mine," said Virgil. "I'd give you all of mine. I hate oysters."

"Ha!" said Dr. Adams. "I dare say your grandmother wouldn't approve of that."

"Yes she would," said Virgil.

There was a brief awkward silence as they considered Virgil's firm assertion that his grandmother would not object to his passing along his oysters to Dr. Adams, and Ruthie, who was infected with the spirit of the season, suddenly saw herself, like Jo in *Little Women* as she contemplated giving away their Christmas breakfast, as divinely appointed to extend largess.

"Oh," she said brightly, "but she would be so glad to have you come for supper. Both of you. After all, it's Christmas Eve."

"No, no, no, my dear," he said, patting her arm. "How could we get out in all this snow?"

"My dad could drive you in the Packard," said Virgil.

"You must come," cried Ruthie, who saw excitement rising in the fluttering Mrs. Gibbs and the hesitant Dr. Adams. "We would all be so pleased."

When they escaped from the stone house they began to run, the sled thumping along behind them. At the crossroads they cut over the fields, racing on hard crust to Webster's Hill and going along the fenced pastures of Berry Bay Farm. When they could see the house and the barn and a dark figure that was Ruby going along the back porch to the shed with the kerosene bottle, they stopped running.

"You'll get it now," said Virgil. "Grandmother's going to skin you."

"Why shouldn't they come to supper—it's Christmas Eve."

"Wait and see."

"You said they could have your oysters, Virgil Beane. You started it."

"You asked. Not me."

Ruby put a platter of red flannel hash on the table and another of sliced corned beef. "Past noon already," she muttered, "I'll never get done," and she plunked Homer's plate down on the kitchen table.

In the dining room Mrs. Howard gave thanks and began to serve the hash. "It's beets and potatoes, Virgil," she said. "Stop mumbling and sit up. Three bites, at least."

What a terrible day, thought Virgil, *beet hash and oysters.* He made a face at Ruthie and mouthed the word *oysters.*

"We delivered everything," said Ruthie in a high nervous voice.

"Thank you very much," said Grandmother Howard.

"You're good children," said Granny Beane possessively, implying that she had had a share in this spreading of Christmas cheer.

"Well," said Ed, "tonight's the big night." Ed's encounter with Mr. Bruce had buoyed his sagging spirits and he ate with an appetite. His work in the barn made him hungry.

"I love Christmas Eve," said Dorothy, "we used to go caroling. Up and down the river road. I remember one year we went to Dr. Adams and woke him up. It was the year Richard . . ." She stopped because whenever she mentioned Richard Currie, Ed got quiet and she never liked saying that Richard was just a friend and had meant nothing to her, because it wasn't true. All the same she appreciated Ed's understanding. Even if Richard had lived she would still have married Ed. She paused and said, "We can have our carol singing right here."

"I hope you like oysters, Mrs. Beane," said Grandmother Howard. "In this house we always have oysters for Christmas Eve."

Before Granny Beane could say that ordinarily she liked them if they were sufficiently cooked, Ruth broke in and said, "Oh, Grandmother, when Dr. Adams heard we were having oysters and Virgil said he could have his, he was so excited and so I said Daddy could drive the car and he and Mrs. Gibbs are coming for supper."

She finished in a rush and then began to butter a slice of bread with such care she might have been frosting her own wedding cake.

"Ruthie dear," said Dorothy, "are you telling us you invited Dr. Adams and Mrs. Gibbs for supper tonight?"

"Well," said Ruth defiantly, "it's Christmas Eve. I thought you were supposed to do things like that at Christmas."

"Of course you are, dear," soothed Granny Beane. Her tone seemed to suggest that if this were her table Ruth could invite the whole town if she wanted to.

Vera suddenly thought of the teapot and got up quickly, saying, "Excuse me, I'll just get our tea."

Ed put down his fork. *Oh God,* he thought, *a man ought to have his own home.* Actually, had they been at home in Holyoke he might have said, "Don't you ever do that again without asking your mother first," but they weren't in Holyoke, they were at his mother-in-law's table, and Mrs. Howard's face was flat as stone and as unreadable.

"Well," she said finally, "if Ruth has invited guests for dinner, she'll have to be responsible for them. As for me, I have always enjoyed Dr. Adams and since it is Christmas, I think Mrs. Gibbs should have been included."

Dorothy reached over and squeezed Ruthie's hand and smiled, and Ruthie swallowed the bite of bread she'd taken a year ago. Virgil muttered, "Well, I meant it. They can eat mine." And Vera poured tea.

That evening the dining room was lighted with candles. In the center of the table polished apples gleamed in a large silver bowl and in the wavering streaks of yellow light produced by the candles on the sideboard nine shadows bobbed against the dark walls.

Grandmother Howard glanced soberly around the table and as she said, "Shall we bow our heads," Dr. Adams lifted his hands to grasp the hands of Ruthie and Virgil, who occupied the chairs on either side of him. He remembered the days at Willowbrook when some boys had tried to crush the hands of their neighbors in this ritual, and smiled. It was surprising how often his old boys mentioned it in their letters, recalling it nostalgically as a good influence on their lives.

As Virgil's hand was taken by Dr. Adams he reached automatically for Vera's, and so it went around the table, a chain of fellowship and good will that brought a lump to Granny's tight throat. In a silence that seemed blessed, Mrs. Howard's voice rose warmly to include "friends and family gathered here on this sacred night."

In the kitchen Dorothy ladled Virgil's stew carefully and when she set it down in front of him she whispered, "There aren't any in yours, Virgil," so he put in a handful of oyster crackers and ate it all.

Following the stew came the scallops, and when Dorothy appeared with the plates, Mrs. Howard said, "Put them in front of Edward, Dorothy, if he would be good enough to serve."

Ed looked up in surprise, but he said "certainly" and he lifted the serving spoon as though it were a daily occurrence. He served Virgil last when it was possible to avoid the oysters and the meal progressed without event to fruit and cheese and culminated with the glorious steamed pudding, mahogany colored, bursting with fruit, redolent with spice and topped with hard sauce.

The appearance of Christmas pudding, a proper one flamed with cooking brandy, reminded Dr. Adams of other Christmases. He took off his glasses and wiped his eyes with his handkerchief, as if to do so would clarify those visions of remembered joy, and Granny Beane, who was moved by his stories of past pleasures, said, "There's a great deal of kindness in the world."

With these words she meant to thank Mrs. Howard for her generosity to them all. It had pleased her when Ed was asked to serve, and she said, looking pointedly at Dorothy's mother, "We have so much to be thankful for this Christmas."

This was as close as Granny Beane could come to expressing herself, and Mrs. Howard, who was not insensible to her meaning, said generously, "Dorothy tells me you always read aloud on Christmas Eve, Mrs. Beane. Won't you read for us now?" Rising from the table she led them out of the dining room and into the parlor, where they all sat down in a circle around Granny, who opened the large Howard Bible to the familiar passage and began to read.

As she read a feeling of peace crept slowly around the room, seeking and finding the hard core of self-pity and anxiety that lurked within each of them. Even her own voice seemed to change, to modulate from minor to major, to lose its bitter tone. Granny Beane read more and more slowly until in the silent room there actually seemed to appear the glory of the Lord, shining all about them.

When she finished and closed the Bible, Mrs. Howard, who found herself strangely moved, said, "And now, Dorothy, please play for us. I would like to hear some of the carols we used to sing."

Dorothy wanted to protest, she hadn't played the piano in a long time, they didn't have a piano in Holyoke. *It's been years,* she thought, but even as she thought it she felt drawn to the piano as the past and present fused curiously and a young, hopeful Dorothy took the hand of the troubled and discouraged Dorothy, leading her to the piano stool and guiding her cold fingers along to the hymnal and then, with a small triumphant crash of chords, she began. Hark the Herald Angels Sing. Everyone sang. Like moths drawn to flame Virgil and Ruthie sidled up to her, she felt Ed's hand on her shoulder, and as she plunged on she could hear the cracked uncertain voices of the old women, a sweet thread of sound that was Vera and a reedy undertone that came from the chair where Dr. Adams sat. Then she thought gratefully that in spite of everything it was going to be one of the best Christmases ever.

In January Virgil and Ruthie went back to school. Miss Norris had arrived early and taken down the stars and snowflakes the children had pasted on the windows, and she disposed of the Christmas greenery they had twined up the flagpole and over the top of her desk. Then she took a piece of chalk and wrote in large round letters on the blackboard—*January 8, 1936.*

For Miss Norris the date—1936—was terribly significant because over the holidays she had become engaged. She was very happy. Of course she didn't know when she and Harold could be married because he was earning only eighteen dollars a week and that wasn't enough for them to live on unless they moved in with his mother in Greenriver. If she went on teaching it would be different and she had said to Harold "Why not?" as they walked hand in hand down the dark street to her parents' home. They had been to see a movie in which Joan Crawford and Clark Gable were lovers. It had made Miss Norris feel hot and cold, just the way Clark Gable looked at Joan Crawford was almost too much for her, and she said urgently to Harold, "I can go on teaching, Harold, until you get a raise. We could be married at Easter and I could finish out the year in Havenhill and then try to get a school nearer Greenriver for next year."

"My wife is not going to work," Harold said flatly.

They were passing under a streetlight and he stopped and confronted her. In the ring of light they could see each other's faces and in her imagination they became Clark and Joan standing center stage under a pale spotlight. Harold's voice even took on profundity as he said, "When we get married, Grace, I'll be able to support you and we will have a place of our own."

"Yes, Harold," she replied meekly.

Now, with the sun brilliant on the snow outside and the sounds of stamping and scuffling in the entry as twenty-four boys and girls pulled off coats and overshoes, she thought sadly that it might be 1937 before Harold got a raise because times were hard despite what Mr. Roosevelt said. Harold worked as a bookkeeper in a lumber yard—what was Mr. Roosevelt going to do for him?

She turned, smiled brightly and said, "Good morning, children." Glancing around she saw that most of the seats were taken. Some of the Martins had chicken pox and she supposed Mary Finley was sick again. Striking her ruler sharply on her desk she said, "Please stand for our salute to the flag."

Following this she took a harmonica from the top drawer of her desk and with a quick nod began to play "America." As the children sang, it occurred to her that she liked teaching, and by the time they finished, trailing off with "Of Thee I sing," she was wondering what was wrong with working. Why shouldn't a wife work?

All of this went through her mind as she sat down, waiting for the scuffling to stop and then bowed her head as they recited the Lord's Prayer. It was a good way to start the day, she decided. She could almost feel them settling down as they gave up to the inevitability of arithmetic and history.

Miss Norris wrote assignments on the blackboard for the upper grades and then she turned her attention to the little ones, who were drawing snow men with tall black hats and carrot noses. The wood stove kept the room warm, almost too warm, but every now and then she made them all stand up and breathe deeply ten times and that helped. The heat made her sleepy too and she jumped groggily from the Continental Congress to the multiplication tables. If it weren't so cold she'd send them out early for recess. The truth was she was the one who needed recess. Her mind kept going in circles as she thought about Harold. The more she went over it, the more unreasonable it seemed for him to say his wife wasn't going to work. Why shouldn't she work, at least until they had a family, and she hoped that wouldn't be right away.

At three o'clock when school let out, Virgil raced for the pond in the meadow at the bottom of Webster's Hill. Every day since Christmas he'd taken his skates to school to save time. John Currie from Berry Bay, who went to boarding school and had long vacations, was usually there by the time Virgil appeared. Ruth went slowly along the edge of the road, hoping for a glimpse of John and if she saw him she would wade through the snow and stand at the edge of the pond watching them. This irritated Virgil, who skated in circles, swatting at John's hockey puck with a bent stick, and eventually Ruth went along home for her sled and crossed the fields to the Madderns (she and Shirley Maddern were now best friends) to slide on Great Hill. Ruthie had told Shirley all about Mary Catherine, and showed her the cross and said she would never forget Mary Catherine, and Shirley understood.

In the clear air the sound of their voices rang with the purity of church bells all the way down to the river and off to the blue and lavender hills beyond. As he skimmed around the pond it seemed to Virgil that his skates had wings and that he was actually flying over the ice. His blood pounded through his body and the wind whistled in his ears.

Ruthie, belly flopped on her sled, heard the hissing sound of runners cutting crust and felt light and bodiless as she swooped down the hill and sailed across the meadow below. In that pristine world they were like negatives receiving the print of a memory they would later call ''Winter in Havenhill.'' In this memory icicles flashed, bare branches hung gray webs against the bright blue of the sky, life was beautiful and nothing ever changed.

In their grandmother's house the long cold days of winter began before dawn when Mr. Godwin shoveled coal into the furnace and Vera stumbled into the dark kitchen to start the coffee. For Virgil's sake they now ate Ralston every other day instead of the usual oatmeal. He had three more box tops and he sat at the breakfast table every morning describing the premiums he was considering to anyone who would listen.

Dorothy would be glad when spring came, but sometimes it seemed to her that it never would. If Ed was ever going to find a job he'd find it in the spring, not in the dead of winter, and while things were working out better than she had thought they might, it wasn't like having their own home. In many ways it seemed to her that her real life had stopped. The time passed, one day like another, with a monotonous procession of chores and events until she almost forgot she was married with a family of her own.

In her mother's house the years peeled back and she was a girl again, with nothing changed except perhaps her mother, who had mellowed in many ways. Sometimes Dorothy wished they might have the kind of row she could remember and that she could pound up the back stairs and slam her bedroom door. But what would it prove or how would it help?

What had become of the reality of Holyoke, where she had been in control? In that house no meal was cooked unless she cooked it, no clothes washed, no mending done. Here, in her mother's house, life would continue without interruption whether she lived or died. If she fell down the cellar steps and broke her neck today, the children would go off to school to-morrow carrying lunches Vera packed. Ruby would scrub po-tatoes at the kitchen sink as though nothing had happened. Her mother would pay the bills. Granny would darn stockings and read the Bible. Ed would spend his days in the barn building stanchions for nonexistent cows. Mr. Godwin would carry out the ashes and shovel the paths. Now and then someone might say, "Poor Dorothy," and, for a while, she would be missed. Then life would go on. The Holyoke house would be forgotten. Everything there would become a fading memory and here, in her mother's house, life would go on unchanged.

Every afternoon at precisely three-thirty she and Vera set the tea wagon and rolled it into the sitting room where the two grand-mothers, now in afternoon dresses, sat waiting. Once in a while someone from the frozen world outside stopped to visit, causing

58

a stir of excitement in the midst of their isolation, but generally the four of them sat alone, speaking occasionally about people who had died or remarking on the latest drop in temperature.

Then one day late in January, Mable Cooper came stamping up onto the porch carrying a brown leatherette case and wearing a green wool coat with a thin fox fur slung over her sloping shoulders. As she unbuckled her overshoes she panted, and then, straightening up majestically, she unfastened her fur and hung it over the newel post. It had been handsome once, but now even its glassy eyes were dull. To fasten it around her neck, Mable would pinch the fox's pointed nose and jaws like a clothespin, and it occurred to Dorothy to give thanks that Virgil and Ruth were skating. They would have wanted to snap it open and shut until they had worn the yellow teeth to nubbins, something Mable would surely have objected to even if it did spoil her chance of selling a magazine subscription, which was the object of her visit.

"You're just in time for tea," said Dorothy.

"That's good," said Mable, taking up her case and stepping into the parlor where it was warm. "My, don't that fire feel good," she said.

"Lemon or milk, Mable," asked Mrs. Howard, although she remembered from past visits exactly what Mable preferred.

"Milk," said Mable, "and two sugars. I'm about froze."

"The winters get colder," said Granny dolefully. "Every year it's worse."

"I've got a cure of that," said Mable, snapping open her case to take out a copy of the *Country Gentleman*. The cover showed an orchard in full bloom. "There," said Mable triumphantly, "look at those apple trees. Don't that make you feel warm, Mrs. Beane?"

"Where?" said Granny. "I can't see that far. What's that you're holding up?"

"We don't need the *Country Gentleman*," said Mrs. Howard.

"Well then, how about the *Farm Journal?* It's only a dollar twenty-five a year."

A dollar twenty-five, thought Dorothy. Suppose she got it for Ed. Would that be a good thing or a bad thing? He spent enough time as it was in the barn and what was the use in encouraging him to think about farming? Even so . . .

Mrs. Howard handed Mable her cup and said, "We get the *Boston Herald* and the *Atlantic* and the *Saturday Evening Post.* That's enough."

"Well, if you change your mind," said Mable, helping herself to a piece of fruit cake, "you can let me know anytime. I guess you know Grace Norris is engaged," she said.

"Poor girl," said Granny, "she'll learn fast enough that running a school is no shakes to running a house."

"Who is she marrying?" asked Dorothy.

"Her old sweetheart, and I hear," said Mable, "they're planning to be married at Easter and move in with his mother. I don't know as that sounds so good."

There was an awkward moment of silence and then Dorothy laughed and said, "Well, that's not the worst thing in the world that can happen to somebody."

"Not everybody's like you and your mother, Dorothy," said Mable. "Feelings can run real hard sometimes. I'm glad to see you folks getting on so well. You'd be surprised what I see some places I go, particularly in weather like this. Winter don't bring out the best in a person."

"Let me replenish your cup, Mable," said Mrs. Howard, who found personal remarks and gossip distasteful. She had no desire to see into the lives of her neighbors and certainly nobody was welcome even to speculate about hers.

Quite to the contrary, personal observations stimulated Granny and she said, "Mr. Beane always used to say February and March were the devil's months. Sickness. Children cooped up for one reason or another. Tempers sharp. Winter gets longer every year."

"Well," said Mable, "I'd best be on my way. That sky looks black to me. I'd say we were in for more snow."

She buckled her galoshes, put on her coat and hat, arranged

her fur and sailed out into the cold world, marching resolutely on to her next stop where, she hoped, people wouldn't be as stiff backed as Mrs. Howard and might be tempted by the sight of apple blossoms on the cover of the *Country Gentleman.*

The snow held off for a day or two and then one morning when Dorothy came down to the kitchen she saw white ash in the air.

"Snow," she said in disgust, "you'd think we'd had enough for a while."

She poured herself a cup of coffee and sat down wearily. Virgil had kept her up half the night with his ear. In another minute she'd have to pack Ruthie's lunch, but she was only making one lunch today because Virgil wasn't going to school.

"Virgil always has earaches," Ruth said. "It isn't fair."

"Be thankful it's not you," said her mother.

Glancing out the window, Dorothy saw Ruby crossing the barnyard, hurrying along in unbuckled arctics that flapped like wings around her ankles. Wearing Jack's plaid mackinaw that hung below her hips, she looked as though she'd wrapped herself up in an old horse blanket. Her head was covered with a brown scarf, looped twice around her neck.

"My stars," she gasped, coming into the kitchen, "I thought we'd finished with snow."

"Won't stick," said Homer, settling down at the table. It didn't matter to him that Ruby was late. Waiting for meals was something Mr. Godwin did with infinite patience.

By the time Dorothy fixed Virgil's tray the snow was thickening, almost like cheese coming to curd, she thought, as she spooned cereal out of the double boiler and poured cocoa into his Tom Mix mug.

"There," she said, setting it down on his bed stand and plumping up his pillows. "How's that? Want to give it a try?"

61

"OK," said Virgil, pushing himself up on his elbows and surveying the food on his tray. He picked up a piece of toast and bit into it, winced and set it down.

"Try the cereal, it's soft," said his mother. "It's Ralston."

"I don't like Ralston," said Virgil.

"I thought you loved Ralston. Why do we eat Ralston all the time if you don't like it?"

"I want the tops."

"Well, eat it anyway."

Virgil ate his cereal and looked at his cocoa.

"It's got skin on it," he said.

"That's not skin," said Dorothy, "it's just a little skim. It always gets like that when it cools. Drink it, Virgil. It's good for you."

He drank half of it. "It hurts to swallow," he said.

"TRY," said Dorothy. "I'm going to make the beds. I'll be back in a minute."

She went down the hall humming. If he could complain, he was better. She pulled the bottom sheet of their bed straight and tucked it tightly. Ed was so restless. She tried to remember how he slept in Holyoke, but it was different there. He was tired, he'd worked all day. All he did here was prowl around in the barn and talk about his ideas for repairing it. She didn't call driving into Mumfert and going to garages looking for work, "work." A man is easily discouraged, she thought. Perhaps in the spring it would be different.

Virgil heard his mother walk down the hall and call out to Granny, "Want me to make your bed?" and then, faintly, his grandmother's indignant voice announced that her bed had been made since six.

He looked out the window. He could see way down the lane, an unbroken expanse of white, and then suddenly a dark mound in the distance became a dark figure moving slowly through a swirling curtain of white. It was Mr. Godwin, gone to the mailbox probably. There sure is a lot of snow, Virgil thought. He'd never seen so much snow. Fields and hills of snow, and not another house for as far as he could see.

Dorothy put Virgil's dishes in the sink. Glancing out she could see that the snow was coming down faster, making with fury. She could hardly see the barn. The drive had disappeared. The stone wall along the lane was now only the soft curl of a wave. Snow collected on the black bark of trees as though it had been painted there and suddenly she thought of Ruthie. How would Ruthie get home, she wondered, and where was Ed? Dropping the dish towel, she ran through the back entry and across to the barn, dancing along in the snow and oblivious to the cold.

She found Ed laying plank to reinforce the barn floor and she called out, "Ed! What about Ruthie? She's at school, how can she get home in this?"

He looked up, noticing for the first time that the snow was making fast, and he shouted, "Get back inside, Dorothy. I'll go with the truck."

In five minutes the truck was down the lane and out of sight. Dorothy watched until it disappeared and then she went back upstairs to Virgil's room. If he hadn't had an earache he'd be at school too, she thought, and then she would have to worry about all of them.

There had been storms in Holyoke and she could remember standing at the kitchen windows watching and wondering where the children were. But in Holyoke there were streetlights and lights in all the houses, which stood like dominoes up and down the streets. There was the trolley, you could hear the bell when it came to the crossing and see its lights flashing. In Holyoke Ruthie and Virgil would have come home together, cutting across the backyards of the houses that faced Summer Street, playing as they came and jostling up the steps with red faces, panting and out of breath, their mittens frozen to their hands and the buckles on their overshoes caked with snow.

She put her hand on Virgil's forehead, decided he wasn't any worse, and went down to the kitchen to fill his hot water bottle. Ruby was getting ready to leave, tying the brown scarf across her face and knotting it behind her head. She said she could find her way blindfolded. Ruby's conviction that there wasn't a storm so bad she couldn't wade through it straight to her own front door was reassuring, although Dorothy knew that in any blizzard a good man, losing his way in from the barn, could freeze to death within ten feet of his own back door. She and Vera watched until Ruby was nothing but a wavy line in the swirling white outside.

Virgil wanted her to read again. He turned to the marker in *Black Beauty* and handed it to her. They had come to the part about the fire, and as she read she could see the horses crazed with fear, straining at their halters and screaming in terror as they kicked in the partitions of their stalls. When she was a little girl she had covered her eyes and ears through this part. She could almost see the flames, hear the rush and crackle of fire, the pounding of hooves and splintering of wood and the shrill terrified whinny of trapped animals. Her voice droned relentlessly on and her throat began to ache. She heard the clock in the parlor below strike two and she thought desperately, *Where are they?*

"Mother," said Virgil, "you're not listening to me."

"I'm reading," she said. "I thought you wanted me to read."

"I do," said Virgil, "but I was thinking about horses and I was thinking maybe when the snow's gone I could have a horse. I could keep it in the barn and I could learn how to—"

"You can't have a horse," said Dorothy. "Don't waste your time thinking about it, Virgil."

"Why can't I?"

"Hundreds of reasons."

"Name one," said Virgil, "just one."

"Horses eat."

"They eat hay," he said, "and this whole place is hay. He could eat his way down to the river and drink river water. I could saddle him myself once somebody had showed me how, and—''

"He would have to have oats and harness and a saddle and all of that costs money.''

"I could get a job and earn it. I could pick strawberries and beans and—''

"You'll have to do that anyway, and besides, when you have a horse you're responsible for it. You have to go out to the barn early in the morning, and you have to exercise a horse and rub it down. Not once in a while but every day. Do you think you are old enough to be responsible for that?''

"Yes,'' he said. "I'll be twelve in July. In the old days boys of twelve went hunting so their families wouldn't starve. They shot Indians. I'm plenty old enough to be responsible. Dad thinks so too.''

"How do you know?''

"He said so. I asked him and he said so.''

"What did he actually say, Virgil? Stop and think now.''

Virgil didn't need to think. He thought about it all the time. Ed had said, "I don't see why not, Son. Horses cost money and you have to take care of a horse if it's going to be worth anything to you. We'll see about it.''

"Ah,'' said Dorothy, "he said we'll see about it, Virgil. He didn't say we'd buy a horse, he said we'll see about it.''

"Well, we will. We will, Mother.''

Dorothy sighed. She was worried and she didn't want to get Virgil upset. Why did Ed have to say things like "we'll see''? Why did he give Virgil hope when he knew perfectly well they couldn't afford a horse and all that went with it?

"Well,'' she said slowly, "if he said we'll see about it, we will. But don't set your heart on it, Virgil. Now close your eyes for a while and try to rest.''

In the kitchen Granny Beane sat at the table picking out hickory nuts, a long, tedious job that suited her. Ordinarily she would have been in her room snoozing, but it was not an ordinary day and while no one said very much they were all thinking about Ed and Ruthie.

When Dorothy came into the room, Granny looked up and said, "I used to get earaches, too. My, I'll never forget the time my mother made a hot poultice and tied it over my ear. I can still feel it up there against my ear, fit to burn my skin off . . ."

Suddenly she realized what she was saying and she stopped abruptly.

Vera, who was sifting flour for the cake she would make with Granny's nuts, said, "Poor Virgil, there's no pain like an earache."

"There's always Dr. Tupper," said Mrs. Howard, "but I don't know how he'd get out in all this."

With one accord they turned to the windows, through which they could see the gray curtain of the day billowing and waving like washing on a line. Surely beyond it, on the road, snowplows were out and telephone wires up above were sketching their black tracks against the roiling gray of the sky.

"Virgil's sleeping," said Dorothy.

She didn't say that it was late, that Ed and Ruth should have been home hours ago and that she was sick with worry. She poured herself a cup of coffee and sat down at the table beside Granny and stared out the window at the blowing snow. It was building up on the window ledge and would cover the lower pane before long.

Through the long afternoon she sat with Virgil. He was tired of *Black Beauty* and they turned to Kipling. By five the Elephant's Child had learned his harsh lesson and now Rikki-tikki-tavi held Nagina's future in his mouth. The flowing waters of the great gray-green greasy Limpopo River and the steaming heat of the garden where Teddy played made her yearn for summer. She read on and on, until her voice grew hoarse, until the pale light of afternoon faded with dusk, until the power line broke, and then she stopped and put down the book and said, "It's all right, Virgil. I'll bring a candle."

Vera stood on a stool in the pantry taking down kerosene lamps for Mrs. Howard to fill.

"I've no doubt Ed and Ruth are perfectly safe, Dorothy," her mother said, as she wiped the lamp chimney and filled the base with kerosene.

Mrs. Howard spoke with authority, and Dorothy, who had heard the conviction in her mother's voice before, thought irritably, *What does she know?* Taking a lamp she went back upstairs, where Virgil and Granny, who had started a game of Parcheesi, were sitting in the dark with the board spread out on the bed between them. She could hear the rattle of dice as she left them.

Downstairs in the sitting room her mother's pen scratched an entry in her line-a-day book and Vera's knitting needles clicked. The lamplight shone, each lamp making its own pool of light on the dark floor. When the clock struck eight, Mrs. Howard said, "You must be worn out, Dorothy. Why don't you go up to your room and lie down? I'll listen for Virgil."

"I'm not tired."

"It wouldn't hurt you to rest."

How can I rest? thought Dorothy. Wasn't it better to sit with her eyes wide open, staring at familiar things, than to risk the inner vision of her imagination?

In the dim lamplight most of the objects in the room were only half visible. To her tired eyes the ivory elephants Cousin Gertrude had sent from China became almost animate, their shadows weaving across the white wall as they moved, trunk to tail, along the bone from which their ponderous feet had sprung. The marble Madonna that her grandfather had brought home from Italy all those years ago stretched out her arms as though to embrace troubled souls, like herself, drawing them together for support in the warm glow of lamplight that shone in the room.

If I were Edith I would be saying my prayers, thought Dorothy, and she wished she were Edith saying Hail Marys instead of herself praying Dear Gods. But was there a difference, she wondered. She thought of Mary Catherine's cross and wondered if Ruth had put it on that morning, and she wanted to go up to Ruth's room to look for it because if the cross was missing

67

it would mean Ruth was wearing it and that would be a good sign.

"Dorothy," called Granny, "Virgil wants you."

"Don't hurry, dear," said Granny, leaning over the banister, "he just wants to say his prayers. I'm going to bed now. I won't close my door."

Downstairs, Dorothy moved from window to window, peering into the darkness. She could imagine how the house looked from the outside, like a ship with lanterns glimmering faintly through a miasma of drifting fog as it rocked at anchor. Now and then she heard the sharp crack of a limb snapping in the cold, and as the hours passed and the others went to bed, the stillness seemed to grow and swell, pulsing like a live thing as it moved through the dark rooms of the house.

At midnight her mother emerged from her bedroom. She carried a candle, its light flickering on her calm, lined face and illuminating her white hair, which was braided and coiled at the nape of her neck. Moving silently she crossed the room and put her hand on Dorothy's arm.

"Come along, dear," she said, "let's make some cocoa. It would do us both good."

She poured milk into a saucepan and touched a match to the burner. Instantly, the room came to life as the spoon scraped softly on the edges of the pan and the faint aroma of burning kerosene drifted through the room.

"I've lived through a lot of storms like this," she said easily. "People make out."

"It's been hours," said Dorothy dully, "they could be anywhere."

By anywhere, she meant buried in the snow, frozen as the ice on the pond. Dead as men lost in an Arctic expedition.

"They're at the Smiths' or the Martins'," said her mother

confidently, "or they might have had the sense to stay at school."

"Suppose they left the truck and tried to make it across the fields?"

"Your cocoa's getting cold," said her mother.

"I can't remember a storm like this," said Dorothy. "All day I've been trying to remember what it used to be like, and I can't. I can't remember being snowed in here or at school, or even going to school on days like this. I should have known enough to keep Ruth home. Ed doesn't know about snow like this. He's never lived in the country. He's always lived in town."

"Ed's a grown man," said her mother. "He isn't a fool."

Dorothy nodded, but she kept thinking about Holyoke, where there was a familiar light, or post, or porch, or trolley wherever you put your hand or turned your face, and she wondered if the night would ever end.

Eventually she went back to the rocker in Virgil's room. The clock below struck two, and three . . . and then, suddenly, she saw that there was daylight edging the shades. She had not heard the clock strike four or five. How was it possible for her to have fallen asleep?

From below she heard faint sounds and felt warm air rising from the register. She closed her eyes again, listening to the utter silence of the outside world, which told her the storm was over.

From the kitchen windows she could see the frozen world outside, stretching away in unbroken sheets of white. She could hear her mother moving in her room. Coffee began to perk and Vera stirred cereal in the double boiler. Mr. Godwin came stamping up onto the porch and into the back entry. And then, suddenly, coming along the road and turning at the lane, she saw two dark figures wading toward the house.

Her mother, coming up behind her, said, "There you see,

Dorothy, here they come." And Granny Beane, pushing up to the window, cried, "Thank God, thank God."

But Dorothy couldn't say anything at all, she simply stood, watching as they approached, her eyes aching, her throat tight, her hands clenched in the pockets of her bathrobe and her heart beating wildly. She didn't listen to Granny Beane and she didn't turn around to look at her mother. If she had she would have seen Mrs. Howard's drawn face and the hands that shook as she tied her apron, all of which would have told Dorothy her mother's abrupt tone only masked the depths of her feelings. In the midst of this Ruth danced around the kitchen, shedding mittens and scarf and telling everyone that she slept three in a bed at the Smiths and that Ed had rolled up in a buffalo robe by the fire in their living room.

Suddenly it was too much and Dorothy began to cry. Then Ed crossed the room and pulled her into his arms. "There, now," he said, "there now. That's enough, Ruth," and holding Dorothy tightly he said gently, "none of that. We're here. Everything's all right."

By the end of the week the sun had melted most of the snow on the roof. Ed went back to his tools in the barn, Virgil was better, Ruthie walked to school, Vera made two pumpkin pies and Dorothy wrote to Edith Callahan to tell her all about it.

"I though about you, Edith," she wrote . . . and then she paused. Now that the sun was out and the Packard making tracks in the lane and Virgil's ear better and everyone safe at home, it was hard to put into words what she had felt during that long, dark night, so she didn't even try.

The second of February dawned cloudy and the groundhog, nosing up through his nest of dead leaves beneath the stone wall, emerged into a bleak world. Under the lowering sky the snow looked dingy and on its smooth crust his coarse round body left no shadow whatsoever. He raised his flat head and stared with rodent eyes over the gray sweep of pasture. If spring was coming early he failed to sense it, and he scuttered back through layers of wet leaves and sharp twigs and burrowed deep into his hole.

In the house Mr. Godwin sat idly at the kitchen table, looking out at the snowy yard and observing the clouds.

"Won't see his shadow today," he said to Ruby.

"Ayah," she replied.

She'd be glad when spring came and she could get Homer out of her kitchen. Between him and the plants lined up in the south windows, things were a bit tight. Spring couldn't come too soon for Ruby.

Mr. Godwin's gaze went across the yard to the maples along the drive and he said carelessly, "Well now, I'd say 'twas getting on time to tap the trees."

"If you think I'm going to boil sap in this kitchen," said Ruby, "you've got another think coming."

"Don't see as how it would be much bother," said Homer.

No one had tapped the maples at Havenhill for over ten years, and he had a notion there were some there who wouldn't think it was such a bad idea.

When Mrs. Howard heard Ruthie and Virgil talking excitedly about making maple sugar she took up her cane and marched out to the kitchen and said, "What's all this about?"

"Time to tap the trees, Mrs. Howard," said Homer. "I can remember when Howard syrup won ribbons at the Tipton Fair."

"They don't have a fair at Tipton anymore," said Mrs. Howard, "and besides that, collecting sap is hard work. I thought you had enough to do."

"Ruthie and I would do that part," said Virgil.

"And who's going to boil it down?" she asked.

"Not me," said Ruby, "not on my stove."

Mr. Godwin scratched his head. Thinking for Mr. Godwin always included scratching. "There's a wood stove in the shed," he said. " 'Twouldn't hurt a thing out there."

"Please, Grandmother," begged Virgil.

71

When the time came and Mr. Godwin had bored his holes and the white meat of the maples curled out in long streamers, and Virgil and Ruthie hung up the pails and old kettles and jars Vera had found in the pantry, and the reality of maple syrup began to seem possible, no one complained. At first, the sap oozed out slowly, carrying bits of bark and pith until at last it began its slow drip, drip. Then Ruthie looked at Virgil and shrugged. "It's going to take forever," she said.

It had turned mild by the time Homer tapped the trees. Mild enough to set Ed to thinking about job hunting again, and when he left the house one morning in mid-February he could see patches of dirt along the lane. He drove the truck (nobody was going to believe a man in a Packard needed work) and he headed north, threading his way in and out of the network of little towns that were strung along the river.

As he rattled past small farms he saw cattle in the pastures, standing there in the last of the snow, waiting for the sun to melt it away from the brown clumps of dried grass that began to emerge in tufts here and there. It occurred to him that if there were cows in his mother-in-law's barns he would be spared the futility of stopping at rundown garages and machine shops to ask for work. It was degrading to beg for work, but he was willing to do it. He'd do almost anything to get Dorothy a house of her own, although in all his ramblings he hadn't seen one he thought she'd have and supposed he wouldn't until they could go back to a place like Holyoke.

Tarred state roads were showing black. It wouldn't be long before side roads turned to mud. As he drove through Mumfert he saw slush along the streets and yards stubbled with dead grass. There wasn't any town around he would have wanted to settle in, he thought, but he didn't feel that way about the farm. He would have started a herd at Havenhill in a minute and put an end to all of this, if he had the money.

He drew in beside the post office to pick up the mail. Dorothy kept looking for a letter from Edith Callahan, but all he pulled out of the box was the *Saturday Evening Post* and a newspaper. As he came out the door, he almost collided with Dr. Adams who, with his cane for an antenna, moved crablike up the stone steps. When he looked out from under the brim of his hat and saw Ed, he smiled. "Well, well," he said, "nice day."

"Nice enough," mumbled Ed, holding the door for the old man. In his opinion it had been a poor day, raw, cold, wet and muddy—it matched his mood. He had asked four men for work that day and none of them had done much more than shake his head. Of course Dr. Adams didn't know that.

"Come along to the house and have a cup of tea," said Dr. Adams. "Just let me take a look in my box," and he hobbled over and squinted into his box, rubbed the glass with his fingers and looked again, saw nothing and turned away.

"Mrs. Gibbs baked today," he said, "come along and sit by the fire and give her the pleasure of seeing her labors appreciated."

Ed didn't want a cup of tea, but he wasn't eager to get home either. Every day Dorothy greeted him with an expression of hopefulness that changed to sympathy when their eyes met. He could see pity where he wanted to see approval, and so he followed Dr. Adams into his house and down the dark inner hall to the study, where a fire crackled and the pale sun of late afternoon shone in through the windows.

"Oh, my," cried Mrs. Gibbs, "a visitor. I've made a cake, don't you know. Thursday's my bake day," and she disappeared down the passage to the kitchen.

Ed sat beside the fire where the warmth of the blaze conspired with the tranquillity of the room to produce a rare feeling of peace in his troubled spirit. He knew that Dorothy, who loved to read, would be right at home here. There were books everywhere. Shelves of books that went up to the ceiling. Books too high for Dr. Adams to reach, although in the past he surely had been able to get up to them. Books too high to dust. They stood in ranks obscured in a kind of gray haze overhead, solid and reassuring. What truths and secrets did they hold, Ed wondered. There were books on tabletops as well. In the lamplight and

73

firelight a warm glow pulsed and shimmered through the room and suddenly the raw edges of his day with its anxiety and frustration seemed, as by an unseen hand, to be smoothed away.

After a bit there was a rattling in the hallway and the door swung open to admit Mrs. Gibbs, who pushed a tea cart on which silver shone and china danced. Mrs. Gibbs's cake was a high yellow cake with lemon glaze dribbled down its sides.

As they ate Mrs. Gibbs's cake and talked of trivial things, Ed began to feel miraculously restored. Was Virgil's ear better, they wanted to know. Did he know this last blizzard was the worst since the one in '88, or was it '87? What were these fireside chats of Mr. Roosevelt's? Did Ed think they should have a radio even though they didn't like all that popping and static? And then Mrs. Gibbs said, "Such a time as we're having with the milk. Thin as water one day, rich as cream the next."

"That's too bad," said Ed.

"It's old Mr. Purvis," she said, "moved to Clinton to live with his daughter. Think of it, he's been working for the Curries since the nineties. All these years."

Ed didn't know that he'd ever heard of Mr. Purvis or given a thought to the creamery at Berry Bay where their milk came from. "I wonder if they've taken on a new man?" he said.

"Now there's a thought," said Dr. Adams, his glance sharp. He knew Ed was looking for work though he didn't say so, but Mrs. Gibbs, who had spent her life in service and assumed security was the business of others, said insensitively, "Well, I hope so."

"Why don't you swing by there on your way home," said Dr. Adams. "John Currie's a hard man to work for, I hear, but he's a fair man. He can't do any worse than say no."

When Ed drove into the yard at six and pulled in under the shed he looked around, almost as though he'd never seen the weathered beams overhead, or the remnants of harness hanging on pegs before. For reasons he didn't question or try to understand, he was suddenly acutely aware of his body, almost as though he were taking possession of it again after an absence. He could feel the breath going in and out of his lungs. He was aware of the pumping of his heart, a steady strong thump thump. For weeks he had moved like someone afflicted with an undiagnosed illness, and when he crawled out of the truck after those other fruitless expeditions, it was as if he were sliding out, his bones turned to rubber. Tonight was different.

It occurred to him briefly that he was entitled to a swallow from the bottle he'd left in the grain bin, but Dorothy would smell it. Still he savored the moment as if he had had a drink. The thought of Berry Bay was intoxicating. It was the kind of place he wanted, a farm with cleared fields, tight barns, a whitewashed cement creamery that was like a clinic, with steel equipment and storage tanks where milk cans submerged in cold water clanged together as they bobbed against blocks of ice. Across the barnyard a carpenter from the lumber company in Mumfert was building a dog run and he saw a girl in slacks chasing a child around a pile of planks. From where he stood she looked like any other young woman, but he'd heard Mr. Currie's daughter was home from New York and going to be divorced. People didn't know when they were well off, he thought.

Vera and Ruby looked up as he brushed through the kitchen, but he didn't have time tonight to lift the lids and smell what they were cooking for supper. He was in a hurry to see Dorothy and the minute their eyes met she said, "You didn't!"

"I did."

"Where?"

"Right here. At Berry Bay."

"At the Curries'?" she said, as though she didn't know who they were.

"I can't turn it down, Dorothy. It pays twenty a week."

"Doing what?"

"The creamery."

"The creamery? What do you know about a creamery, Ed?"

"How much do you have to know about a creamery?" he said. "I'll get the hang of it soon enough. Things are different from the way they used to be. They don't just put milk in cans and bottle it up for delivery. I have to run the pasteurizer and cooler and the separator. If there's anything I do know it's machines. You should see it, Dorothy. It's like a clinic up there.''

"I'm glad you've got a job," she said, "but how will it change things? We'll still be here, Ed. We won't have a place of our own. It's not going to be any different."

"Money," he said.

"I thought we'd be moving."

She had imagined them going somewhere, just the four of them, and Granny Beane of course, with all their furniture on a truck, moving to their own house, like the one in Holyoke, with neighbors who would have children too, where she would have a social life, a study club, a women's group.

"We will, Dorothy," he said, "just give it time."

"What do you know about separators, Ed? Did you ever see one working? The cream shoots out in one direction and skim milk in the other and if it isn't set right the cream comes out thick as butter, and—"

"Maybe you ought to run it yourself, Dorothy," he said.

"I didn't mean that, Ed. I just meant it would all be strange. You're a machinist. You're skilled, Ed. Everything about cows is different."

"I'll have the herdsman," he said. "Mr. Currie said he'd work with me until I get the hang of it."

"You won't like it, Ed."

"What do you want me to do, Dorothy? Burn up gas going in and out of body shops looking for work where there isn't any, or taking on night watchman at someplace like the Railway Express down to Clinton?"

"No, I don't mean that, Ed."

"What do you mean?"

"I don't know," she said miserably.

"Look," he said, "this is just a beginning. It will lead to something better. It will be a paycheck." He put his arms around her and said, "We've got to start somewhere, Dorothy."

"I know it," she said, "and I am glad, Ed," but even as she said it, she was thinking about Richard Currie, who had taken her to her first dance and ridden across the fields to call on her when she was fifteen and too young to think about the things he wanted her to think about. The last time she saw Richard he was in uniform . . .

Granny Beane wrote to Evelyn in Hollywood and told her that Ed was going to be in charge of the creamery at a big dairy farm, and by the time Evelyn finished reading the letter Berry Bay Farm had taken on a whole new character.

The house, approached by a winding drive, was actually a large white New England farmhouse with lilacs along a stone wall that separated the front lawn from a hay field. In the back, Rachel Currie's flower beds were laid out in neat rows screening the house from a large vegetable garden.

As she read this, Evelyn imagined an English garden surrounding a great stone manor house, and all the Curries drawn by Granny's facile pen began to resemble stock movie characters in the fantasies of Merry Olde England that the films created. John Currie, hearty, matter-of-fact, hard working and widowed, became in Evelyn's imagination Sir John, aloof, stern, imperious and self-sufficient. His herdsman, who was going to teach Ed all about the creamery and had a Polish name, was a quiet, tireless man, good with cows, who became in Evelyn's mind a Polish count driven into exile by the Russians after the Great War. Louisa Wright, John's daughter, an energetic young woman who had left her husband for undisclosed reasons and was now dabbling in breeding collies, was transformed by Evelyn into a seductress who would tempt Ed with her body and her wealth. Louisa's daughter, Amy, age five, a robust, curious child, metamorphosed into the pale, delicate, nervous heir of the property, undoubtedly threatened by something or someone. Granny's letter hadn't, after all, described all the persons who lived and worked there, and it hadn't even touched on the most important of the Curries, at least in Ruth's and Virgil's eyes, who was named John (for his grandfather), because John spent most of the year away from Berry Bay in boarding school and Granny hadn't realized yet that there was such a person.

Evelyn folded her mother's letter and sighed. Ed had all the luck, she thought. Maybe she ought to go home. Being an extra, and that was all she'd been to date, wasn't much, even if it did mean she'd been up close enough to see Connie Bennett's makeup, including the false eyelashes that looked real on the screen. It was possible, Evelyn thought, that her mother had failed to mention an unmarried son of Sir John and the deceased Lady Rachel. If there were such a son, and there always was in the movies, she might go home for a visit . . .

And then it occurred to her that home was a house owned by Dorothy's mother in which her own mother resided by sufferance, and she dismissed the thought and began to work on her fingernails with a cuticle stick. Waiting table was hard on her hands and who knew when they might be in a close-up of one kind or another.

Water ran in the ditch at the side of the road, gathering speed and splashing into a gully at the bottom of Webster's Hill. Over the dark and muddy fields crows flapped black wings and cawed raucously. Midafternoon sun beat down hotly and Ruthie unbuttoned her jacket and pulled off her cap. Virgil dragged his feet. Rubbers pulled like weights on their feet as they squelched up the lane toward the house. Fields were bare and brown, but north of the barn and along the stone wall snow lay in dingy ridges. It would be rubber weather for quite a while yet, and Ruthie said irritably, "It wasn't like this in Holyoke."

Driving home from work Ed noted the brown fields and muddy lanes and a show of yellow along the wands of the willow trees down by the river. It wouldn't be long, another month or so, and the orchard would be in bloom, and his glance took in the straggling rows of the Howard orchard. At Berry Bay, where the trees had been regularly renewed, the rows were straight and Mr. Currie was already ploughing in the meadow along the river. If Ed could have things the way he wanted them, he would have his own herd and his own tractor. And, besides that, they would have a horse for Virgil. It was all Virgil talked about, a horse he could ride, and it wasn't Tom Mix and his horse that Virgil wanted. It was Virgil Beane on his own horse, riding across the fields to the river, crossing through the wood lots, riding the lines, marking the property that would in all probability be his one day.

By God, he thought, *that's one thing I can do for him.*

As he drove into the yard and saw Homer Godwin sitting on a bench in the sun, backed up against the side of the barn whittling, with white chips flying out like snow and settling at his feet, Ed exploded.

Slamming on the brakes he got out of the truck and roared, "Homer! How come that's all you got to do? I told you last week to start pruning the dead wood down in the orchard. I don't see as you've done a thing."

Homer goggled up stupidly. "Well, now," he said, "I'll get to it, Mr. Beane. Apples is a long time off yet."

"That's just the beginning of the things need doing around here," said Ed.

"Don't get me wrong, Mr. Beane," said Homer, "but Mrs. Howard don't seem too concerned about the orchard."

"You leave Mrs. Howard to me," said Ed, "and when you finish up in the orchard you can walk the south line and let me know if that fence is still tight."

"Yes, sir, Mr. Beane," said Homer. He didn't like taking orders from Ed. He had his own work, he'd been doing it for ten years before Ed and Dorothy came to Havenhill.

Ed could hear Homer muttering. *Lazy bastard,* he thought, and he walked along to the house to look for his mother-in-law.

He found her in the sitting room and when he finished saying

79

what he had to say he stopped, took a deep breath, and added, "I know this is your place and I've no right to interfere, but the orchard isn't dead yet and maybe someday we could have cattle in the south pasture. I could manage that much and hold a job too. All I need is a little help."

"I see," said Mrs. Howard.

Granny Beane sat in her chair, sputtering silently to herself. If Ed said Homer Godwin was lazy she didn't doubt he was and any fool knew an orchard neglected was a sin and a waste. Fortunately she had the wits to keep still.

While Mrs. Howard considered, Ed went on. "These days with men out of work you could hire a dozen men glad to do all Homer does and the little I've told him as well."

"He's almost sixty and he's been faithful," said Mrs. Howard. "All the same, it would seem to me you aren't asking much."

That satisfied Ed and he went upstairs to wash and change for supper. He didn't hear what followed, but if he had he would have known that Homer, cap in hand, came into the sitting room and told Mrs. Howard he couldn't go on working for her if he was expected to take orders from Ed Beane.

When he made this announcement his face, which was already flushed, grew mottled with anger and his voice jerked like a schoolboy's and after he'd finished, he stood there, impotent with rage, as he waited for her verdict.

"I see," she said. She had already realized that what Ed wanted done was summer work when there was no furnace tending or snow shoveling, but it seemed reasonable to her to get started even if it was early, and she said slowly and kindly, "If you feel that way you're right to say so, Mr. Godwin, and if you can't work with Mr. Beane you're free to leave. I'll be sorry to see you go, but I'd not want you to stay under the circumstances."

Granny Beane ducked her head and restrained the impulse to nod in joyful triumph. Her fingers moved furiously and silently over her crocheting.

Homer stood there, staring at the floor, unable to speak. He wasn't sure what he had expected to happen, the truth being he hadn't thought at all. To leave Mrs. Howard would mean leaving his room over the garage, leaving the Packard, leaving Vera's chicken dumplings and Ruby's doughnuts. *How did I get myself in a fix like this,* he thought stupidly, and facing the walls of the box he'd made for himself his mind skittered around helplessly. Suddenly a brilliant thought occurred.

"Well now," he said, "if you was to ask me to do them things, Mrs. Howard, it would be different. I never said no to what you wanted done, did I now?"

"That's true," she said, "you've always done a good job for me, Mr. Godwin. Just what do you have in mind?"

"The orchard and south field could do with a little tending," he replied.

"That's so," she said. "I would like you to prune in the orchard and repair the fence around the south field if it needs repair."

Homer nodded and said he would be glad to do that, and then, feeling he'd managed a touchy situation with great diplomacy, he proceeded to the kitchen to see if Ruby was ready to feed him.

The grandmothers said the days were getting longer, but Dorothy couldn't tell it. She stood at the kitchen window, staring into the blackness outside and waiting for Ed to come down to breakfast. He was up at five these days and gone by half past.

She broke three eggs into a pan and put some bread in the toaster. The coffee was just beginning to perk. It went schlop, plop, schlop, plop . . . one of the best sounds she knew, and she turned the toast as a curl of smoke appeared.

There was a line of pink along the tops of the hills and she said, "Look, Ed, it's almost light."

"So, 'tis."

"Spring's coming."

"I knew it would," he said.

81

She smiled and lifted her face. Things were easier, she thought, not right, but easier. They'd opened an account in the First National Bank in Mumfert and there was already over eighty dollars in it. Ed said it wouldn't last long, not if he bought the parts he needed to rebuild the tractor, but there would be another twenty going in every week. That was something.

"Time to go," said Ed.

"I was thinking about calling on Louisa one of these days," said Dorothy. "I could ride back with you after dinner some afternoon, Ed. What would you think of that?"

"Fine," he said, but he didn't think much of it. He'd watched Louisa Wright hanging around the men in the yard and it didn't look good. From a distance you would have thought she was Ruthie's age, but up close was different. You couldn't miss that she was a woman up close. She came into the creamery off and on looking for Amy, who was five, and if Ed saw her coming he turned on the hose and began to wash down the floor. Stan Kisloski had warned him about her. "Currie's a good man to work for," Stan said. "I've got nothing against her, but I'd steer clear all the same."

"Thanks," said Ed.

"Too bad," said Stan, "she's got a nice kid."

Ed hadn't mentioned it to Dorothy, but now he said, "She's getting divorced, you know."

"I know that," said Dorothy, and as she watched the truck disappear down the lane she thought, divorce is worse than death, worse for children, terrible for women left on their own.

She'd try to get up there soon, she decided. If she had a house of her own she could invite Louisa in for tea, but she wouldn't do it here. Sooner or later the conversation would turn to family, and the grandmothers, who were, she thought, unaware of Louisa's situation, would want to know where her husband was and what he did for a living.

She could imagine the scene when Louisa announced that she was in the midst of a divorce. Her mother would say, "Oh—is that so." And then she would straighten her shoulders slightly and reach for the teapot. "Let me freshen your cup, Louisa," she would say.

Granny Beane would flutter, her teaspoon rattling in her saucer as she bit into a cookie, shattering it and scattering crumbs in her lap, saying, "Oh, dear, oh, dear, look what I've done."

Neither would know what the correct reaction to divorce would be, although divorce was growing more and more common.

Of course the grandmothers couldn't or wouldn't accept this. They were quite capable of accepting tragedy in its many forms. Death, bankruptcy, illness, all sad but acceptable, could be accommodated, but not divorce, which represented change. Things were changing all over the world, thought Dorothy, but not in this house. Nothing would ever change here.

On the first day of school after Easter vacation Miss Norris wrote in large letters on the blackboard, *April 13, 1936. I am now Mrs. Baker. Welcome back, children.* She wore a blue skirt and a starched white blouse with a round collar. If she had put on an apron she would have looked like a housewife, which is what Harold wanted her to be. Only the color in her cheeks and the expression in her eyes indicated the agitation she was feeling.

She couldn't understand Harold. First he wanted to wait to get married. His wife would never work, he said, as if being married wasn't work, and then his mother broke her hip and all of a sudden Harold wanted to get married right away so that they could move in with his mother and take care of her.

Well, she thought, *I did it this vacation and I'll do it this summer, but that's all I'll do and I've told him so.*

She walked up and down the rows of desks as the children took out books and paper, but she wasn't thinking about the multiplication tables or the names of the state capitals, she was thinking about Harold's mother, who was large, immobile and morose. Mrs. Baker required attention, cups of tea, strips of hot buttered toast, the bedpan, the paper. She complained incessantly. Her neck hurt, there were lumps in the bed, where was the sugar, hadn't Grace heard her calling?

Martha Harris, who was a nurse before she married, came in three times a week to give Mrs. Baker an enema. She rolled the old woman onto her side and spread a rubber sheet and towel under her, said in a brisk voice, "Now take a deep breath, Mrs. Baker, and hold it." And then she turned to Grace and talked about plans for her garden, ignoring Mrs. Baker's moans and protests as soapy water entered her body and then threatened to explode all over the bed and the walls of her room. Afterward Mrs. Baker groaned, "Don't get old, Grace. Nobody treats you right once you're old."

What was the alternative, Grace wondered. Was she supposed to pray for the deliverance of an early death? It wasn't fair. Harold's sister wasn't working and her children were old enough to take care of themselves.

Well, thought Grace, *I'll do it this summer, but if she's not better in the fall Velma will have to take over and we'll get our own place*. It occurred to her that when she'd said this to Harold he had complained about money and asked her how she thought they could afford a place of their own.

"I'll come right back up here to Sunnyside," she said. "Mr. Robbins said they'd have a hard time finding another teacher and I can live at the Cutters' and come home on weekends."

She could hear the children pushing and laughing outside and she was tempted to let recess go for an extra ten minutes. It was such a pretty day and maybe an early spring was a good sign, she thought. It made her want to stay at home and plant her own garden, but, she wanted it to be *her* home and *her* garden, not Mrs. Baker's.

How could these hard feelings have arisen in just two weeks' time? It seemed to Grace she had hardly been a bride at all. She and Harold had gone to Boston for two nights and then back to Mrs. Baker's house, where they slept in a room next to her room, and the morning after they got back there Grace was in the kitchen packing Harold's lunch as if they had been married ten years.

At the end of the day she washed the blackboards with a wet rag and took the erasers outside where she stood on the steps, hating the feel of chalk on her hands as she pounded them savagely, raising a cloud of dust that swirled around her. Suddenly she saw a troupe of women coming across the school yard, and she peered through the dust she had risen to see who it was. It looked to her like every mother in the PTA, with hats and bundles, descending on her en masse, and she brushed back her hair and braced herself. *What is it now,* she thought in dismay.

"Helloo," someone called, and she recognized Dorothy Beane leading the others. "Hello, Mrs. Baker," she said, "we've brought you a party."

When Grace realized it was a shower, she began to cry and Eunice Brewster thumped her on the shoulder and said, "There, there, dear, it's just a party. You're still a bride, you know. Come on in everybody."

Someone spread a white linen cloth on Grace's desk and set out a cake and a jug of lemonade.

"Now," said Dorothy, "open your presents, Grace. You're only a bride once and you might as well enjoy it."

Grace began slowly, untying all the ribbon carefully and winding it up so that she could use it again. "An apron," she said, "and hemstitched tea towels. They're too nice for dishes, I'll use them for bureau scarves."

"Do anything you want to with them, dear," said Mrs. Finley.

"And napkins," said Grace, "how beautiful. I always wished I knew how to tat. Look at that lace, isn't it lovely."

"Anybody can tat," said Wilma Martin, "wouldn't take me two afternoons to show you how that's done."

Grace folded tissue paper carefully and reached for the last box. She suddenly felt better. Weren't people good and kind. She wished Harold could find work up here somewhere and that they could find a little place of their own around Havenhill and then she could go on teaching forever.

"Open it," said Dorothy, "so we can cut the cake."

Grace tore it open, suddenly forgetting about saving paper and ribbon and pulling a bib and baby's kimono out of the box.

"Oh, my," someone said, and Ethel Forbes spoke up quickly. "Mercy, what have I done now? That's for my sister in Worcester. What will she think when she sees I've sent her a pair of pillow slips."

Everyone laughed, but Grace rose to the occasion and said, "Well, Mrs. Forbes, if you don't mind, I'll keep these for good luck."

Good luck, she thought. She wasn't even sure she wanted a baby. Ever. Things just weren't the way she thought they'd be, back when Harold was Clark Gable and she was Joan Crawford. She thought lovemaking was supposed to be gentle and beautiful, but it wasn't. It was grappling in the dark and Harold's hard body invading hers, suddenly and savagely, and then his heavy breathing and nothing else, no words, no tenderness.

She folded the kimono carefully and placed the bib on top of it and then she put the cover on the box. "Thank you all so much," she said. "This is the nicest thing that's ever happened to me." Her lips trembled and her eyes filled with tears, but Eunice Brewster put her arm around Grace and said heartily, "There, there, here we go again. Somebody cut the cake so Grace can stop crying."

It was a lovely day to walk, and as Dorothy went along the state road she saw clumps of bluets springing up in the grass and pussy willows along the creek. On the south side of the house there was even a show of yellow in the forsythia and as she came up the lane she felt as though she ought to be carrying her lunch box. Havenhill didn't change, she thought, and in this instance found some comfort in the fact.

There was nothing to mar the serenity and beauty of the day except her own restless feelings, and even when she found Vera kneeling over Angus's box she was too preoccupied to recognize the small tragedy in the scene. There was Vera, her hand stretched out to Angus and her hair, with hairpins slipping loose, falling in scallops around her thin white face. *Why*, thought Dorothy in surprise, *Vera's pretty*, and she thought how sad it was for Vera to be spending her life with two old women and another woman's children. Why hadn't there been some nice man for Vera, but, of course, there was William who had been killed in France in 1918. She never thought about William, but probably Vera did.

"What's wrong with Angus?" she asked.

"I don't know," choked Vera, her finger tapping gently on his skull as though to draw his attention, although he was surely dead, already stiff, his coat coarse and wiry with death.

"What's happened?" asked Ruth, coming in and dropping her lunch box with a clatter and bending down. "Oh, poor Angus," she said, "he's dead, isn't he? We'll have to have a funeral."

Vera gave a little cry then, as though she couldn't bear to hear the word *funeral*.

"Why don't you go and find Homer, Vera," said Dorothy. "I'll finish tea, and Ruthie and I will take care of Angus."

Vera turned obediently and went into the shed, where she stopped and put her face into an old garden coat and cried. Then she wiped her eyes on her apron and went out into the yard. "Mr. Godwin," she called.

Dorothy put on the tea kettle and laid the tray. "Go out into the back entry and find a box, Ruthie," she said, and then they lifted Angus in, quilt and all, and closed the flaps as her mother came tapping through the hall to inquire for tea.

"Well," she said, touching the box with the tip of her cane, "what's this?"

"Angus," said Ruthie, "he's dead."

A flicker of sympathy crossed Mrs. Howard's face. "Vera will be upset," she said. Privately, she felt it was a mistake to become attached to anything or anyone, except for one's children, because affection rendered a person vulnerable to pain.

Poor girl, she thought, *she was foolish about that little dog*, and she went back to the sitting room and informed Granny Beane that Vera's dog had died and tea would be delayed.

Into the kitchen clumped Mr. Godwin. "Well, now," he said, "what's all this?" Of course he knew perfectly well what it was. It was a dead dog in a box for which he was expected to dig a grave.

"Would you rather have tea in your room, Vera?" asked Dorothy, but Vera thought not. She would have tea with the others. She didn't want to upset Aunt Alice or Mrs. Beane. Angus could wait.

In the sitting room Mrs. Howard poured out as usual. She knew each one's preference when it came to milk or lemon, but she asked anyway because in her opinion it was in the performance of ordinary ritual that civility was created, which in turn distinguished the society of men from the savagery of beasts. She said, "Lemon or milk, Mrs. Beane? One or two lumps?"

Dorothy passed the biscuits Vera had put into the oven just before discovering Angus, and Vera declined. To think Angus had been lying there dead at her feet while she was sifting flour and cutting in lard. It was too much.

"I am very sorry about Angus, Vera," said Mrs. Howard kindly. "He was a nice little dog."

"Thank you, Aunt Alice."

Granny Beane put jelly on her biscuit, breaking it in the process, and she busied herself with crumbs and bits of sticky scraps. Then she turned to Vera and said placidly, "Well, dear, it's always hard to lose a pet. I know. I remember when Ed's dog died. That was old Jupiter, Dorothy. He was old as the hills, poor fellow, blind and stiff, but Ed was only nine and you know how boys are at that age."

Vera stirred her tea, taking care not to rattle her spoon on the side of the cup. She didn't know how nine-year-old boys were. She knew very little about boys and less about men, but she tried to look interested in what Granny Beane was saying.

Dorothy wished Ed's mother wouldn't always dwell on

things, relating them to herself and the past and her family's past.

"It was a blessing of course when Jupiter died," continued Granny, "poor old thing, he'd lost most of his teeth. I tried to tell Ed, but what can you say to a little fellow who loves his dog?"

"The less said the better," remarked Mrs. Howard acidly, and turning to Dorothy asked, "did you happen to read the article about the Hoover Dam?"

Neither Dorothy nor Vera had noticed it and Granny didn't read magazines except to look at the illustrations. On the other hand, Mrs. Howard believed in keeping abreast of things and this had prompted her recently to accept an offer of membership in the National Geographic Society.

"There are several interesting pieces in the new *Geographic*," she said.

"I always liked the *Geographic*," said Granny, "and Mr. Beane liked the stories about Africa and India. Of course there were all those photographs of bosoms. Such collections of naked brown bodies," she said with distaste, "but of course it showed the need for our missionaries. I daresay Gertrude is accustomed to seeing naked heathen, but we never put the *Geographic* out in our Sunday school room."

A short silence followed as no one felt inclined to comment on the naked of the alien world or to remark on the efforts of Gertrude, who was a distant cousin of Mrs. Howard's, to transplant Christian values into their heathen hearts.

The conversation turned comfortably back to grape jelly. Mrs. Howard spoke more than usual and Vera less. Eventually tea was over and Dorothy and Vera wheeled the tea cart back to the kitchen where they found Ruthie and Virgil waiting patiently. Ruthie held her Bible and Virgil held out a bouquet of forsythia, which Vera accepted with the grace of a visiting dignitary.

Dorothy said, "The children can manage alone, Vera." But Vera put on her floppy hat and holding Virgil's flowers like a bridal bouquet she marched ahead of them down the lane to the

89

place by the stone wall where Mr. Godwin had buried Angus in his box.

When it was all over, Vera hung up her hat, changed her dress and never mentioned Angus again. He was buried, just as her other loves were buried, laid to rest in unmarked graves along the narrow paths of her life. She supposed that there might be a cross somewhere in France with William's name on it and a faded American flag stuck in an iron holder fluttering over it. If she had known William's family better and been able to ask she would know, but no one had bothered to tell her.

When she went to bed that night, performing the usual rituals of hair brushing and prayers, she ventured a small word in Angus's behalf. She hoped he hadn't suffered. She sat at her dressing table in her long white nightgown, a ruffle of eyelet at her throat and wrists, and she took the pins out of her hair and brushed and brushed, but in the dim light of her bed lamp her hair seemed dull and her eyes, looking out of her narrow white face, were ashy with resignation. The last thing she saw as she turned out the light was the ceiling of her room. It stretched over her head, a perfect square, as white and empty as a page on which no one had ever written.

By early May Ed had the tractor running and one Sunday afternoon he put on the mower and cut the south field. It was hot for May and sweat ran down his bare back. It soaked his head, plastering his hair to his skull. Insects rose up in clouds as the mower cut through the tall grass and undergrowth, but as the dead grass and nettles fell away the shape of the past began to emerge. Even Mrs. Howard, who stood on the side porch shading her eyes to watch his progress, glimpsed in the opening sweep of pasture a glimmer of what the land had been and might become again. It occurred to her that Ed was working double shift and it might do to hire a crew to clear out the thickets to the north. Curiously, as she thought of these things she was reminded of her last will and testament. She ought to call her lawyer and ask him to come out from Clinton one day soon so they could go over things again. All she wanted to do was add Ed's name and have him and Dorothy joint heirs. Then, of course, she would set up a trust of some sort for Vera, although she was sure Ed and Dorothy could be counted on to do the right thing.

Dorothy came onto the porch with her mending basket and sat down in a wicker rocker. She had a dozen socks to darn. Virgil's were so bad she was darning darns onto darns. She watched as Ed went back and forth across the field. *He might have kept his shirt on,* she thought, and she said, "I know it's Sunday, Mother, and I'm sorry."

Inside the house Granny Beane was thinking the same thing. He ought to know better than to mow on Sunday, but it was Ed's health, not the Lord's commandment, that troubled her. She muttered, "He works all week and half a day on Saturday. The Lord said that on the seventh day thou shalt rest. It's not right." She looked vaguely around the sitting room for someone to confirm this, but no one was there.

Vera was on the back porch gazing through the trellis where morning glories would soon be twining in profusion. She stared with fascination at Ed. She'd never seen a bare-chested man before and even at a distance she was acutely aware of this. Suddenly she realized in horror that she was having carnal thoughts about Dorothy's husband, something she had scarcely even allowed herself to imagine about William, and feeling ashamed of herself she retreated to the kitchen.

That night when Ed stretched out beside Dorothy he said, "Did you ever see a prettier sight than that field? We could start our own herd out there."

"And what about a house of our own?" she replied. "I thought we were saving up for the time we could have our own place. I can't understand you, Ed. You're not a farmer. I don't want to even think about turning this place into a farm again. One of these days you'll get a job like the one you had in Holyoke, and we'll move into our own place again."

"I like it well enough here," he said.

Moonlight shone through the trees, a breeze stirred the curtains, and from the woods and fields where water collected in dark hollows he could hear the shrill throbbing of the peepers. It had been a good day, but there had to be more and he put his hand out to Dorothy, felt her body lift with a small receptive thrust, and with a moan of pleasure, he took her with the last burst of strength that was his to command.

Dorothy lay awake staring at the black ceiling. She wondered how Ed could sleep and why they never talked anymore. She touched his arm, but his breathing was already deep and regular. It wasn't that she wanted to talk, she decided—she needed to talk. Marriage had to be more than working and sleeping, coupling like squirrels on a tree limb, still for a moment then drawing apart abruptly and darting off in separate directions. It would be different if they could talk, but as she lay there, wide eyed and troubled, she wondered what they had to talk about. The children were happy, Holyoke was all but forgotten, even Granny seemed content. One would have thought she'd spent her life in Ruby's kitchen shelling peas.

Why do I feel empty and useless, she wondered. *Why do we need our own house?*

This house was big enough for three families. Her mother rarely interfered with the children, and it certainly wasn't her mother's fault that she and Ed were losing touch. There he was, right beside her; why did she think so often of Richard? Her throat tightened and she swallowed rapidly. She hadn't thought of Richard in years, but ever since Ed had gone to work at Berry Bay memories of him had come rushing back and when she looked across the fields to the Currie farm, she wasn't thinking of Ed, she was remembering Richard. Remembering the time they'd met on the hill . . . Richard's son, John, was a constant reminder. Richard too had disappeared behind the walls of a private school, and like Vera's William, Richard too had been killed in France.

And then one day in 1920 a girl named Millie came to Berry Bay with a child named John who was her son she said, hers and Richard's, and no one doubted it because John was the image of his father. Millie didn't stay long, and when she left she left without John, riding off with a man in a yellow convertible, the wind blowing her red hair and her scarves out behind. No one was sorry to see her go.

What did it matter now, thought Dorothy wearily. Richard was dead, his son seemed like a nice boy and she loved Ed. She was Ed's wife, the mother of his children, thirty-four years old, sleeping in the house she'd grown up in, safe and surrounded by family. To be discontented was a sin, and in times like these, who but a fool would have felt anything but gratitude?

During the long cold days of winter when they were all prisoners of the weather, Dorothy had almost begun to think differently about having a house of their own. She had looked out over white fields to distant hills and wondered where they could find as beautiful a place to live. She thought of the houses in Clinton, square boxes lining the streets that bordered the now defunct paper mill, identical two-story houses with small porches, set so close together the occupants could look into one another's windows and, in summer, share the sounds and smells of their neighbors' lives, and she knew there wasn't any reason compelling enough, not the furniture in the attic or the lack of privacy in the bedroom, that could make her move to a house like that.

Maybe it wasn't so much a house that mattered, perhaps it was the thing, whatever it was, that had been growing between them, like a weed that sends out runners and tentacles to strangle good growth and flourish unproductively. If they did find a house, would they move this "thing" with them, along with the towels and the Poole rocker and the children and Dorothy's kitchen cabinet?

Well, she thought, *we have money in the bank and our bills are paid.* Momentarily she felt cheered. The creamery was better than nothing. Let Ed mow every field there was. Mowed fields didn't hold you. People held you. People and the things that mattered to them. Where would Virgil skate if they moved? Where would he and Ruthie go to school? Where would they find another house big enough to hold them all so comfortably?

Moving was hard. There were some who thought it made life fuller, but she knew differently. Moving took away from life. A part of yourself that could never be reclaimed was left behind. Maybe that was the trouble with her and Ed. The two people who had been close were two people who had become ghosts occupying a house on Elm Street in Holyoke. It hadn't taken long, had it, for life in Havenhill to claim them. And hold them. But it didn't silence the feeling in her that life was no longer her own, because Ed had changed, and the children were pulling away, and others were taking a portion of what was hers, leaving her the poorer for it.

On Sundays Mr. Godwin drove the Packard to the front of the house and out came the two grandmothers, Vera and Dorothy and the children. Mrs. Howard and Vera sat in front with Mr. Godwin and the others sat in the back. Virgil, who was squeezed in between his mother and sister, stuck his legs out at an angle and said, "I don't see why I have to go to church."

He always said it and his mother always replied, "Because you do, that's why."

Grandmother Howard added, "It will do you good, Virgil."

Granny Beane snorted, "What! Not go to church? The idea. People who don't go to church don't go to heaven."

"What about Daddy?"

"That's different," said Granny Beane, although in her opinion it wasn't.

When they were all settled, Mr. Godwin drove them three miles down the road to the Congregational Church, where he parked as close to the front as he could. Then from the car emerged the old ladies in their black silk with black hats and veils (and in winter black coats), carrying black string bags, which they held in their black gloved hands. With the family behind them, they marched up the gravel path to the entrance of the white spired church that had been attended by Howards since 1820.

As they made their way up the walk they encountered friends and neighbors. No one hurried to get inside, except on rainy days, because everyone knew exactly what awaited them there. Mr. White, a kind man, gave deadly sermons that bored most of his congregation except those like Granny who approved of quoting scripture. People a generation ago had found the Bible more sustaining than they did now, and Mr. White clung to it tenaciously, for the thought of addressing the real issues that affected the lives and stunted the spirits of his congregation terrified him.

Dorothy wished he would speak out on the terrible conditions in the country, the unemployment, the gaunt, hollow-eyed gray figures who stood in long lines waiting for something to eat, the desperate need of farmers whose homes were being buried in drifting soil that had become in the searing droughts the sands of a new and desolate desert. Perhaps Mr. White hadn't seen the pictures in the newspapers and magazines that she had seen, or if he had, perhaps he didn't know what to say about them. Could he assure anyone that God would provide for the hungry, homeless masses captured for eternity by the lenses of a Kodak camera? If it hadn't been for her own mother, where would they be now, Dorothy wondered. And yet the fact that week after week Mr. White spoke on the parting of the Red Sea and the parable of the talents and ignored the thousands for whom no seas parted and no talents were given, had to be wrong.

Mr. White is a good man, she reminded herself and she let her attention drift. Across the church sat the elder John Currie, John's grandfather, wearing his Sunday suit, the white of his collar like paper against his weathered neck. Beside him squirmed Amy, her braids tied with blue plaid ribbons, and next to Amy sat Louisa wearing a blue suit, her head turned toward the windows. Probably Louisa suffered at the prospect of a

95

divorce, but how could one tell? People whispered and speculated and raised their eyebrows when divorce was mentioned. Perhaps all Louisa saw was the sun streaming through the small paned windows to fall with almost celestial radiance on the first three rows of the congregation.

Dorothy put her hand on Virgil's knees and shook her head at him. He glanced in her direction and mouthed the word "horse." She shook her head again and he replied silently, "Why?" She took a deep breath and suddenly realized that they were in church so she put her finger to her lips. "Later," she whispered.

Virgil scuffled restlessly and she turned away with a sigh. Mr. White was now describing Moses' flight through the desert with the Israelites, plagued by hardships that drove Moses up the mountain to pray, beyond the sight of the glinting golden calf.

How much longer was he going to go on, there were forty years of wandering and her throat was tickling. She had had a cold and she couldn't seem to get rid of the cough. It rumbled in her chest and tormented her sore throat. She was so tired, but she reminded herself sternly that it was spring. The world came to life again in the spring and things were getting better. Ed was earning enough money to put in the bank. They were lucky, all considered, but for the moment Dorothy simply prayed the service would end before she was strangled.

"That's a bad cough," said her mother later in the week. "I think I should call Dr. Tupper."

"My cousin Ezra had a cough like that," said Granny Beane. "His mother used to say he would cough up his tonsils, but it wore off in time."

Mrs. Beane's opinion had not been solicited and was not welcome. Mrs. Howard said sternly, "I want you to go upstairs and lie down, Dorothy. There's nothing here Vera and Ruby can't do."

But Dorothy didn't want to lie down. She wanted to write to

Edith, and she wanted to see what all the commotion in the barnyard was. Ed had gone off in the truck to Clinton for lumber, Virgil was . . . where was he, she wondered, and she went rapidly through the house and out the side door and was just in time to see something she had never expected to see.

There was a truck and trailer coming up the lane, and as she came across the yard she could see that it was Ruby's husband, Jack, and inside the trailer was a horse. All she could see was a wisp of tail and mane, but Virgil was dancing around wildly as the truck rattled to a stop. He seemed to go mad as the tailgate went down and a black colt emerged. To Virgil the colt shone with the radiance of Bucephalus. With nostrils flaring, black coat gleaming, Virgil saw Pegasus or, better still, Tom Mix's wonder horse, Tony.

Dorothy watched in silence. She saw Jack pass the halter to Virgil. She couldn't see the expression on Virgil's face but suddenly, as she watched, she didn't see a horse and a boy. She saw a truck and a tractor, a mowed field, rebuilt stalls, a tightly fenced pasture, and she wondered bitterly what Ed had paid to make this part of his impractical dream come true.

"Forty dollars," she said. It was two weeks' pay.

"Now, Dorothy," Ed said gently, "we've got the barn. I'll be cutting hay soon. Jack's going to train him. If he does well at the track he will more than earn his keep. Racing is two years off yet, but by then I'll be able to pay the fees and Virgil wanted—"

"Virgil's only a boy," she cried. "Of course he wants a horse. Every boy wants one, but what about us, Ed? Are we ever going to have a place of our own?"

"In time."

"How much time?" she said bitterly.

"What do you want me to do, Dorothy, go out west and hunt for gold? I could try the coal fields. I read somewhere there's always jobs in the mines. Maybe I could get more down in a hole somewhere. Is that what you want?"

"No," she said, "but there'll be another job somewhere, sometime. A better one."

He stood at the window staring into the darkness, as though he might see something out there in the blackness that would help. A dog barked and in the distance an owl hooted.

"Have you seen a rent house near here you'd live in?"

"No," said Dorothy. "Come to bed."

Ed moved restlessly beside her. "What do you want me to do? We're saving some, which is more than we did in Holyoke. Do you want Virgil to go through life wanting and never getting, like we have?"

"Virgil has all he needs," she said bleakly.

Ruthie's graduation from Sunnyside in June was an "event" for which Dorothy made her a white dotted swiss dress and everyone in the family, except Virgil, gave her a present. Virgil forgot, but of course he didn't have any money and Ruth knew it. Wrapped in white tissue and tied with colored ribbon, her presents from the others lay beside her place at the dinner table. Granny Beane gave her a lace-trimmed hankie and Vera gave her a box of notepaper. Her parents gave her a brown leatherette bookbag for high school. It had a gold-colored metal clasp with a lock and key. She said she loved it and she did, *actually* love it. Last of all she opened Grandmother Howard's gift, a gold pin shaped like a leaf. It was solid gold with a safety clasp and her grandmother said, "That's for Sundays, Ruth."

"I'll treasure it," replied Ruth dramatically but sincerely. "I love all my presents. Oh, thank you all."

She might have gone on and on, this singular attention was so intoxicating, but Virgil said he was hungry in a loud voice, and Vera and Dorothy went to the kitchen for the serving dishes. As they passed each other, Dorothy said, "It's lovely paper, Vera," and Vera replied, "I always wanted a bookbag like that. I had to carry an old carpet bag that was raveling. I hated it."

On the platform in the Havenhill Town Hall the five graduates sat on straight chairs placed beside tubs of mountain laurel, and after Mrs. Baker had expressed her appreciation to the school board for the new flag and the World Book they had purchased in the spring, she called on the graduating class, one by one, for what she said were graduation exercises.

Shirley was the first. She had written a poem that she called "Life" announced Mrs. Baker, who nodded encouragingly as Shirley rose and took her place at the podium, where she began to recite in a sweet, breathless voice.

"LIFE," she said.

> When I see life ahead of me
> I think of all the joys I've known.
> The family and friends I see,
> Have strengthened me as I have grown.
> I hope that I will always be
> Honest in my life ahead.
> Let no one ever say of me,
> 'Twould be a better place if she were dead.

At this point several men coughed and a number of ladies took out handkerchiefs and patted their flushed faces. No one would have considered laughing, and if anyone smiled, it went unobserved by Shirley, who continued earnestly,

> So as we face the world tonight
> We promise we will do our best
> To show our loved ones gathered here
> That we can pass life's test.

The minute Shirley sat down, there was a wild burst of applause and when that was over, Dianne Holeman rose to recite the poem she had memorized. Dianne had no imagination, but she was good at memorizing and she had chosen Joyce Kilmer's "Trees," which everyone knew and liked. There was a pleasant gentle clapping when Dianne sat down.

Next, Alfred Wilson gave his thoughts on What School Meant to Me.

"Mostly," said Alfred, "school means good friends and learning things."

During Alfred's spontaneous remarks, Mrs. Baker kept her eyes fixed straight ahead and smiled vaguely at a tub of laurel. She wondered if anyone listening would question just what sort of "things" Alfred had learned at Sunnyside. Alfred never could remember two consecutive lines of poetry or the names of the presidents, but she was sure he would make a good lumberman, and since his father owned a mill, she foresaw a creditable future for Alfred.

When Alfred finished, people clapped again and then Brewster Smith, who was the class valedictorian, read a paper he'd written on a subject Mrs. Baker had chosen for him. It was The World Today.

Brewster began with the words, "It was the best of times, and it was the worst of times." As soon as he'd said that much, an electrified silence came over the gathering. Those who failed to recognize the quote thought it sounded very impressive and true, and those who knew the author of those words were amazed that a product of Sunnyside School would have thought to apply the opening of *A Tale of Two Cities* to the current situation in the world. The assembled families and friends sat in respectful silence as Brewster continued.

"Our country is a great country," said Brewster. "As a people we have pushed our frontiers from the great Atlantic to the wide Pacific. We have more land and better resources than any other country in the world, and yet within this great land of ours thousands go hungry and hundreds are out of work. We cannot sit idly by when there are things we can do. Our great president in Washington is starting up programs that will help all Americans. He is doing what he can for the veterans who fought for this country to try to bring an end to war. He is doing things for young men who have no jobs. We must support him in his work to save this country and its people."

When Brewster finally sat down there was a pause and then

hard, prolonged applause. Dr. Adams nodded his head. He'd had boys like Brewster at Willowbrook. They were God's bright lights of the future and he felt reassured to know God was still on the job.

Mr. White, to show his approval, nodded at everyone whose eye he happened to catch. The boy was right. Times were hard. He could use the address as a text for his next sermon. He would start with "inasmuch as ye do this unto the least of me, you do it unto Me," and he drifted off in a happy haze.

Dr. Tupper remembered when he'd delivered Mary Smith of her only son thirteen years ago. He came into the world squalling and he was still at it. Good boy, thought Dr. Tupper.

The buzz of approval continued for a moment and then Ruthie, the last to rise, went to the podium. She had thought she was going to be nervous, but she wasn't. What Brewster said was right. It was a great country and they all needed to do something to keep it that way. It was people like Mrs. Baker, who taught in little schools and planned Christmas pageants and made sunshine boxes for people who were sick, and told you the meaning of history, those were the people who mattered. Ruthie said in a firm, clear voice, "My talk tonight is about memories of our school days, and I was going to tell you about all the things we'll remember about our life at Sunnyside School. But instead of that, I'm going to tell you about our teacher, because without her there wouldn't be any good memories at all."

Mrs. Baker looked up in surprise and blushed, then she smiled as Ruth talked on, describing how Mrs. Baker started every day with a salute to the flag and then a prayer and singing "America." How Mrs. Baker took books and lessons to pupils who were sick. How she planned birthday surprises and games. How she made them learn about geography and explained that you couldn't think of the world as just the place you lived, or the state you were in or even just your own country, because people all over the world were alike and needed things from one another's countries, and most of all they needed to help and love one another.

"Without a teacher like Mrs. Baker," she concluded, "I

wouldn't have learned enough to go to high school and I wouldn't have wanted to anyway. Mrs. Baker is a great teacher because she made us want to learn.''

With that, Ruthie turned red and sat down hurriedly. Everyone clapped happily and Mrs. Baker came over and gave her a hug. Then she presented each of them with a paper tied with green ribbon on which Mr. Robbins, the school superintendent, had written—Promoted from the Eighth Grade, Sunnyside School, Havenhill, Massachusetts.

There were punch and cookies in the basement of the Town Hall, where everyone milled around congratulating various people for numerous accomplishments, including such things as having peas ready to pick and ripening strawberries. When it was all over, people got into their cars, unless they lived close enough to walk, and went home. By then, it was after nine and getting chilly. At home, June bugs bumped the screens and Virgil and Ruthie were almost too excited to go to bed.

"Come along, children," said Granny Beane, who stood at the foot of the stairs, leaning heavily on the newel post. "Come help me up the stairs. It's been a nice time and now we all need to get rest.''

As Vera passed Ruthie she kissed her, something she had never done before, not even when they first came to Havenhill, and she said, "You did a lovely thing, Ruthie. You made someone very happy tonight.''

"Well," said Grandmother Howard, "another milestone. You spoke very well, Ruth. I was proud of you," and she stumped off to her room, saying as she went, "turn out the lights, Dorothy.''

And then suddenly Dorothy and Ed were alone, the lights were out except for a light at the head of the stairs. The screen doors were hooked and the outside doors closed. From Granny Beane's room came faint sounds as she opened and shut bureau drawers, but Ruth and Virgil had finished scuffling for the bathroom and all was silent. In the distance an owl hooted.

"We're a lucky family," said Ed.

"Yes," she replied, reaching for his hand as they started up the stairs together.

"Strawberries, strawberries," said Granny Beane, who sat at the kitchen table hulling berries. The ends of her fingers were turning red. Enough jam and jelly and canned berries for a year stretched out ahead of her, and hulling berries was a good job for Granny.

Dorothy brushed the hair away from her face with the back of her hand. It was a hot day, hotter than usual, and she didn't feel well. She and the children had picked all morning and now Ruth and Virgil had put on their bathing suits and gone off to Webster's Pond to swim. There were blood suckers in the pond, people said, but it was safer than the river. Still, she wished they'd waited for Ed. The river was cleaner and in weather like this he was usually glad to go.

"Whew," she said, "is that the last of them? I think I'll go up and take a bath."

"Go on," said Vera. "As soon as I'm through here I'm going down to the river and see what's biting."

As Dorothy pulled down the shade upstairs she caught a glimpse of Vera in her floppy hat with her fish pole over her shoulder, heading for the river. If she weren't so tired she might have gone along, but suddenly she was tired all over, and pulling off her dress, she lay down on the bed and closed her eyes.

At Berry Bay Ed finished early. Heat had invaded the creamery where steam rose in hot waves from the sterilizer. In the storage tanks milk cans bobbed among blocks of ice, but when the lids were lowered the atmosphere thickened. Warm milk, rising steam, and the roaring motor of the separator gave him a headache. He finished up and hung his black rubber apron on a peg, took off his boots, and closed the door behind him.

The haze of the day shimmered over the fields and when he

came to the fork in the road Ed turned toward the river. The thought of a swim tempted him, and as he walked toward the river he pulled off his shirt. When he saw Vera's hat dangling from a branch he said, "Damn." What was she doing here? Fish didn't bite in weather like this. If she wanted to fish she could have gone on down below, he thought angrily as he put his shirt back on.

He stood, glowering at her hat, and then it occurred to him that she might have gone below the bend and that he could risk a dip. He was undoing his shirt again when he saw a ring of bubbles on the water and coming up through them was Vera, like a beaver, her head sleek, her hair a thick black tail swinging sinuously down her back.

Except for the hat, he wouldn't have known it was Vera. She wasn't wearing her glasses or much of anything else for that matter, and Ed watched in fascination as she came out of the water. Vera was slim, delicate, graceful, all the good things. She stood up, shaking herself slightly and passing her hands down her arms and legs to shed the water that clung to her body. She wore an undershirt and she took the edge of it, twisting it to wring out the water. The shirt was plastered to her body like white paper and Ed saw a Vera he didn't know existed. She was feminine and girlish. The breasts she hid under shapeless dresses and dark sweaters were the white breasts of a statue with nipples that nodded like the blossoms of flowers. Her hips curved gently forward, ready and receptive. He could see the dark triangle of her pubic hair and he turned away quickly and plunged back through the bushes to the truck.

When he got home, he went around to the side of the house and turned the hose on full. The cold spray hitting his body made him gasp and he tipped his head back and began to drink.

Dorothy stood at the clothesline, watching him curiously.

"What on earth are you doing, Ed?" she called. "You've got your clothes on."

He turned off the water. "They were already wet, Dorothy."

"You'll have to change for supper."

"I know it," he said.

104

Summer suppers were simple. Onto the table came bowls of sliced cucumbers and tomatoes. Dishes of strawberries now, blueberries in July, peaches in August. New peas, fresh bread and butter, a pitcher of milk, a block of cheese. In August it would be corn. Dorothy made hot rolls. Ruby's tuna fish salad appeared with sliced hard-boiled eggs, and dishes of relish and pickled beets and piccalilli went around the table.

Lately no one had had much to say, except Granny Beane who prattled continually. It was never too hot for her, she said. The green tomato relish wasn't quite right. Where was the summer going? She could remember when her father brought home a bushel of peaches for canning and her mother took off her apron and said, "Amos, I canned my last peach yesterday. You can just take them peaches out and give them to the pigs."

Dorothy wished Ed's mother wouldn't talk all the time. There was always something wrong with the relish. Who knew where summers went? Did anybody actually care what Ed's grandmother had said to his grandfather on that long ago day when she decided she had canned her last peach?

The heat made her tired and her head ached. It made everybody tired, she supposed, and she would be glad when September came and Ruthie and Virgil went back to school. She would be glad when the dishes were done and it was time to go upstairs to bed. What was Granny saying now . . .

"I recollect when it was so hot the Sawyers, you remember the Sawyers, Ed, they lived in one of the mill houses down by the river . . . well, one of their young ones had convulsions it was so hot and Carrie Sawyer picked that child up and ran all the way up along the river to the ice house and carried it in there and sat in the sawdust on a block of ice all that time with the whole town out looking for—"

"Now, Ma," said Ed, "no one here knows who the Sawyers were."

That night Dorothy slept fitfully and in the morning when she took her temperature it was 103. She shook the thermometer down with trembling hands, as weakness washed around in her head draining down through her trembling body to her feet. She tottered back to bed. It occurred to her that she never got sick, but with her head and stomach reeling that was absurd. She was sick now, yet the habit of years told her she couldn't be sick. Mothers with houses to keep and children to feed couldn't be sick.

"Well," said her mother, "you're sick this time," and she went downstairs and called Dr. Tupper.

Dr. Tupper had first seen Dorothy Howard's chest when her breasts were only a soft fleshiness around her small pink child's nipples. That was twenty-five years ago. When he put his hand on her forehead, saw her cracked lips and put his stethoscope on her chest he said, "Well now, Dorothy, what did you want to go and get sick for?"

He shook down the thermometer and put it in her mouth and lifted her wrist to take her pulse. Dorothy had been one of the prettiest girls he could remember.

"Had a little cold, haven't you," he said, and she nodded.

"And a cough and bad throat? How long have you had that cough?"

She nodded again. "It comes and goes," she said. "Six weeks."

"Let's unbutton that gown now and let me have a good listen." He helped her sit up and began to thump her back. Eventually he said, "Well, Dorothy, you're up to your old tricks. It's sitting right there in your chest. I'm going to write out a prescription and I want you to take it just like it says on the bottle. Will you do that?"

"Yes," she said.

"And drink a lot."

He turned to Mrs. Howard. "You keep her drinking, Alice. At least eight ounces an hour and go on with the aspirin. Sponge her if the fever doesn't go down."

Grandmother Howard accompanied him down the stairs and when they reached the lower hall she paused and said, "Tell me the worst, Doctor."

"Pneumonia. If it is pneumonia. She's been sick for some time, and we can't be sure. It could be some sort of streptococcal infection, I don't know. Her throat is bad. I can try her on something new, one of the sulfa compounds. There is one . . . I think it would be available in Clinton."

They both knew what pneumonia meant and Mrs. Howard looked at him steadily, and then she said, "If it is pneumonia?"

"If it is this won't help, but it won't hurt. In any case I would tell you to keep on with the fluids and aspirin and sponging."

She nodded

"Call me any time," he said, "day or night."

Through the long hot afternoon Granny Beane sat in her rocker just down the hall from Dorothy's room. She read the Bible and snoozed. Whenever Ruby or Vera came up the stairs she stirred, lifted the round gold watch that was pinned to the front of her dress and noted the time. Then she promptly forgot it again. She was distressed to discover on one of these occasions that it was almost five. She smoothed her hair, tucking stray wisps under her hair net and then she went slowly down the stairs to see if there was anything she could do for anyone.

She found Ed on the porch sitting in the hammock and staring across the yard at the barn. He gave no indication that he was thinking anything, although his mind was spinning wildly. It seemed to have broken out of his body to move in the orbit of his imaginings in a frightening way. Through the dark aperture of the barn he thought he could see full hay mows. He seemed to hear the clanking sound of cows locked in their stanchions, and the clop clop of hooves on the wood floor of the barn.

It had been a mistake to come back here. Dorothy was right. This wasn't their place and never would be. All his ideas about a herd of his own and farm machinery and tight fences were just ideas, nothing more. Thinking about it now, he wondered why they had come back here to Havenhill, and for a while he persuaded himself it was because he had let others do the thinking for him. In the middle of June it was hard to remember that in Holyoke in November the coal bin had been empty and he hadn't had a pay check in a month and a half. We shouldn't have come, he thought, knowing that there hadn't been a choice.

"Ed?" said Granny, "is that you out there, Ed?"

"Yes, it's me, Ma."

He ought to be in Dorothy's room, he thought, but he'd spent half the afternoon watching his mother-in-law wring out wet washcloths to sponge Dorothy's white inert arms and legs, and the longer he sat there and watched the more useless he felt.

Granny was muttering about herbs, things she remembered from her childhood, bunches of dried leaves and twigs and roots from which her mother had produced colored brews that were forced on people who shook with fever or trembled from retching. In her anxiety, she rambled on until Ed said, "Please, Mother, not now," and then she rose and drifted out to the kitchen, where Ruby put her to work peeling potatoes.

Birds flashed and twittered in the twilight, but the house was silent. Virgil and Ruthie sat and stared at the five hundred unplaced pieces in a jigsaw puzzle and wondered when their mother would be better. Ed sat on the porch and watched as fireflies appeared, swarming in the bushes, flashing over the lawn as darkness came. Vera sat at the kitchen table eating supper. She had been with Dorothy all through supper and she sagged wearily as she ate. From the porch, Ed could look into the kitchen through one of the back windows and it seemed to him that in her flowered house dress she looked like all the women he had ever known, tired and colorless. If he were a good man, he thought, he would be able to wipe that other Vera right out of his mind, but he hadn't been able to, and it had almost begun to seem to him that life at Havenhill was like that. Underneath, there was something glowing and possible, but up front and on top it was just an old house and a sagging barn and fields grown up with thickets and nothing much to hope for.

The hammock chains creaked. They needed oil and he thought about looking for the oil can, but he didn't. He went upstairs again where the children were getting ready for bed, and his mother was already in her room.

There was no use in going to bed. He wouldn't sleep. He'd lie there in the dark thinking of all the ways he'd failed Dorothy. Anybody looking at them would have said they were a lucky family, but somewhere along the line they had taken a wrong turn. All Dorothy talked about was a place of their own and he should have managed it somehow.

He said good night to the children and went to his mother's door. She sat now in the Poole rocker with her Bible on her lap, but he could tell she wasn't reading. Her head nodded back and forth as the rocker, appearing to move of its own volition, marked off the seconds and the minutes that would spin out the night.

He moved stiffly along the empty hall and down the stairs and out onto the porch. The moon was full and the sky bright with stars. The roof of the barn looked like buttermilk, silvery gray in the moonlight. He stepped off the porch into the wet grass and crossed to the barn. For a while he prowled around, going at last to the grain room and lying down on a pile of gunny sacks.

Eventually he fell asleep and he slept heavily, starting up suddenly to realize that he was cold. Through a break in the wall he could see to the outside where moonlight transformed all that was familiar into something pale and grotesque. Fog hung over the garden and gathered on the grass, entering the barn as mist. He sat up abruptly and stumbled to his feet. Standing in the yard he could see the house, where only the light in the hall window shone. There would be lights on all over the house if things had turned for the worse, and with a feeling of relief he crossed the lawn and entered the dark house where, suddenly and unexpectedly, he encountered Vera.

She gave a little cry and he whispered, "Vera?"

"Ed?"

"I didn't mean to scare you. I've been in the barn."

"She's better," said Vera. "I'm going up now."

She passed in front of him, brushing against him in the darkness, her bare arm touching his, so close he could smell the lavender toilet water she used. It had never particularly attracted him, but in the dark kitchen where they were both accustomed to being, he suddenly felt as though he had touched a faulty light switch, felt a shock and brought the kitchen alive with light. *Oh my God,* he thought, and all the deprivation he had felt with Dorothy, the nights when he had wanted her, but "someone would hear." Nobody would hear now, but if she were there instead of Vera she would draw away, and for just a moment Vera paused, as though she had come to a crossroads to catch a bus and then, as she turned to look both ways, there he was.

She turned toward him. He could see only the pale oval of her face, sense her slender body, know the soft ins and outs of it, her breasts, her wide, shocked eyes, her open mouth struggling to breathe, for she knew and he knew and he knew that she also knew that this was not the time or the place, that there would never be a right time or place, that people like them couldn't slip, for if they did there would be only a few moments of joy to be paid for by years of anger and regret.

"I'll go up," he said, his voice husky but steady. "It's time you got some rest."

"She's better," whispered Vera. Then Vera gave a little gasp and turned away.

Dear God, he thought, *Dorothy, Dorothy,* and he stumbled up the stairs and down the hall.

Hot, hot, hot. The hottest July since 1915, said Mr. Godwin, who claimed he could remember. Under the burning sun tall grass swayed lifelessly in the heat and fields turned from green to gold to amber to brown. In late afternoon, thunder rumbled in the distance and heat lightning flashed, white against the sky. Vera's chickens scratched in the hen yard or sat on their nests, their necks bent like squashes' crooks, and refused to lay. In the garden, cucumber vines withered and crackled, tomatoes no bigger than Ping-Pong balls drooped on the vine, the corn was stunted and muskmelons looked like tennis balls.

Dorothy was up and dressed now. She sat on the porch in the shade shelling beans or sewing. Now and then her mother stepped out to inquire if she needed anything, but, inasmuch as Dorothy was well enough to come down for meals and able to shell beans she didn't see that she needed anything. Mrs. Howard knew this, but sat down anyway to talk about the years when Dorothy was Ruth's age, even referring to Charles, the brother Dorothy had never known because he died before Dorothy was born. It seemed significant to Dorothy that her mother would talk now about Charles, when she had never referred to him in the past. Her mother had changed. There was a new closeness between them and in the heavy heat of summer, after illness, it seemed unsurprising.

That afternoon at teatime Mrs. Howard rummaged through her bureau looking for Cousin Gertrude's fans. She had forgotten all about them, but they had to be there, because she had put them there. Sure enough, wrapped in tissue and tied with a gold silk cord, she unearthed enough for them all, and taking them into the sitting room she said, "Look what I've found."

"Oh my," said Granny, reaching out with a shaking hand. "It never gets too hot for me, but that's a pretty thing, isn't it?" and she clutched the carved bone handle of the Chinese fan in her thin veined hands and leaned back, fanning her flushed face so fast it looked as though she had captured a bird that was beating its wings frantically against her pale transparent skin.

Cousin Gertrude was Mrs. Howard's sister's daughter who had gone out to China in 1918 to take the Reform Church to the heathen in northwest China. Gertrude had been there ever since except for a furlough in 1923, which Mrs. Howard remembered vividly as a time when they had subsisted, at Gertrude's insistence, on tea, rice and half-cooked vegetables. She hoped that if Gertrude took another furlough, she would be content to visit her Cleveland cousins. Nevertheless, she admired Gertrude's dedication and wrote to her faithfully and kept a box in the sewing room for things to send to China. The Ladies Aid met once a month and twice a year they sewed for Gertrude's mission, turning out little white flannel gowns, bellybands and receiving blankets for Asian infants. Twice a year Grandmother Howard packed several cartons of these things and sent them to Gertrude in Luliang, China, a place so small no map showed it, and every Christmas a box containing fans, ivory pins, packets of green tea and chopsticks arrived from Gertrude.

"Just a little bit of China," wrote Gertrude, and then proceeded to describe a China of dead babies floating in rivers, of bound feet and famine and honored ancients who slept on top of their own coffins. This was meant to show the good ladies of Havenhill how much their efforts were needed and appreciated, and they listened to Mrs. Howard reading Gertrude's letters with wide eyes and sharp intakes of breath, in a state of exhilarated horror.

As July advanced people complained that it was too hot to do anything, all except Homer who was glad not to have to mow grass that had shriveled to nothing. Most of the time he sat in the shade of the shed, whittling. Inside the house, window shades were lowered, bedspreads put away and white counterpanes, like dust covers, were spread over the beds. Ice was guarded like gold. Ruthie lay on the floor reading *Gone With the Wind,* a book Louisa Currie had sent home with Ed. When she finished it she gave it to her mother, who had wanted to read it for a long time and Dorothy sat on the porch hoping for a little breeze and turning the pages rapidly to see what would happen at Tara next. Her heart went out to Melanie as the wicked, but fascinating, Scarlett flounced her way through the Civil War. The pages fluttered through her fingers and as the heat dragged on she felt almost uplifted as that distant wind from the South stirred through the hot tedious days at Havenhill.

In the evening Ed and the children swam in the river, stepping over the cracked mud of the riverbank to put their feet among

the roots of trees that spread bony fingers along the bare ground
and down into the mud as though hanging on for dear life. For
a while, after swimming, they felt refreshed and went to bed
clean, lying without even a sheet over them and listening to the
katydids as they sawed through the heavy heat of early night.

Virgil stood in the sun, revolving slowly as the colt ran in circles
at the end of a rope. Beau had worn a path that looked like a
giant doughnut in the field. From where Dorothy stood at the
sewing room window she could see little puffs of dust, like
balloons, strung out behind him as his hooves hit the dirt.

What is the use in it, she thought wearily. Virgil and his
dreams. How simple it was when all he thought about was
saving Ralston tops for Tom Mix premiums. If they had given
him a dollar or two then he could have sent for a gun, belt and
holster, or a pair of leather cuffs. For five dollars more he could
have had leather chaps. Maybe then he would have been content
to sit on a sawhorse in the barn and imagine all the rest.

While she watched, Jack came up the lane and crossed to the
fence. Jack was a fence watcher and, gray as dust, he slouched
against the rails in the hot sun, his hat pushed back as he
watched the colt run. He was as indifferent to the heat as a piece
of wood.

As he watched Jack thought, *That's a nice little horse I put
Ed onto, what we used to call a good buggy horse,* and he pulled
a rag out of his pocket to mop his face and neck, then he
sauntered back to the barn where Homer sat in the shade whittling.

"When Mr. Beane comes in," he said, "you tell him I was
here and told you that colt's as pretty as any I ever seen. Virgil's
got him a nice piece of horseflesh."

"You tell him," said Homer.

"Will if I see him."

"You're looking at him," said Ed, coming out of the shed.
"I hear you. You recollect you said you'd take a hand in his
training?"

"Did I say that?"

"You did."

"Well now, what sort of training was we talking about? Looks to me like Virgil's doing a good job on his own."

"You said that colt was bred to trot," said Ed. "We were talking about sulky racing."

Jack rubbed his chin. He appeared to be contemplating a shave or trying to stimulate his brain, which in his case, thought Ed, was probably located somewhere near his jaw.

"Well," said Jack, "that's a nice colt. He was bridle broke when I brung him. He's four months short of being a two-year-old and you can't tell much before that. He's all right for Virgil who don't weigh too much. Has he got a saddle on him yet?"

"What do you think," said Ed. "He had a saddle on him the first week."

"Long as it's only Virgil that's all right. Don't want too much weight on a colt until he's filled out and growed up so to speak."

"You said the colt was a trotter," said Ed.

"I heard you the first time," said Jack.

"What about it?"

"Now, Ed, you'll get your money's worth out of that fellow in the end and I may be wrong, Mr. Beane. Don't take it from me, but he's no trotter."

"How do you know?"

"I don't." Jack shook his head and backed off. "You can ask anybody you want to. I go by the chest. He's got a good chest, don't get me wrong, but it's a mite narrow. I don't see him with a sulky out back."

"You said I could race him."

"I may have," said Jack, "but I didn't mean for you to take it serious. Ask Homer. He's been around horses. He ought to know."

Ed didn't ask Homer. One Saturday in August he went down to Tipton and studied the horses on the track and watched them in the ring and what he saw didn't help much because he was no judge of horses. If he'd had the money he would have hired a trainer anyway. As it was, all he could think about was fees, not to mention sulkies, silks and drivers. He'd been a fool, but he wasn't sorry. The colt meant everything to Virgil. Racing was a sorry business anyway and there was no guarantee of winning. The thing he dreaded was telling Dorothy he'd paid for a horse that wasn't good for anything except to make Virgil happy, and he walked away from the track in a black mood. Damn, he thought, if a man wanted to give his son a horse and he had a place to keep it and hay to feed it he ought to be able to do it. The next time anybody said ''race'' to him, he'd let them know what he thought about people who had money to bet on horses, or anything else for that matter.

Would the weather ever break? ''Two years in a row,'' people said, as though the heat were a personal affront and not to be tolerated, and they checked their almanacs for signs of relief. The men were haying at Berry Bay. Corn swayed in the heat, rustling and dry, drooping and wilting for lack of rain. If it didn't rain soon, the garden wouldn't amount to much and he'd be buying hay come winter, thought Ed, and knew what Dorothy would have to say about that.

And then one day lightning split the sky, thunder exploded overhead and the rain came, first just a splatter that sent Dorothy and Vera running to the clothesline to snatch up sheets and towels. By the time they got to the porch the wind was blowing and raindrops hopped like a carpet of crickets in the dust.

They stood at the kitchen table folding the clothes, listening to the welcome sound of rain on the porch roof, and suddenly the clouds opened, a torrent hit the house, doors slammed and Ruby screeched, ''Oh Lord, the windows.'' All of them raced through the house closing windows just as the rain slashed against the glass panes.

Ruthie was reading in her room and, jumping up, she closed her windows and ran down the hall to Granny's room. Granny didn't like thunder and as it crashed overhead she reached a shaking hand out to Ruthie. "Oh dear, oh dear," she cried, "I hate storms."

"It's only clouds bumping together up in the sky, Granny."

"Humph," said Granny, clutching Ruth's hand. "Help me downstairs, Ruth. If we're all going to die, I'd rather be down there with the others."

The sitting room was dark, for the rain had blotted out the sun and the power had gone with a loud pop. As Vera scurried around for candles Mrs. Howard sat, rocking comfortably, and said, "We're perfectly safe. The house has lightning rods. Stay away from the fireplace, Ruth."

Candlelight improved the situation and Grandmother Howard who, despite her outer calm, disliked storms as much as Granny, sent Vera off to the kitchen for their tea.

Vera found Ruby huddled at the table with her hands over the ears and she said, "You're perfectly safe, Ruby," just as thunder exploded in the yard and a great tearing sound told them a tree had been struck and would fall on the house in another minute. Vera's hands began to shake as she set the tray, but inasmuch as the tree did not crash through the roof she proceeded with the kettle and cups and when things were ready, she poured a cup for Ruby, added milk and two sugars and set it down firmly. "There now, Ruby," she said, "there are lightning rods everywhere and it never strikes twice in the same place." Then she wheeled the tea cart into the sitting room where the others waited in semidarkness with their hands gripped together in their laps as they talked about other storms and how much everyone needed rain.

Eventually the rain slackened and thunder rumbled away. Dorothy, who was worried about Virgil, began to feel easier because Ruth said she had seen him go into the barn.

"The barn is perfectly safe," said Mrs. Howard. She could remember the lightning rod salesman who came through years ago and sold her husband lightning rods for every building on the place, including the outhouse.

Although thunder rolled away like Rip Van Winkle's ninepins, Granny's hands still shook and she put her cup on the table beside her. She had always been afraid of lightning and she crumbled a cookie without thinking and then ate the crumbs.

When the power went out at Berry Bay all the machines in the creamery stopped. In the barn, the milking machines had stopped too, and the cows would have to be stripped by hand. Chunks of ice bobbed in the water of the storage lockers, and as Ed lifted in milk cans, they knocked against one another, clanging like bells. He wasn't afraid, but he'd be glad to get away from all this metal and put his feet on a dry floor again. He hoped the rest of the family was at home where they belonged.

When Ruthie saw Virgil go into the barn that afternoon, the sky was blue, and if it was going to rain nobody knew it. Inside the barn it was so hot Virgil felt as though he were stepping into an oven, and he threw a blanket over Beau's back, bridled him and rode him across the field, through the meadow and down to the river. A little breeze stirred in the grass along the bank and below this the water moved lazily along. It was the only place he knew where Beau could get cool, and he sat there, stroking Beau's neck, with the water lapping at his knees. He didn't notice that the sky was getting dark or that the breeze had quickened and the temperature dropped.

Suddenly there was a crash of thunder and lightning zigzagged brilliantly toward the earth, disappearing on the other side of the river.

Beau reared and whinnied and Virgil jerked on the reins. For an awful moment he thought he was going to slide off Beau's back and into the river, but he didn't, and he said loudly, "Whoa boy, whoa there, Beau," and swinging his head around he turned the colt toward home. As they scrambled up the bank, loose stones and dirt rattled down behind them. Wind whipped through the trees along the riverbank and the rain started to fall. The meadow stretched ahead and across from that rose the north wood lot. It was the shortest way home.

By then the rain blinded him. Thunder exploded overhead and lightning flashed in the black sky on all sides of him. Under his knees Virgil could feel Beau's heart pounding as they raced across the meadow and went dodging through the trees. When they came to the old lumber road Virgil flung his arms around Beau's neck and pressed his face flat against the colt's mane. By then the wind was roaring in the treetops and thunder burst all around them. And then suddenly all sound stopped. The rain, the wind, the trees bending and hissing above him, the thunder, all of it ended as Virgil went sailing over Beau's head. Behind him, with his leg in a stump hole, Beau screamed and thrashed in the muck.

By the time Virgil came to, Beau had stopped struggling. Rain fell steadily, drenching them and the ground under them and the foliage over them. Virgil's head hurt and he wondered where he was and what he was doing there. He put his hand up to his head and felt a lump on his forehead, and he wiped at his eyes, trying to get rid of the water and blood that poured down his face, obscuring the tangle of underbrush and the forbidding aspect of the trees. He could hear thunder rumbling in the distance, and as he groped around he wondered what Beau was doing on the ground. Tottering over, Virgil grabbed the bridle and pulled. "Up, boy," he said in a croaking voice that didn't sound like his own, and as he tugged at the bridle Beau threw back his head and whinnied shrilly. Then Virgil saw Beau's leg. He reached down and as he ran his hand along Beau's flank the little horse screamed and began to plunge in futile agony.

When Virgil reached the house he stumbled onto the porch and burst into the kitchen just as Ruby opened the oven to take out a cake, and as the door slammed behind him Ruby's cake fell. She whipped around in a fury, said "Virgil" in a terrible voice and at the sight of his bloody face ran to the front of the house for Dorothy.

When Virgil saw his mother he began to cry and babble incoherently and she put her arms around him and tried to quiet him. Looking up, she saw Ed in the doorway. "He's hurt," she said needlessly, Ed could see that much for himself, and he bent down to Virgil and said, "Now, Son, just stop crying and tell us about it."

Dorothy began to bathe his face, sponging carefully at the blood and saying, "Look at his head, Ed. He has a terrible bruise."

"Just be still, Dorothy," he said and bent down again. "Tell me about it, Son."

"I think he's broke his leg," gasped Virgil. "He's all doubled up, Daddy, and he can't get up."

"You're sure his leg is broken, Son?"

"He's in a hole. It's all bent up. He was screaming," said Virgil and he began to cry again.

Ed patted him gently. "It's all right, Virgil," he said. "We'll go out and get him. You just let your mother look at that place on your head." Then he turned to Ruby and said in a low voice, "Where's Jack?"

"At home."

"Go find Homer and tell him to get the Packard and drive you home," he said, "and tell Jack to meet me in the north wood lot. Tell him I think the horse broke his leg."

Ruby nodded.

"Does he have a gun?"

"Yes," said Ruby.

"Better tell him to bring it with him."

Ruby went out the back and in a few minutes they heard the Packard and saw it disappear down the lane.

"He can't go back there," said Dorothy, holding a cool washcloth over the knot on Virgil's forehead, "it will start to bleed again."

"I'm all right," said Virgil, pulling away. "I'm going."

"No," said Dorothy.

"You can't stop me," sobbed Virgil. "Tell her, Daddy."

"It's all right, Son," said Ed, "we'll go together," and he took the towel from Dorothy and put it over Virgil's shoulders and they went out together, down the steps and across the yard, moving slowly and silently toward the woods.

When Ed saw Beau he knew what had to be done, but he made a pretense of examining the colt, running his hands gently over Beau's head and neck, giving Virgil the impression that there might be some hope.

"Well, Son," he said, "we'll do what we can. Now you go on back. Your mother's worried you're hurt, so you go on back and do what she says."

Virgil shook his head. He wasn't going to leave Beau. It was getting dark, water dripped from the trees, clumps of ferns drooped with wetness, it was dank and eerie in the half light and he didn't want to leave.

"What are you and Jack going to do?"

"Whatever we can."

"Can you get him back to the barn?"

"We will if we can, Son. Now you go on home, Virgil."

Virgil sat down beside Beau and began to stroke the colt's face. Pain had stupefied the animal. It lay motionless on the ground, breathing heavily, occasionally rolling its eyes, but Virgil's presence calmed him and Virgil, dazed himself, murmured, "Good boy, good boy," over and over again.

When Ed heard the men approaching, their boots cracking branches and sucking mud, he said sternly, "Now, Virgil, you go home. I mean it, Son."

Virgil stood up, but he didn't move away and when he saw Jack's pistol he dropped to his knees and putting his arms around Beau's head, he began to cry again. Swallowing as though he were going to choke, he said, "You can't shoot him."

"Get up, Son," said Ed, taking Virgil's arm.

"No," sobbed Virgil.

"There's no other way."

"What about splints? It's only his leg. Put on splints."

"If horses can't stand, they can't live," said his father.

Jack and Homer came closer and bent over to look. They saw jagged bone ends sticking through the skin and Jack said, "It don't hurt, Virgil. He won't feel a thing."

"No," screamed Virgil.

Homer Godwin backed off and kept still, but Jack went on in his flat voice as though shooting horses was something he did every day. "Longer you wait, more pain he feels. Go on, Virgil, just shut your ears and your eyes and get on home."

Virgil looked at Ed and Ed nodded. Then Virgil put his face down on Beau's. His tears ran into the black silk of the colt's coat, but when Ed put his hand down, Virgil stood up and they went off into the woods together, not looking back.

When they heard the shot, Virgil jerked and then he began to shake. Ed patted him gently and they stood under the trees for a while, then they went along home.

Later that evening, before it was full dark, Ed got on the tractor and went across the field and up the lumber road. There was a gully near where Beau lay, and when Ed had pulled off the blanket and taken the bridle, he worked a chain around the carcass and pulled it to the edge of the gully. Then he lowered the blade and pushed it over.

He worked until dark, burying the remains of Virgil's dream under the rocks and stumps and loose dirt the plow scraped up. He'd come back and finish the job later, but what he did was enough to keep down the stink and keep away scavengers. After that he went back to the house.

Virgil had a bath and went to bed with an ice pack on his head. He looked like an invalid and he turned his face to the wall when Ed sat down on the edge of the bed.

"Life is hard, Son," said Ed. "As you go along there are good times and bad times. It's that way for everybody. All you can do is face it as best you can and remember the good times."

Virgil lay like a stone and Ed reached out and touched his hand. "I know," he said, "there are some things it's no use to talk about. That's all right." He paused. "There was nothing else to do, Son," he said. "I'm sorry."

Down the hall his own bed was turned back and Dorothy was waiting for him. "I'm going to sit with Virgil," she said.

"He's all right."

"You never know with head injuries," she said. "I'll have to keep waking him up."

"God," said Ed.

"There's no need to be profane," she said coldly.

"I'm sorry."

"I never wanted him to have a horse," said Dorothy.

"He wanted one."

"And look what it's got him," she said bitterly. "What a cruel thing. What a terrible thing for a little boy to have to go through."

"I'm sorry," said Ed, "but if that's the worst thing he ever has to go through, he'll be lucky."

"Next time you get a bright idea like buying a horse, just ask me first."

"I will, Dorothy," he said wearily.

"Have a good night," she said, and closed the door.

One Saturday in September Ed drove home at noon and asked if anybody wanted to go up to the Curries' to pick apples. "Twenty-five cents a bushel," he said, and Dorothy, who wouldn't have picked apples at the Curries for any price, said, "Who were you thinking of, Ed?"

"Who do you think? Ruth and Virgil."

It occurred to Dorothy that picking apples meant ladders and she knew it wouldn't do for Ruthie to pick in a dress, so she went upstairs and found a pair of Virgil's overalls.

The Curries' orchard covered a hillside and despite the summer drought there was a good crop. Virgil and Ruthie bouncing along in the truck counted their money in advance and felt wonderfully happy. It was a gloriously bright day. Leaves were turning. One good frost and the trees would burst into flame. There were cornstalk wigwams in the fields, and orange pumpkins lay in the brown stubble like giant gold beads scattered carelessly over the ground.

In the orchard a man called Hollis gave them canvas bags and showed them how to pick. The trees were contorted with fruit; their branches bent almost to the ground forced them into curious poses so that the trees seemed to have become knobby little people staggering about the orchard.

Ruthie worked rapidly and carefully, but Virgil's apples went into his bag plop, plop, plop, and pretty soon Hollis came along and said, "Mebbe you'd best pick the drops, Sonny. It takes somebody little like you to get in under the trees."

"Do I get twenty-five cents a bushel for that?"

"Nope," said Hollis, "but it goes a sight faster. You'll get more apples and it will end up even."

Ruthie moved in one direction and Virgil another. She marked the bushels she filled with red string, which was what Hollis told her to do, and she had filled two and a half when she saw John Currie coming along through the trees. He was wearing riding breeches and if Ruthie's Aunt Evelyn had seen him she would have sighed in satisfaction—his appearance was so exactly correct for the young lord of the manor, and he was making his debut perfectly on cue.

Ruthie experienced a spasm of self-consciousness when she saw him, probably because she felt painfully ugly in Virgil's overalls. She couldn't have said why she felt ugly or why it bothered her, but it did. Shirley talked about boys all the time and what you were suppposed to do to make them like you, but Ruthie couldn't remember anything Shirley had ever said that fit this situation and she ducked her head as far into the branches as she could.

"Hi," said John, "what are you doing up there?"

What a dumb question, she thought, but she said, "Picking apples."

123

"I can see that," he replied.

"Why aren't you?"

He shrugged. "I've been riding. I'm home for the week-end."

"I can see that," she said. Shirley couldn't have done any better.

"Come on down."

"I can't."

"I'll hold the ladder."

"That's not it," said Ruthie. "I don't want to. I'm getting twenty-five cents a bushel," and she picked faster, although she suddenly felt embarrassed to have admitted that twenty-five cents meant something to her. She couldn't have said why because she knew that only a fool treated money lightly, but her face began to burn.

"I'll help you," John said, "tell me what to do."

"Go ask Mr. Hollis. He'll tell you."

"Damn Hollis," said John, and when he said "damn" Ruthie's feelings crystallized. She recognized instantly that he was more man than boy and this thrilled her. She stopped then and looked down at him with a new appreciation and said, "It's all right, John. It really wouldn't be fair if you helped me. Nobody's helping Virgil."

"I heard about his horse. I'm sorry."

She nodded.

"I'm going back to school tomorrow."

"That's good," she said.

"I might come over and see you before I go."

"That would be fine," she said.

When they came in from church the next day they could smell dinner cooking. A pork roast in the oven had reached the brown crackling state and potatoes and turnips were already peeled and ready to go on the stove. Ruthie, for whom the domestic life had few charms at the moment, moved slowly around the table, putting napkin rings where they belonged because by now it was clear that everyone had his own place, marked by his own napkin ring, fixed in the circle of family now and forever.

As she worked she thought about John, wondering when he would come. If he would come. As time passed she glanced anxiously out the window. Probably they were having dinner at the Curries' too, and after that someone would drive John back to school. She decided gloomily that he had probably come over in the morning and she had missed him. If he didn't come it was going to be a long stupid afternoon with nothing to do and she thought dismally that she wouldn't see him again until Thanksgiving.

When dinner was ready and they had said grace and spread out their own napkins and her father had served the plates, and gravy and applesauce were passed around the table, Ruth sat there, pushing things around on her plate. She wondered why they couldn't have spaghetti sometime. The Madderns had spaghetti whenever she went over there to eat with Shirley.

Besides that, Ruth was tired of the conversation at the table. No one said anything interesting. Granny was always talking about dead people. Uncle Charlie, Aunt Annie, distant cousins who lived somewhere, at some time, but were gone now. Vera and Grandmother Howard talked about church and the sermon and missionaries like Cousin Gertrude. Then, of course, there was Virgil, who talked about the pond and Joe Martin and wondered when the ice would be thick enough for skating. And her mother and father . . . well, what did they talk about? Mr. Currie, John's grandfather. Sometimes her father said, "Well, Dorothy, if anybody knows about the Curries you do," and then her mother looked up and said, "What's happening this week?"

The meal progressed and then suddenly Ruth heard her mother say, "Ruth! Are you asleep, dear? It's time to clear the table."

And so she stood up and began to take out the serving dishes, which came, or went, first. Then the plates. Then she filled the water glasses, and it was just as she was pouring Vera's glass that she looked out the window and saw the Curries' car and there was John running across the yard to the front door.

Without even asking permission, she raced to the hall and threw open the door and stood there, her cheeks flaming as she said, "I thought you weren't coming. I thought you'd be on the way back to school by now."

"I am," he said, "I just wanted to say good-bye and see you at Christmas."

Having said that, John stood, twisting his cap in his hands, staring at her with a look of need although he couldn't have said what he wanted or needed, and she, smiling and blushing, was relieved to have her mother come up behind her and say, "Hello, John, can you come in?"

"Thanks, but I can't. I'm on my way back."

"Come to see us at Christmas," said Dorothy, and then she put her hand on Ruth's shoulder and stepped back, saying, "it's getting a little cold, dear."

"I'll see you at Christmas then," said Ruthie.

Then John smiled and bolted and when the car moved off they went back into the house and Dorothy said, "He seems like a nice boy, Ruth."

And Ruth, who had just decided she would marry him some-day, only replied, "He's all right, I guess."

It was a beautiful fall. Foggy mornings were followed by long golden September afternoons. Ruthie went off to high school on the bus that stopped at the end of the lane and Virgil walked to school alone. Dorothy sat in the sewing room working on clothes for Ruth, who had suddenly begun to grow in all directions. In through the open window poured all the pungent scents of fall. She could see Mr. Godwin in the yard burning leaves. The smoke of his fire curled upward and Dorothy, breathing deeply, could smell Halloween. For the first time, the orchard was producing apples worth bothering with, and Homer took the drops to the cider mill in Mumfert. They hadn't had such cider in years, said Mrs. Howard.

One afternoon as Dorothy was upstairs in the sewing room turning the hem on a new skirt she glanced up just as Mable Cooper came up the lane. Mable wore a brown sweater over her orange plaid dress and had a brown felt hat on her head. She moved jauntily along, her briefcase swinging from one hand and a paper shopping bag in the other. When she saw Dorothy at the window she tipped her head back and called out "helloooo" and Dorothy took her foot off the pedal and covered the machine.

This time Mable was selling magazines and Christmas cards, and as Dorothy and Vera went out for the tea cart, Mable spread her magazines on the dining table and set out six boxes of Christmas cards.

"Come and look," said Mable, "I want you to see what I've brought this time."

"We'll look at your things after tea, Mable," said Mrs. Howard, and she poured out, saying, "Well, Mable, tell us what you have this time."

"You'll have to see for yourself," said Mable. "It's Christmas cards, they're in assortments. I have six boxes, all different. I've already sold thirty-two boxes."

"My goodness," said Granny, "thirty-two boxes."

"And I have a special on the *Good Housekeeping* this month. Fourteen issues for the price of twelve. You'd like the *Good Housekeeping,* Dorothy." Mable stirred her tea with a steady hand and said, "All of you for that matter. Not just Dorothy."

Granny looked up and said thoughtfully, "If you've sold thirty-two boxes, Mable, then everyone we know will be sending the same cards. There won't be many surprises come Christmas."

"They're all different, Granny," said Mable, "that's what an assortment is, all different, and the idea is that you send them to your out of town friends."

"I don't know as I have any anymore," said Granny. "Of course there are all those people in Millbrook, but if I sent to one I'd have to send to all and it's just too much."

"Wait till you see them," said Mable confidently, "I've never seen a prettier bunch."

While Mable waited, nervous and impatient, Mrs. Howard discussed the weather and the apple crop. She asked Dorothy about her sewing and remarked to Vera that she hadn't heard from Gertrude in almost four months.

Vera had seen pictures in the *Boston Herald* showing Japanese planes dropping bombs on Peking, and ventured to say so, but Mrs. Howard thought it unlikely Japanese bombs had fallen on Luliang, where Cousin Gertrude was stationed.

"We don't get the Boston paper," said Mable breezily, "it's all I can do to keep up with what's going on in Clinton and Mumfert." She reached for another slice of bread and butter and put her cup and saucer down with a small rattle to let Mrs. Howard know that time was passing.

"By the way," she said, "I guess you know about Grace Baker?"

They all knew that Grace was expecting and Dorothy said, "But it's too soon. She isn't due until February."

"She slipped on the back steps and lost the baby," said Mable. "A perfect little boy. They say Harold's beside himself."

"Poor Grace," murmured Vera.

Mrs. Howard thought instantly of Charles, who had died of the croup forty years ago when he was only two. It would have been easier, she knew, if he had never been born, but she didn't say so.

Dorothy thought immediately of something Grace had told her just last week in a strained undertone. "Harold doesn't want me to teach," Grace had said, "but I can't stand it at home. His mother won't let me alone, Dorothy. It would be better if I stayed here weekends. I dread Thanksgiving when I have to give up for good."

"She'll blame herself," said Dorothy.

"She was carrying out the ash bucket," said Mable, "going down those steep back steps."

"Well," said Granny Beane, "only the Lord knows why these things happen. Grace is young and healthy. There'll be another."

"Not from what I hear," said Mable. "They say Harold blames her. They say Harold said it all came from teaching this fall."

"Well," said Mrs. Howard, who disliked gossip, "I think it's about time we looked at your cards, Mable."

That night Dorothy wrote a note to Grace Baker. She wrote, "These times are very hard, Grace, but I know you and feel sure you'll bear it with good courage. I know it sounds heartless (and I don't mean it to) to say that things do happen for the best, yet so often they do. You are both young and healthy and there will be other babies and the pain of this will fade. Somehow such things often seem harder for men to accept, so be patient with Harold and don't blame yourself. I've always heard a good pregnancy can't be stopped. Think of what the women who crossed the prairies in covered wagons must have endured, yet many of them went full term and had healthy children. Try to believe that it really is true that God knows best."

She stopped and thought about Ed, who would never have blamed her for something like this, then she reread what she had written. "Such things seem harder for men to accept," and she wondered what things she meant? Losses, disappointments, things that were supposed to be women's affairs, babies and sickness, caring for the old, stretching meals and money, things that women were responsible for, things for which women could be blamed and men allowed to grieve.

Who had decided that men would change tires and women change diapers? That men's lives would be insured, but women's not. Why was a man's rest guarded and a woman subject to call at any time day or night?

She put down her pen. Just to think of Harold Baker, whom she had never liked, standing a foot taller than Grace, looking down his thin nose at her, blaming her, made Dorothy furious. What right did he have to judge Grace and, for that matter, why should any man have the right to judge his wife? It escaped her notice for the moment that she was indifferent to half the things that Ed seemed interested in since they'd come to Havenhill, and if that wasn't a judgment, what was?

Sometimes when he thought about it, Ed couldn't see that anything much had changed since he and Dorothy had moved in with her mother. Granny had always been sleeping down the hall from their bedroom, and Dorothy had always been reluctant to show him the kind of affection he craved. "Somebody will hear," she would whisper frantically, and he would think desperately that all the doors were closed, the children had been asleep for hours, his mother was half deaf—who was there to hear?

But it had been better in Holyoke, and discontent moved sluggishly inside him. Dorothy wasn't the only one who wanted a change, he thought. He would give anything to be his own man again. When they had arrived a year ago and Mick had turned up the lane and the truck had bumped along the dirt road to the front of the house, he had seen fields going to underbrush and a barn standing empty and he'd said to Mick, "Look around, will you. Did you ever see a place that needed a man more than this one here?"

Well, he thought bitterly, *looks like it's going to go on needing a man until the woods grow right up to the back of the house and the barn caves in.*

Snow came in October, early, people said. Tiny flecks of white ash danced in the air, barely visible against the slate of the sky. When Ed drove in at six it was making fast, whirling against the windshield of the truck so he could hardly see the road or make out the shed. It reminded him of the night last year when he and Virgil came in from Boston. Well, he wouldn't be cutting trees this year, except for the house, because this year he had a job.

As he drove into the barn, turned off the ignition and stepped out, he experienced a wave of bitterness. Mr. Currie may have been a fair man, but he was not an easy man to work for. There was no future at Berry Bay for a hired man, and Ed knew that's all he was—the Curries' Homer Godwin.

In the half dark he sensed a settling of the swallows overhead, breathed in the dry staleness of vacant stalls and empty hay mows and thought angrily, *This is where I ought to be.*

It had been some time since he'd thought about the bottle he'd left in the grain bin and it suddenly occurred to him that it wouldn't do any harm to check it. He crossed the barn floor, his footsteps ringing hollowly in the emptiness and he paused to listen to the wind singing around the corners of the building. As he stood there in the darkness, he sensed something eerie, almost as though there was a herd locked in stanchions in the milk barn below, shifting, blowing, hooves in the gutters, muzzles in the feed trough. There was life in the barn, swallows in the rafters, hay in the mows. *There could be—Lord yes,* he thought, *there could be.*

Virgil never came into the barn anymore. Beau's blanket and bridle were where he'd dropped them that night in the summer. There was still a scattering of hay in the stall and droppings turned to stone. In the morning he'd sweep the place clean or make Virgil do it. *My God,* he thought, *you can't coddle them.*

He dug the bottle out of the grain and twisted it open, then tipping his head back, he took a swallow. The liquor went along his throat like flame, burning all the way down to his stomach and he suddenly felt warm, free and untroubled. He tipped the bottle up again, then rammed down the cork and put it back where it belonged. Something was coming to him, like a vision, something that would liberate them all, a thought so obvious he wondered why he hadn't thought of it before, a name and a face, staring down at him as though from a lighted billboard, telling him which way to go.

Mr. Bruce.

Mr. Bruce, leaning out of his big car, stretching out his hand and saying, "If you ever need a friend." All he had to do was find that card.

Dorothy found him standing in the middle of their bedroom, turning it over in his hands, a dazed expression on his face as though, now that he had it, he wondered what to do with it.

"There you are," she said. "Where have you been? You aren't even dressed, Ed. Look at you. You know supper's at six."

"Look, Dorothy."

She read the card and dismissed it. "What do you want with that?" she said. "Who is he anyway?"

"When Virgil and I took trees into Boston last year. His car broke down, he gave Virgil the money."

"That's right," she said. "I'd forgotten. Hurry up, Ed. Vera's almost ready to take things up."

"Listen, Dorothy," he said urgently, "I think he'd give me a job."

What is Ed talking about, she thought, sinking down on the bed and staring at him. *Why would a man named Bruce give Ed a job?*

"You've got a job," she said, "and you'd better hang on to it." She stood up and brushed past him, then she turned abruptly. "You've been drinking, Ed Beane," she said, "I can smell it."

"I had a swallow of liquor. That's all."

"Where did you get it?"

"I have a bottle."

A bottle, she thought. *How could he have a bottle without my knowing it? What was happening? Something was wrong,* and she said, "You're not going to Concord to look for work, Ed. It doesn't make any sense. We're here. You aren't really thinking any such thing, are you?"

"Yes."

"Why?"

"Because I'm never going to amount to a hill of beans here. I should have done it before this, only I didn't think about it."

"What about us? What about me and the children?"

"You'll be all right," he said, knowing they would be all right if he lived or died. Most men would give their right arm to know that. "It won't be forever, Dorothy, only until we can get a place of our own."

"What about the creamery, Ed? You can't just leave Mr. Currie. You'd have to give him some warning."

"I guess I could leave any time I'd a mind to," he said.

"What about Thanksgiving and what about Christmas?"

"I'll be home," he said.

"I thought everything was all right here," said Dorothy.

"It is all right," he said, tearing off his shirt and reaching for the one Dorothy had spread out on the bed. "It's the money, Dorothy. What can we do without money? We'll never have our own place at the rate we're going."

"We can stay here. It's better than it was, Ed. I like it better all the time."

"So we stay here," he said, reaching for his comb, "then what? What can we do without money? Suppose I do make this into a going thing. There has to be stock. The tractor's falling apart. There's got to be money before we can even think about building onto what's here."

"What about Mother? Why not ask her?"

"You want to be beholden to your mother for everything, Dorothy?"

"There's no harm in asking," she said.

"I've taken all I mean to take," he said shortly. "Long as there's a way to turn so as I can earn it, I'm going in that direction."

They went down the stairs together, two stiff people braced to meet expressions of impatience and disapproval because it was well after six. What difference did it make, thought Dorothy wearily as she apologized. How could Ed sit there, unfolding his napkin, serving and passing the plates as usual as if nothing had happened when their world was suddenly going upside down?

"Well," he said cheerfully, "day after tomorrow I'm going down to Concord to look for work."

This was met with shocked silence and Dorothy said quickly, "Of course there may not be any work down there, but he thinks there might be."

133

"Well, I never," said Granny, "and I've just written Evelyn. Now I'll have to write to her all over again. What kind of job are you getting, Son?" Clearly it hadn't registered in her mind that Concord was fifty miles away. To imagine Ed looking for work more than ten miles from home was unthinkable to Granny, and she sat, smiling vaguely as she waited for an answer.

"Anything that's offered, Ma," he said.

Mr. Bruce needed a driver. He offered Ed fifty dollars a week, room and board, and time off when he'd been with him two months. It all happened so fast Ed didn't have time to count up days and he'd been there a week before he realized he wouldn't get home for Thanksgiving.

He called Havenhill collect, and Dorothy, who assumed all long-distance calls meant bad news, accepted the charges in a strained voice and said breathlessly, "What's wrong, Ed? Are you all right?"

"I'm fine," he said, "everything's all right. I called to tell you I can't come for Thanksgiving. I don't get time off for two months. That brings me right up to Christmas. I'll be home Christmas."

"But it's Thanksgiving, Ed."

"I'm sorry, Dorothy. That's just how it is."

"Why can't he get somebody else for the weekend? Other people drive cars. Why can't he hire somebody else?"

"He's paying me a lot, Dorothy, and it isn't only the driving. It's the car. That's how I got the job. You can't get the car fixed at any gas station, it's a Rolls-Royce, Dorothy, that's an English car."

"I know it is," she snapped. Did he think she was stupid?

"I don't like it any better than you do," said Ed, "but it's a job. You're the one that wants a house, Dorothy. We weren't getting any closer to it up there. Were we?"

"I never meant for you to be there, and for the rest of us to be here," she said, "that's not what I wanted, Ed."

"We'll have to take things the way they come," he said. "I'll be home for Christmas."

She put the phone down. They had probably talked more than three minutes and there was no telling what the bill would be. Probably her mother had been looking at her watch and counting the time. When Granny heard Ed wasn't coming for Thanksgiving she would fuss, and Vera would shoot sympathetic looks in her direction. Well, she didn't need Vera's sympathy, and straightening her shoulders, Dorothy went back through the hall to the sitting room, where the others had stopped reading and knitting as they waited to hear what Ed had to say.

"That was Ed," she said, "he's not coming for Thanksgiving."

"Well," said Granny indignantly, "do you want to know what I think . . ."

But Dorothy didn't want to know what Granny thought. She went upstairs to the sewing room and began to rip the seams out of a dress she was making for herself. She was so furious she forgot which seams needed altering and tore them all out.

John Currie didn't come home for Thanksgiving either. He went to Boston with a classmate, and his grandfather, who had written permission for the visit, tried to hide his disappointment as he went stoically through the motions of the annual feast for Louisa's sake. He didn't know what ailed her, but he and Rachel had kept their troubles to themselves. Louisa could do the same.

It had been a hard fall. He lost Ed just when things in the creamery were going better than they had in a long time, but he couldn't blame the boy. He'd heard Ed was getting fifty dollars a week driving somebody's car. Well, he thought, I wouldn't be surprised to find out there was a rotten apple in that bushel, one way or another. They'd get along here, he thought. They had before and they could now. He'd asked Louisa if she didn't want to ask Charles to come up for Thanksgiving and she'd said "no," which was her affair and he wouldn't ask again.

Louisa, who nursed a special bitterness of her own, instructed Mrs. Hobbs, who had managed things at Berry Bay since Mrs. Currie's death fourteen years ago, that there was to be a big turkey (not a roast capon, which is what her father said would do now that John wasn't coming) with chestnut stuffing, mashed potatoes, boiled onions, baked squash, cranberries, glazed apples and giblet gravy.

Mrs. Hobbs, who had been cook at Berry Bay since before Louisa was born, took her orders calmly and then proceeded with a small turkey, breadcrumb stuffing and flour gravy. Louisa was always changing her mind. Mrs. Hobbs hoped the divorce would blow over, or blow away entirely, and that Louisa would go back to her husband and have another baby, which would be the normal thing to do, but there was a grim set in Louisa's face whenever Charles was mentioned, and Mrs. Hobbs knew better than to ask questions.

Thankfully, no one had questioned her about Charles, Louisa thought, although her father had a right to and she tried to think about him as infrequently as she could.

For Thanksgiving dinner Louisa put on her black silk and her mother's pearls. She lighted candles (at Berry Bay dinner was served in the evening) and sitting down in her mother's chair, she tried to live up to the occasion. She was more than thankful to be there, but she was lonely, and sitting in her mother's place she felt like the spinster daughter, home to the bitter end for the sake of the old folks.

Candlelight shone on the polished table and the centerpiece of bittersweet. The delicate twigs and berries might have been taken from a Chinese scroll and it occurred to her that it would be a good thing if she could acquire more of what she imagined were oriental graces—patience, submission and acceptance. How distinguished her father looked and how barren his life had been. He rose and went to the sideboard where there was a bottle in a cooler, and when the stopper came out with a loud pop she thought in surprise, *He's doing this for me. To make it festive,* and she almost wanted to cry.

Amy squealed when the cork hit the ceiling and when her grandfather filled the glasses he put a taste in hers. Then he stood with all the calm and poise of Evelyn's Sir John, and proposed a toast.

"To all those loved and absent."

He thought of Rachel and Richard.

Amy thought of her father.

Louisa thought of all three.

December brought more snow, choking the roads and imprisoning them in the house. A bitter wind blew clouds of snow across the fields and windowpanes gathered frost so thick Virgil could scratch his name on it. Webster's Pond disappeared under a featherbed of snow that lay softly over the frozen water below. The pond wasn't cleared for skating until John came home for vacation.

By midmonth the Christmas baking had begun and Mr. Godwin brought in the usual basket of greens. No one felt particularly joyful despite the spicy smells drifting from the kitchen, and Dorothy, sitting at the card table near the fire, tried to write Christmas cards. She had bought two boxes from Mable and sat dispiritedly going through them. Mable was right, it was an assortment, sleighs, white churches and snowmen. The snowmen would have to go to Ruth and Virgil for their friends in Holyoke. It seemed to Dorothy that Mable might have pointed out that half the cards in the box were suitable only for children.

She wrote her first card to their Holyoke pastor. *It's been a hard year,* she wrote, and then, thinking of people with real problems, she added, *but of course we are fortunate to be here.* After all, what was a little sickness and hot weather, and what was there to say about Ed except that he finally had a wonderful job driving a Rolls-Royce for a rich man in Concord.

The truth was, Ed was nothing but a chauffeur who wore a

black suit and a chauffeur's cap, and was paid to do it. He was nothing more in that household than Mr. Godwin was in this, and it was her fault because she was the one who wanted a house of her own. If she'd been more content . . . Guilt burned through her.

Some people might have confessed these feelings to their pastors, but she couldn't. Instead, she wrote about the children, who were both well and looking forward to Christmas. She didn't say that Ed hadn't been home since the first of November and wouldn't be home until the day before Christmas. He would miss the Christmas music at church, and the program at Sunnyside and the pageant at Mumfert High. All she said was that they missed their friends in Holyoke and hoped that things were going well there. She wrote this message to most of the women in her study group and to Edith Callahan too.

On the night of the eighteenth, they all bundled up and went down the snowy front steps and got into the Packard. Their breath rose in spirals of vapor, even in the car, and Mrs. Howard, who sat in front with Vera and Mr. Godwin, spread a plaid steamer rug over her knees, lifting the edge to accommodate Vera as well. In the back, Granny, Dorothy and the children shared a buffalo robe, once thick and warm, now tatty and musty. Dorothy said sharply, "Don't pull on it, Virgil, you'll tear another hole."

Ruth was wearing a plaid skirt and a new red pullover, which was Granny's Christmas present. Ruth wore Mary Catherine's cross around her neck. The sweater had turned out smaller than Granny intended it to be and fit Ruth snugly, showing her developing figure. Since most of the other girls in Mumfert High had well-established figures already, this aspect of Granny's present pleased her.

I wonder if it will stretch when it's washed, thought Dorothy, glad for once that Granny didn't see as well as she used to. The revelation of Ruthie's breasts would have alarmed Granny, whose robust heritage had been sorrowfully overcome either by a ripple from the Victorian pool or by the Mother Hubbard viewpoint of the missionaries her husband's churches had supported so enthusiastically. If Granny had her way Ruth wouldn't be allowed to have breasts at all until she had children of her own.

They rode silently, bumping over roads that had been scraped and sanded, chains clinking, passing now and then the lighted houses and barns that connected the center of Havenhill to the metropolis of Mumfert.

In Mumfert, there was a village green around which clustered a post office, a filling station, a white frame building with a front porch, occupied by an A & P and a hardware store. Across the green, presided over by a statue and a cannon, stood a small brick house, now a library, and next to this, a ten-cent store, a dress shop called The Bonton, and a sandwich shop with a plate glass window framed in colored Christmas lights. A blizzard of snowflakes, made by whipping up Lux flakes and water with an eggbeater, had been daubed all over the window and as they passed, Vera said, "Look at that. Doesn't that look Christmassy?"

"Yes," said Dorothy.

"Where?" said Granny. "What? What looks Christmassy?"

"The window of the sandwich shop, Granny," said Dorothy. "It has lights around it."

Mr. Godwin pulled up at the front of the high school and stopped the car. He got out and went around to open the door for Mrs. Howard. He didn't expect to sit with the family. As a matter of fact, he was looking forward to going across the common to the sandwich shop for a cup of coffee, but he said, "I'll find a place to park and sit in the back."

"That's fine," said Mrs. Howard, taking Vera's arm. "We'll meet you at the door when it's over."

In the brightly lighted auditorium there was a pleasant buzz of voices and the sound of a violin being tuned. The room was suffocatingly hot, and they began immediately to shed their wraps as they went down the aisle to find their seats. Now and then people from Havenhill called out to them, but it was getting late, the violin was lifting its voice in hysterical squeaks, and there was a general scraping, coughing, scuffling unrest that told them the program was about to begin. Eventually the lights dimmed and Mrs. Corliss, who was in her sole capacity the music department of Mumfert High, struck several crashing chords on the piano and the lights went out.

Virgil was squeezed between his two grandmothers who, when they saw Ruth, began to expand with pride and pleasure at the sight of her draped in blue and wearing a gilt paper halo. She cradled one of her old dolls in her arms, rocking back and forth with her head inclined, presenting such a natural aspect Dorothy shivered with a sudden revelation of the future. Even Granny's red sweater had failed to capture what this vision of her daughter foretold, and Dorothy could see Ruth with her own child in her arms. At the same time, she was aware of Virgil and she leaned over Granny and hissed, "Stop squirming, Virgil. Sit still."

"I'm being squashed."

"Hush," she said. "It's just for a little while."

In the library afterward tables were cleared for refreshments. There was green punch made with lime Jell-O, and plates of cookies cut in the shapes of trees and stars. Granny and Mrs. Howard went immediately to chairs that rimmed the perimeter of the room where they, and others like them, framed the event. Old women wearing dark coats and hats and old men in their Sunday suits with black overcoats folded across their knees watched the scene, while youngsters like Virgil trotted back and forth with paper cups of punch and cookies wrapped in paper napkins.

What a picture it presented, the old gazing across years of similar Christmas programs to their own beginnings, crumbling cookies in their swollen, shaking hands and sipping green punch from small paper cups. Fathers congregated in one corner to talk weather and cows. Ed should have been among them, thought Mother Howard. And there was Dorothy with the other mothers, pouring punch, fussing with little brothers and sisters, scolding the boys who would run and the girls who did scream.

Ruth stood in a corner with her friends, and Virgil, cramming cookies in his mouth, looked around for someone his own age. Only Vera seemed to have no place of her own. She stood behind Dorothy, ready to help, although no one seemed to need any help, and Mrs. Howard went across the room toward her.

"There you are, Vera," she said. "Would you mind going over and helping Mrs. Beane into her coat? I dare say Mr. Godwin's already in the entry waiting."

Ed didn't come home for Christmas after all. He had to take the car to Florida for Mr. Bruce, and Dorothy, her hand clenched on the receiver, heard his voice, scratchy and distant, telling her the unthinkable. They had never had a Christmas apart—not since they were married. What would she tell the children?

"I'll be there for New Year's," said Ed. "Look Dorothy," he continued desperately, "I don't like it any better than you do, but it can't be helped. It's a job. I'd never find a better one. Not the way things are now."

"I don't care," she cried. "You don't have to have *that* job."

"We've been through all that, Dorothy."

"Mr. Currie would take you back," she said, "he'd find something for you."

"For fifty a week?"

"There's more to life than money," she said bitterly.

"That's not what you thought last year."

The silence on the line was costing money. Sometimes it seemed to Dorothy that even to breathe cost money. When had money become so important to them? Why had she ever thought she needed a house of her own?

"Oh, Ed," she said, "it won't be like Christmas without you. Are you sure you'll be here for New Year's?"

"Yes," he said.

When the time came, his plans changed again and a bushel of oranges arrived by railway express with a card that said Happy New Year, and when Dorothy saw that, she put the card back in the oranges and kumquats and orange blossom honey, and went into the sitting room, picked up Ed's presents, which were still wrapped and sitting on top of the piano, and took them upstairs and put them on the bureau. She walked stiffly, her face set in hard lines, her eyes shut tight. She wasn't sorry to see the end of 1936. As far as she was concerned, it had been a bad year.

Bored, bored, thought Ruthie, wandering through the house looking for something to do. Other people had parties on New Year's Eve. Even Shirley was going to a party in Northampton. *There's nothing to do in Havenhill,* she thought morosely. She was tired of reading and tired of old people and tired of hearing about the Bible. Her mother said, "Maybe we could pull some candy tonight," and Ruthie retorted scornfully, "On New Year's Eve!"

"Why not?"

"Other people have parties on New Year's Eve."

"We'll have one," said Dorothy.

"Who with? There isn't anybody in this dumb town to have a party with. If we were still in Holyoke there'd be . . ." and she stopped, trying to think which friends would come to a party. Mary Catherine might have to go to Mass and there was no telling about the others. "There's nobody here," she said, and Dorothy didn't bother to reply.

"Well," said Ruth. "I'm staying up until midnight. I'm not a baby anymore, you know," and she stamped up the back stairs and down the hall to her room, where she threw herself on the bed and lay on her stomach looking out the window. Snow, snow, snow. Icicles hung from the roof outside the window and the afternoon sun, striking through them, dazzled her. Then, as she watched, she saw a dark figure emerge from the woods and come swooping down the hill and across the meadow. It was John Currie on skis.

She leaped up and ran to the bureau, grabbed her hairbrush and brushed her hair furiously. He was already in the kitchen talking to her mother. "Why don't you and John go in by the fire," said Dorothy, "he's probably frozen."

In five minutes Ruth was back, her face flushed with excitement.

"He wants to take me to the midnight show in Clinton, Mother."

"Oh Ruthie. That will be so late. Ask him to come here. We can see the New Year in right here. I don't want you out on these icy roads. Clinton is twenty miles away."

"I'm not a baby, Mother," said Ruth. "It's the first time a boy's ever asked me to go to a movie, and he's a good driver. Virgil says he is."

"I'm sorry, Ruth. I don't want you to go out tonight."

"Why not?"

"You're fourteen, Ruth. You're too young."

"I am not too young," said Ruth. "You're just old-fashioned. Everybody at school goes out with boys. There's nothing wrong with it."

"I'm sorry," said Dorothy.

"If Daddy were here he'd let me go."

"I doubt it," said her mother, "and he's not here."

When Ruth looked back on that New Year's Eve it seemed to mark the beginning of her real life because John came after all. He brought his Monopoly game and they (they being John, Ruth, Virgil and Dorothy) spread it out on the dining room table and played all evening. Vera came in from the parlor to look on and Mother Howard stopped on her way to bed to see what all the laughing was about. At eleven Dorothy owned all the railroads, which was quite enough property for anyone to own, she said, and she went to the kitchen and started the taffy. When it was ready she poured it out on buttered platters to cool, and when the new year presented itself they were all standing around with their hands full of sticky taffy. Kissing was impossible under the circumstances. Undoubtedly there was kissing at Shirley's party in Northampton, thought Ruthie in disappointment.

Poor John. He'd never pulled candy and the slippery mass came apart in threads that he clutched in his buttered hands as he hopped around the room in a sort of wild dance. Ruthie pulled in frantic haste until hers was pale and supple and she drew it into a long thin rope for cutting. Then she took John's and pulled it expertly while he watched and marveled.

Why was that such a glorious time, she wondered later. It had been a bleak Christmas. Her mother must have been worried and lonely with her father still in Florida. Why did that night stand out so shiningly in her memory? The Monopoly board, the warm kitchen, the golden candy, the black sky brilliant with stars, the snowy fields, the sound of chains crunching as John drove away and disappeared in the dark, the silence of the sleeping house as she and her mother crept upstairs together. The beginning.

Once more they settled down to the long dull days of winter. The Florida oranges disappeared one by one. Before long Mable Cooper would come tramping up the lane with her magazines or flower seeds. Grace Baker was teaching again. Louisa Currie had left for Reno. There hadn't been a Christmas box from Cousin Gertrude, and occasionally Mrs. Howard remarked on that. It seemed odd to her, but, of course, said Vera, the Japanese were bombing China and it might have been blown up en route.

Dorothy measured everything in relation to Ed. He had now been gone since the first of November. She had had twelve letters and two postcards. She waited for the mail and jumped if the phone rang. She sat in the sewing room making Virgil a pair of pajamas and turning the material she double stitched a seam. It seemed to her she ought to be patient. Most of the women she knew would have thanked God for their husbands to be working anywhere. Her last letter from Edith had sounded worried.

Mick's brother had been laid off and his wife and their three children had moved in with them, wrote Edith.

Dorothy had never felt separated from Ed before, not the way she did now, and she didn't like it. What did it matter where they lived, she thought, or what sort of work he did? Being together was all that mattered, and shaking out the pajamas, she thought, *Good Lord, they look enormous.* Virgil was growing, he'd be as tall as Ed before she knew it. A boy needs his father, she thought, feeling she had recognized a great truth when it was actually rather an unoriginal thought.

He'll come when he can, she thought fiercely, willing it to be true and she slid the jacket into the machine and began to pedal rapidly. And then, with the whirring of the wheel and the clacking of the treadle something occurred to her, something so obvious she wondered why she hadn't thought of it before.

If he can't come here, she thought, *there's no reason I can't go there.*

The next week Dorothy withdrew twenty dollars from the bank and bought a round-trip bus ticket to Concord. She sat down at the desk and wrote to Ed. "Dear Ed," she wrote, "I'm coming down on Friday and if you're there to meet the bus I'll stay until Sunday. I don't like living this way. I know it's not your fault, and if you're going to be off somewhere, just telephone."

She read what she'd written. It sounded short, but what she felt was strong and direct—she wanted to see him and be with him, she needed him. She added, "I can't wait to see you. All my love, Dorothy."

On Friday morning she dressed carefully. The silk blouse her mother had given her a year ago dressed up her old blue suit. Taking her navy felt hat from its box she saw how dilapidated it was. It had been in and out of the rain so often the brim hung in a scallop around her face. *You look old, Dorothy,* she said to herself, and then she thought, *why not?* She was thirty-five years old. If she looked tired there was good reason. She pinched her cheeks until they burned and pinned on her lapel the gold oval pin Ed had given her when they got engaged. Then, picking up their battered suitcase in one hand and her pocketbook in the other, she went down the front stairs with her head up, smiling at the family who were waiting to see her leave.

"You look beautiful, Mother," said Ruth.

"Have a good time, dear,"said Granny.

"Straighten up, Dorothy," said her mother. "That's better."

"Bring me something," said Virgil.

She kissed them all and then without looking back she went straight through the door and into the Packard. Glancing in the rearview mirror she saw that they had all come onto the porch and were huddled together shivering, their breath rising to form a halo of vapor over their heads, and a lump rose in her throat. There they stood, her dear family, and she lifted her hand to wave.

At the bus station in Concord she spotted Ed before he saw her. Pacing up and down in a black suit she'd never seen before, his chauffeur's suit, he looked different to her, alien and exciting, and she pounded on the glass. She had forgotten how good looking he was.

When he saw her, he put his fingers on the window and ran along beside the bus, grinning at her, and when he had her in the car he began to kiss her like a wild man until she broke away and gasped, "We're in town, Ed. People will see."

He laughed. "Who do you think notices?" he said as he backed around and headed for home. If she wanted privacy he knew where to find it.

The Bruce Estate was situated north of Concord and entered through stone gates where a man in uniform sat in a cubicle to inspect anyone passing in or out. He smiled and waved Ed on.

"That's Mike," said Ed. "The guard."

"Why would there need to be a guard?"

"Mr. Bruce is a rich man."

They passed along a drive of evergreen. Here and there clumps of birch trees nodded in the sun and then, beyond a sweep of lawn as broad as a golf course, the house came into view. It was like a scene in a movie, thought Dorothy, the distant house appearing as the landscape unfolded to reveal tennis courts and a swimming pool, gardens just showing green and horses grazing in the field beyond.

"Good heavens, Ed. Who is this man?"

"Now you see why I haven't been able to get away."

"No," she said. "He doesn't own you. Everybody gets time off."

"You have to earn it," he replied. "I've only been here since November."

It had seemed like an eternity to her. To Ed it was only ''since November.'' She looked up, taking in the greenhouses and the well-kept gardens that surrounded them, and as they approached the garage over which there appeared to be living quarters, she noticed a little boy pulling a red wagon around in the drive.

"Who is that?" she asked.

"Jean's boy."

"Who's Jean?"

"His secretary."

Just then a young woman with blond hair appeared and called to the child. When she saw Ed she waved and smiled. What was a girl like that doing here, wondered Dorothy. Wouldn't a man as important as Mr. Bruce have an older woman to do his secretarial work, someone with gray hair? A woman who wore conservative clothes and suitable shoes, not this flashy-looking girl in slacks. It gave her a funny feeling to know that on the other side of the wall from Ed there was another apartment just like his with a girl and her little boy living in it.

"Now," said Ed, his arms around her and the frustration and longing of the past weeks exploding inside him so that he could scarcely control himself even when he felt her stiffen and heard her gasp, "Oh, Ed, please darling, not so fast. I want to get used to being here. I want to talk a little."

He laughed and thought grimly that she hadn't changed, but

he kissed her more gently and took her hand. "Look around," he said, "this is the bedroom."

It was so neat she knew he'd gone to a lot of trouble just for her, and it never occurred to her that he might have maid service. The spread was straight, the dresser top bare. On the bed table there was a lamp and radio, and she said, "A radio! Wouldn't the children love that, Ed. Right beside their beds. They'd never go to sleep."

A small round table in the kitchen was set for two and in the center there was a bouquet of fresh flowers. No one had fresh flowers in Havenhill yet and she said, "Flowers! Oh, Ed."

"They're for you, Dorothy."

"Daisies in the middle of winter," she said, putting her face down, "but you shouldn't have. They must have been expensive."

"Not a penny. They came from the greenhouse. You can see it from here," and he held back the kitchen curtain for her to look. "They even grow orchids there," he said, and he opened the refrigerator and took out an orchid and pinned it on her blouse.

"It's beautiful, Ed."

"That's not all," said Ed, and he took out a bottle of champagne. "This is for us, Dorothy. To celebrate."

Dorothy had never had champagne. She had never had wine or liquor either and the only time she'd tasted beer she hadn't liked it. She was eighteen when Prohibition was voted in and repeal didn't mean a thing to people like the Howards, who had always been abstemious. The idea of champagne both thrilled and alarmed her.

"It must have cost a fortune," she said.

"Mr. Bruce gave it to me for Christmas," said Ed, "it's one of the things his son-in-law imports. The one in Scarsdale."

A picture was forming slowly in Dorothy's mind. "He must be a liquor dealer," she said.

"Who?"

"Mr. Bruce."

"I don't know," said Ed. "In Florida it's horses. Jean says

he made his money during Prohibition. She keeps . . ." Ed stopped. He could see by the look on Dorothy's face that to mention Jean had been a mistake, but Dorothy didn't comment on Jean.

"He must have been a bootlegger, Ed," she said. "Any fool could see that. He made a fortune bootlegging during Prohibition and now he gambles and imports wine."

She said this scornfully, as though she had some sort of superior knowledge of the seamy side of life, which she didn't, and Ed said, "He pays me well and I work hard for it. Selling liquor is not illegal now and the racetracks are there."

"Money isn't everything."

"You didn't say that two years ago when I was laid off."

"That was different."

"How?" he said. "How was it different?"

"It just was," said Dorothy stubbornly. "This isn't real." She waved her hand as though to include in one grand, scornful gesture the orchid, the champagne, the garden outside, the horses in the pasture, the tennis courts, the Rolls-Royce, the house. "It's like a movie," she said contemptuously. "It's like something Evelyn would write about, a huge house and bottles of champagne and an old man betting on horses with a fortune he made bootlegging. It's wrong, Ed," she said. "We aren't like that."

He glowered at her and said, "What are we like?"

"We're just plain people. We don't drink and gamble. We work hard. We're family. We stay at home, and do decent things. You made butter, Ed, with milk that came from the cows right there. Ordinary people bought it and ate it. The cellar is full of canned things from our own garden. Ruthie and Virgil believe in honesty. We brought them up to think gambling is wrong and that making money selling whisky is a sin."

She turned to look out the window, afraid to look at Ed and panting with emotion. *What has happened to me,* she thought. *I want him to come home. I want us together again. I ought to coax him, I ought to be begging him, I ought to entice him.*

149

But she didn't know how to entice anybody. She'd been brought up to think that flirting and luring and enticing were cheap. What she wanted now was just to have him take her in his arms and hold her so tightly she'd know they'd never be separated again.

"Have you finished?" he said coldly.

"Yes."

"Do you know what it's like to lose your job and have a family you can't support? Do you know that?"

"Yes, I know," she said. "I was there, Ed. We were in it together."

"Do you know how it feels to live in your mother-in-law's house, to have to ask her for money to fix up an old wreck of a truck, to have to put on a tie to sit down to supper at somebody else's table, to have to creep around so as not to disturb anybody, to have a wife who shrinks away from you and says 'Oh, no, Ed, not now. Somebody might hear.' "

Ed let his voice go up so that in the telling he mocked her and she said, "It wasn't always that way and you know it. You never could understand, could you? Did you want the children to hear us, and your mother? Whose mother was it, Ed? Yours or mine?"

He turned his back and gazed out of the window, seeing the same view he'd seen for ten weeks, no longer imagining how it would be if Dorothy were there with him because now he knew and it had been better alone.

"Fine thing," he said slowly, "all this time I've wished you were here, and when I couldn't get home I'd think about it and plan how it would be if you were here. We've never had even one bottle of champagne, or anything else," he said, "but even if we had it wouldn't have mattered, would it, because we never celebrated anything. Somebody was always sick or it cost too much, or you were too tired."

"Or you were."

"What difference," he said bitterly. "We had my mother and your mother. We were never like other people, were we, Dorothy? Other people let down sometimes, and if they make too much noise they don't even know it. Other people can open a bottle of champagne and it's not a sin, it's a party."

"Like with Jean, I suppose."

"Jean who?"

"Your Jean," she said, "next door. With the blond hair, who waved at you. That Jean. With her it would be a party."

"Oh, God, Dorothy. What does that mean?"

"You know what I mean. Why haven't you come home all these weeks? I suppose she goes to Florida too. What do you do with yourself, Ed, alone all those evenings?"

"Stop it, Dorothy."

"I won't stop it," she said. "When did you ever put flowers on a table before, Ed? Or talk about champagne, and act as if you thought gambling bootleggers were decent people, and had a blond floozie sleeping just on the other side of the wall and—"

"That's enough," he said.

"Am I right?" she cried. "Have I hit home, Ed?"

"No."

"Ha!"

The small dramatic "ha" was so unlike her she laughed. She could hear a hysterical laugh that became a sob and she turned her head quickly away and pressed her hands to her ears as though she could shut away all that had been said or might be said.

"You can forget about Jean," said Ed. "Just forget her. She sleeps with the boss. That's what she's here for."

Dorothy's hands dropped to her sides.

"Satisfied?" he asked. "Want to know how I found out, Dorothy? You know Mike at the gate. He told me the day I was hired. I took the car to meet the old man in town and Mike stopped me at the gate. He put his hand on my arm and he said, 'Let me tell you something, Son. You got a nice little piece of ass living right next door to you up there, but take my advice and leave her alone. She belongs to the old man.' "

"Stop," said Dorothy in a low voice.

"I can tell you more than that," said Ed. "Want to know about the girls in Florida?"

151

"No."

"Are you satisfied?"

"Why do you stay?" she said, and he didn't reply. "Money isn't that important."

"It's not only the money."

"What is it?"

"It's you and me," he said, "even now. Here we are alone. You won't let me near you. Who's going to hear us now?"

"I'm sorry."

"Would it be any different if I came home?" he said, shaking his head.

"Oh, Ed," she cried, reaching out to touch his arm. In the half dark it was easier to look at him. In the growing shadows the pain they had inflicted on each other was less evident.

"I'm sorry," she said.

"It's all right."

He didn't move toward her but stood away, as if he were still alone and she hadn't come and none of this had happened, and she moved closer, shivering, running her hand slowly up and down his forearm until, at last, he reached out to reassure her and then a terrible ache and desperate longing took possession of him. He seemed to see her as he'd seen her a thousand times before, her body a soft blur glimpsed through her gown, her hair down, her arm brushing, brushing, and suddenly he crushed her to him. His hands went to the buttons of her blouse and in a daze of feeling he was surprised to feel her hands at his belt, tugging at it and sobbing softly as she kissed him.

He carried her into the bedroom and put her down on the bed and began to love her gently, his fingers barely touching her, as though he were afraid that she was some wild thing that might spring away at any moment, until at last he grew sure of her and found her breasts, her belly, the soft velvet between her legs.

Afterward they lay in the dark, half asleep and half awake, their naked bodies together. In all the years it had never been like this before and the thought went in and out of Dorothy's mind, a strange fuzzy question that puzzled her. Why now, after all this time? Why hadn't she ever felt this way before?

She closed her eyes and sighed. Oh beautiful darkness and silence, she thought, with no one here but us, and she reached over and began to stroke Ed absently and gratefully.

"Oh, Ed," she murmured, rolling against him, "what do you want? What do you really want, Ed?"

"You," he said roughly, burying his face against her. "You. Just you."

Cars passed along the drive, their headlights slashing into the room and the sound of their great motors purring as they passed and were gone.

"I don't mean that," she said, "you've got me. But the other. Where do you want to be? What do you want to do? How do you want to live?"

"With you," he said, his arms tightening around her, "with you, Dorothy, and the children. Anywhere. Wherever you say. In a house of our own. At the farm. I don't care."

She sighed. She might not have thought so a year ago because she simply took it for granted, but now she knew that all she cared about was being together, and curiously, the only house she could visualize when she thought of going home was the house in Havenhill.

"I don't need a house, Ed," she said, "we have a house. I like the house we live in, but what do you want, Ed? What do you really want?"

"I want to farm," he said.

He didn't add that it was the only thing he thought about when he thought of going home. A herd in the pasture, another horse for Virgil, the orchard replanted, corn in the flats along the river. What was he doing here if that wasn't what he wanted, and he said, "I have over four hundred in the bank, Dorothy. In another six months I'll have fourteen hundred more. That's close to two thousand dollars. I could do a lot with that much money."

"What would you do with all that money?" she asked sleepily, suddenly too tired and content to care very much. "How would you spend it, Ed?"

"I'd buy you a mink coat," he mumbled.

"I don't want a mink coat. And I don't want a diamond ring." She reached out and touched his face, stroked his cheeks, traced the line of his chin with her fingers as she said, "I don't want anything but you."

"I'd buy me a bull," he said slowly, "and a new tractor."

"Ah . . . ," she sighed as she imagined a bull chained to a stake, tossing its head and pawing the dirt, blowing steam from its wet nostrils, a bull that would beget calves. Something flitted into her mind. *Beget* was one of Granny's words and she amended it. A bull that would sire calves. Calves that would become a herd. And a tractor with a harrow that would break the earth, opening it in ribbons to accept seed and drink rain and become long even banners of green that would stretch for as far as anybody could see.

For a moment she wondered what the family would think when she told them Ed was going to come home as soon as he had two thousand dollars, and that he was going to take the farm and wake it up from its long, idle sleep and shake it hard until apples rained from the trees and cattle multiplied and every seed that touched the ground burst with goodness.

What would they think, she wondered dreamily, not really dwelling on it because in her last hazy moments of wakefulness she knew what the answer would be. They wouldn't wonder anything at all. They would simply nod and smile and go on about the usual things, because as far as she could tell all of them had accepted long ago that Havenhill was where they belonged.

Interim

Ed came home from Concord to stay the following Christmas, and early in January he bought a bull and four heifers. In February he bought a tractor and hired a man named Oscar Koehler from Mumfert to work for him. Between the two of them they plowed and seeded the south pastures and put in enough corn on the flats that lay along the river for silage in the fall. By summer there was water and electricity in the barn, Ed joined the Grange and the Holstein Dairyman's Association, and the following spring, in 1939, all the heifers calved. There wasn't a bull in the lot.

The Dairyman's Association had a publication that was filled with information about dairy farming, and at Christmas they sent a calendar to their members. Dorothy hung it on the kitchen wall between the two windows that looked toward the barn. For every month there was a picture of a Holstein bull or cow or herd. Black and white cattle covered the pages of the calendar, up to their teats in snow or mud, depending on the month— grazing among the dandelions and buttercups of spring, wandering over browning pastures toward a backdrop of brilliant fall leaves. Lord Lavender, prize Holstein bull of AppleDrop farm in Utica, New York, captured the month of June. Thornhill

Meadows' prize milker, Nancy, averaging forty pounds of milk a day for all of 1937, decorated the month of August.

Meanwhile, on other calendars wonderful things were happening in the world outside of Havenhill. Beyond the cultivated fields, far from the orchard, as days fluttered away and drifting clouds gathered, seasons came and went with the rapidity of water flashing down a brook. Life within the walls of the house moved serenely along at its own pace while that other world, the great wide world outside, pressed in frantic haste to embrace its destiny.

In the course of 1937, while Ed saved money in Concord, two little princesses dressed in purple robes witnessed the coronation of their father. That same year, FDR, cigarette holder clamped jauntily between his grinning teeth, embarked on a second term. Under black caterpillar eyebrows, John L. Lewis raged at the savage injustice that was the lot of coal miners, while spinning around in organdy ruffles, a curly-headed live doll tapped her way into the hearts of all America.

In 1938 a man under an umbrella waltzed with death in Europe. The New York El, transformed by magic of the Japanese, continued to fall with bursts of smoke and flame on the sleeping Dragon of the Orient. Soldiers goose-stepped into Austria by invitation, and a girl named Brenda Frazier was the first debutante to be heralded with all the fanfare usually reserved for a movie star.

In 1939 there was a world's fair in New York City to which fifty-eight nations sent exhibits, and in Atlanta, Scarlett O'Hara, in vivid Technicolor, said "Fiddle di dee." Germans massed on the Polish border, people fussed about Lend-Lease and women worried about whether or not the seams of their silk stockings were straight.

Howard, named for his maternal grandmother's family, was born in February 1939, and Dorothy and Ed moved into the room over the west wing. For the past thirty years it had been used for storage, but now Mrs. Howard decided there was enough room in the attic to take care of all the old trunks and broken furniture and called Wilber Smith in the village to come out and put in a closet and repaper the room. Besides that, he cut a register in the floor for heat and put a door through the wall into Ed and Dorothy's old room so that they could have a sitting room. When the baby came, Dorothy said they needed a nursery more than they needed a sitting room and that's where Howard's crib was put.

"No more babies in the bedroom," said Ed, and Dorothy settled for leaving the door cracked.

Ruthie and Virgil couldn't believe their mother was going to have a baby. Old people didn't have babies, they assumed, but they got used to it. The baby carriage came down from the attic, and on cold winter days Howard, wrapped up tightly and wearing a bonnet, had his nap on the porch.

In those short years, Virgil changed from a boy to a man and everything about him began to seem too big. His nose was too big for his face. His hands dangled like baseball mitts at the ends of his arms. His feet grew too fast and he was out of his shoes before they were worn through. His voice croaked at unexpected and embarrassing times. In the summer, he drove a skittish horse called Ginger hitched to the hay rake and under the burning summer sun his bare back tanned to the color of strong tea. As soon as the snow fell, he built a lean-to at the edge of the pond so that when people put on their skates they could sit on a dry log instead of outside in the snow. He and the older Martin boys now had hockey sticks and a regular puck and played hockey after school.

Meanwhile, Ruth fell in love. Since it was something she had been doing ever since she was fourteen, Dorothy didn't pay too much attention. John Currie came and went, from one vacation to another, and Ruth watched the mailbox for letters in between. Letters weren't like dates, however, and she and John had progressed from holding hands and good-night kissing to parking after the movies. Sometimes she would fold her arms over her chest and say flatly, "No. Not until you promise to write me. You never write unless you have to."

"Who says I have to," John said, "but I promise anyway. I will write you faithfully this time."

"Prove it."

"How am I going to prove it?" he said. "Be reasonable, Ruth," and he reached out and twisted his finger in her hair, curling a long strand of it around and around as he slowly drew her face to his and kissed her until she thought she would suffocate. Then she pulled back and gasped, "No, John, please," but her heart pounded wildly all the same, and if it hadn't been for knowing what was right and wrong, and being scared to ignore that, she would have let John do anything he wanted to do.

Dorothy, who suspected how things were with Ruth, went into Ruth's room one day and sat down on the edge of the bed and said, "You wouldn't do anything foolish with John, would you, Ruth?"

"What do you mean by foolish?"

"You know what I mean."

"I'm going to marry him, Mother."

"You think that now, dear, but you may feel differently when the time comes. John has four years of college ahead of him and you're too young to make up your mind about things like that. You have your own life to think about and you may change your mind."

"I won't."

"I hope not, dear. We all like John, but marriage is a long way ahead. You've got to be careful, Ruth. I mean it. Boys, even nice boys, will take advantage of willing girls."

"If you mean go all the way, Mother, why don't you just say so?"

"Well, don't," said Dorothy.

"I'm not stupid, Mother," said Ruth. Sometimes her mother amazed her. "I wasn't born yesterday," she said.

Vacations came, vacations ended. In June 1940, Ruthie graduated from Mumfert High School and that fall she went to Katharine Gibbs Secretarial School in Boston. John was at Harvard and Dorothy tried not to think at all about what they might be doing on dates. Howard was now going on two, a robust, noisy little boy who had four women, not counting Ruth, to spoil him. Virgil helped with the milking before he went to school. He got on well with Oscar, who had never finished high school but knew about cows. For Oscar, milking thirty cows a day was a simple matter of getting to it. He ate more than Mr. Godwin, Ruby said, but then, she added, he earned it, which was more than she could say for Homer.

There would come a time when Dorothy would look back and see her family as it was in 1941, a vision that radiated joy and contentment. By then, the farm was beginning to take its final shape, reemerging from the thickets with furrows running straight to the river. In 1941 Ruthie was in Boston finishing the course at Katharine Gibbs that she imagined would take her wherever she wanted to go, providing it was ever necessary. With John at Harvard, Boston was the only place she had considered. Virgil was at home, doing a man's work for his father. Vera studied McCalls dress patterns, wondering which would be the best for Ruth and never asking herself why, exactly, she had a special feeling for Ruth. The grandmothers scarcely seemed to change, although Granny forgot things with irritating frequency and then denied stoutly that she had. She misplaced her glasses, which didn't matter much because her cataracts were almost as thick as milk glass, but she did tat, when she could remember where she'd set her work basket. She called Vera, Madelaine (Madelaine was her sister's daughter whom she hadn't seen in forty years, who seemed suddenly to have become very real to Granny). But everyone understood. Granny was the oldest. She was going to be eighty that fall, and she didn't miss a chance to tell people, as though she could actually remember, exactly what kind of world it had been when she was born.

"You can't believe that, can you?" she insisted to anyone she encountered. "It was right in the middle of the Civil War. And I'll tell you another thing you won't believe. I was forty when I had Ed. Thought I was an old woman at the time, but what did I know? Not anymore," she sighed, "not anymore."

Granny was going to have a birthday party. It was meant to be a surprise, but of course it couldn't be because she had to have a new dress and blind as she was, she could see what was going on in the kitchen and through the rest of the house.

And it did look beautiful, Dorothy thought later. Ed and Virgil went into the woods and cut yards and yards of running cedar. It was twined all the way up the banister from the entry to the second floor. After the first frost, Vera nursed along a dozen pots of mums and asters, keeping them in the greenhouse, and then brought them in for the party, bursting with gold and white blooms.

"That was the last time things were the same," Dorothy said out loud, as she stood at her mirror pinning up her hair, and spoke to the stranger in the mirror who looked out at her with a sad, bleak expression, almost as though she didn't know what Dorothy was talking about, when of course she did, since they were one and the same.

Dorothy could remember the day of Granny's party vividly. As a matter of fact, the memory was so clear it was almost as though a photographer had captured it on film and there they were. All of them. A family portrait. Her whole dear family.

Her mother, wearing black silk with white lace at her throat and wrists, seemed to regard her benevolently, but sternly, from her seat in the wing chair on one side of the fireplace. Across from her sat Granny, gazing vaguely about with a little smile, appearing ready to make an observation that would diminish something or someone. On the ottoman beside Granny sat Vera, wearing a green dress made from Chinese silk sent by Cousin Gertrude. Vera's eyes were focused on something beyond the eye of the camera and she smiled her small, shy smile. Her hands were clasped in her lap, and although it wouldn't have been evident if the scene had actually been photographed, Vera held them so tightly together the knuckles were turning white.

Grouped in the center was Dorothy's own family, smiling happily. Ed held Howard, who was dressed in a navy sailor suit she had made for the occasion. He'd had his first boy's haircut and he looked older than two. One of his small round arms was around his father's neck—not actually around Ed's neck, but reaching up Ed's lapel toward his collar, as though he clung to the sturdy trunk of a familiar tree.

Ed wore his Sunday suit, a white shirt and blue tie. His thick hair was gray and his face lined, but he was better looking than he'd been when they came to Havenhill. Farming agreed with him.

She stood beside Ed in this imaginary photograph, and she couldn't see herself clearly, but Ruth and Virgil, who sat on a bench in front of them, were painfully clear. Ruth had just turned nineteen. She wore a plaid skirt and white twin sweaters, and she was beautiful. Ruth was naturally, unconsciously beautiful and it tugged at Dorothy's heart to see the vulnerability in Ruth's expression. Where had all that trust come from? How had it happened, wondered Dorothy, although she knew the answer. Ruth had lived in a gentle world where in the limits of her experience she had known only what was good and beautiful. Dorothy imagined that at Katharine Gibbs Business School in downtown Boston Ruth would see something of the world that would open her eyes, but to date all she ever seemed to see was John. Maybe she'd be one of the lucky ones, her mother thought, and never have to glimpse the sordid, cruel, indifferent world that existed just beyond the curtain of her own innocence.

Beside Ruth, Virgil throbbed with life. He was seventeen, but he looked twenty. They couldn't keep him clothed. From where Dorothy stood behind him she could see the seams of his coat straining against his broad back. He had just had his hair cut, but at the nape of his neck it was already thick and would need trimming in a week. Virgil smiled broadly and looked boldly into the camera. Goodness shone in him, yet through that shield of purity a knowing look flashed. Virgil had felt life's cruelty and was wary.

On the day she remembered, the day when such a family portrait would have been made if she had paused long enough to think of it and engage a photographer no matter what it cost, something special was going on and the house was in an uproar. Granny Beane's birthday had finally arrived. Actually, Granny would be eighty on the next Sunday, the seventh, but they celebrated the week before because it was the only weekend before Christmas that Ruth was free to come home.

Ruth took the bus to Mumfert and Homer drove the Ford to town to meet her. When she stepped down from the bus and saw that the only one there to meet her was Homer, she knew things must be wild at home, and sure enough, as soon as she was settled, he said, "You'd best put on your apron right now, Ruthie, they've asked the whole town."

There was a light cover of snow on the fields, but the road was bare. As Ruth gazed out at the familiar landmarks she saw the hills rising in the distance. Evergreen and birch stood out sharply against the gray sky. Cows stood in rutted barnyards, their warm breath rising in the cold air in thin, white spirals. Black stone walls, some tumbling, some as straight and solid as when they had been placed there two centuries before, marked the stubbled fields. The flag fluttered in the wind outside the post office, and in the Martin's yard, old tires and rusting farm machinery formed a barricade of debris around the house. Webster's Pond was already frozen, and she saw what she presumed were the younger Martins playing about on the ice.

It was good to come home. She hated leaving John in Cambridge and wished he could have come too, but, she thought cheerfully, Christmas is coming, and she turned her attention to her own family as she glimpsed the house through the trees. There was smoke rising from both chimneys.

Homer was right, everyone in the village was invited and Granny said fretfully, "Oh, dear, so many people. What will we do with all those people in the house? Suppose I die before next week? All that fuss for nothing."

Dorothy turned her head so that Granny wouldn't see her smile and Ed said, "Now, Mother, you're not going to die."

"Humph," said his mother. "Eighty years is too long for anybody to live. When you get to be my age, Ed, you won't feel any more like celebrating than I do."

All the same she tried on the dress Dorothy was making her and preened in front of the oval mirror in the sewing room, and although she couldn't really see the dress, she did know her own figure flaws and she said, "If you could just put a few gathers here, Dorothy, on the shoulders," and she picked at it nervously, "see, here. Then I wouldn't look so round shouldered."

Actually, Granny looked very pretty sitting in the parlor in the Poole rocker, which Virgil had brought downstairs for the occasion. She sat there to receive, like royalty, and Dr. Adams and Mrs. Gibbs were among the first to arrive. As Dr. Adams guided Mrs. Gibbs into the parlor, he said loudly, "Here she is. Here's the birthday lady."

Mrs. Gibbs, now very deaf, extended her hand and Granny reached up, sensing more than seeing, and grabbed it. All three of them began to talk at the same time in their thin, rasping voices, filling the room with a chirping brightness that created an air of festivity. What Granny was actually saying was that she was sad and hurt because Evelyn hadn't been able to come, although they all knew, of course, that California might as well be the moon when it came to visiting family. Dr. Adams said he was very sorry, life was full of disappointments, and he was pleased to see that she was rallying so splendidly. Mrs. Gibbs, distracted by the crowd, squeaked pleasantly that no one would ever guess to look at her that Granny was eighty, and the occasion being what it was no one observed that to Mrs. Gibbs, who was now almost as blind as she was deaf, all faces were identical oval blurs.

Ruth took Mrs. Gibbs by the arm and led her into the sitting room and established her on the sofa. "I'll bring you some punch," she said and returned to the dining room where the table, stretched to its limit with all its leaves installed, was spread with refreshments. There were two punch bowls surrounded by glass cups, one at each end of the table, and in between were plates of sandwiches cut in fingers and circles and triangles. There were trays of cookies made in the shapes of Christmas stars and bells, and tiny cakes frosted with pink and white frosting. There were dishes of nuts and butter mints and on the sideboard stood a tiered birthday cake, decorated with pink roses and green leaves. Eighty unlit candles stood at attention all over the top.

Everybody came.

John's grandfather, wearing his dark suit and carrying a cane. For his lumbago, he said. It was cold and he couldn't take the cold the way he used to. With him was Louisa, strikingly handsome in a red wool dress . . . they had heard she was going to be married soon to someone she'd met at a dog show.

Suddenly Dorothy saw Grace Baker, now divorced, who was accompanied by a bearded man with melancholy eyes. *Oh dear,* she thought, wondering what this meant, and she said brightly, "I am so glad you could come."

"I've brought a friend," said Grace, "I didn't think you'd mind," and she introduced him by a name Dorothy couldn't remember, and later, when she mentioned it to the family she said, "I think he's Austrian. He must be one of the refugees."

Across the room Ruth was talking to the Smiths. As Dorothy passed them, Ruth spoke up. "Brewster's in the army and stationed in the Philippines, Mother. Isn't that exciting?"

"Oh, my," said Dorothy, "you must miss him."

As she passed through the room, she thought about Brewster Smith, half a world away. She wouldn't like having Virgil over there, but the world was shrinking. One had to accept it. To think that in their own house they were entertaining a refugee from Austria and that one of Ruth's classmates was already in the army, and he was such a bright boy too. She would have thought he would be in college.

Glancing around the room she saw that Granny was enjoying herself, sitting happily in the midst of the guests and expressing opinions with respect to the attainment of great age, as though it was something she had managed through good living and careful foresight. She prefaced each remark with the words "when you get to be eighty." It didn't seem to matter what was said. If someone had good news Granny stated that at eighty nothing much surprised her anymore, she'd seen all of life there was to see. It was no wonder, Dorothy thought, that her own mother found Granny tiring. Querulous and self-centered, there was nothing to do about Granny but try to laugh at her, although, she admitted, it wasn't always easy.

People nodded and smiled, only half listening. The men wandered in Ed's direction, drifting eventually toward the barn. The young people stood together at one end of the living room, talking in low voices. The older women sat in chairs with plates and cups balanced on their sloping laps while the younger women moved in and out of the kitchen replenishing trays. Howard wriggled through a forest of legs and cried when he couldn't find Dorothy. Ruth heard him and picked him up and Dorothy, coming through the hall looking for him, had a sudden feeling of dismay because it looked so natural and right to see Ruth with a baby in her arms.

When it was all over, Granny hobbled up the stairs, leaning on Ed, and she paused at the landing to regard the rest of the family as they stirred about in the ruins of her party. Then she said in a voice that quavered, "My dear, dear family. I thank you all for a lovely birthday."

Pausing, she dabbed at her eyes with her handkerchief and then in her usual way she said, "I just hope that when the rest of you get to be eighty, you'll feel better than I do. You don't know when you're young what it's like to be eighty years old."

On the following Sunday, Granny announced the obvious. She had survived. Her actual birthday had arrived. December 7, 1941.

"Happy birthday, Granny," mumbled Virgil, who had been to a square dance in Tipton the night before and could have slept all morning. He didn't see why his presence at breakfast on Sunday morning was necessary and he thought his head would split as Howard beat his spoon on the tray of his high chair.

Ed said, "That's enough, Howard."

Vera poured Granny's coffee and passed it to her, saying, "Happy birthday, Mrs. Beane."

Mrs. Howard took up her grapefruit spoon and said calmly, "Congratulations, Mrs. Beane."

Dorothy went to the kitchen and returned with a coffee cake, which she passed first to her mother-in-law, saying, "Happy birthday, Mother Beane."

Ed said, "Now, Mother, one birthday's enough. You had yours last week."

It had snowed in the night and the sun, reflected from the white world outside, flashed at the windowpanes. It would be a pretty drive to church. Vera's Christmas cactus was in bloom. Dorothy spooned oatmeal into Howard's mouth. The vegetables were peeled and before they left, she would set the table and put a pork roast in the oven. It was going to be an ordinary Sunday. Ed and Virgil would find things to do in the barn as they always did, and the rest of them would go to church. After dinner, Granny would go up for her nap and Dorothy would put Howard down. Mrs. Howard would retire with a book. Ed would take his pipe and go off to read the latest state agricultural bulletin, and when she and Vera had cleaned up in the kitchen she would go into the sitting room and lie down on the sofa to rest.

That afternoon Vera retreated to her room and turned on the radio. Every Sunday afternoon she listened to the symphony and that afternoon, in the middle of Beethoven's Fifth, the program was interrupted by an announcement from Washington. Japan had bombed Pearl Harbor.

Vera dropped her embroidery and leaned forward to listen as static crackled in the speaker and a voice that seemed to come from the inside of a bottle repeated, "A surprise attack by Japanese war planes on Pearl Harbor this morning has left the battleship *Arizona* sunk and . . ." She had heard enough and she went quickly down the hall to the living room.

"The radio," gasped Vera, clasping and unclasping her thin hands. "There's been an attack on Pearl Harbor."

"What sort of attack? Where is Pearl Harbor?"

"Hawaii, I think. They've sunk a battleship. The static was so bad. . ."

Dorothy rose and went quickly upstairs and down the hall to their bedroom, where Ed had fallen asleep with a pamphlet on his chest. She shook him gently. "Ed," she said urgently, "wake up, Ed. There's been an attack on Pearl Harbor."

When he was awake enough to know what she was saying, he got up. One would have thought he was going somewhere immediately to do something, but all he said was, "Oh, my God."

The news stunned them all. The war couldn't be in Hawaii, they thought, that paradise of leis and grass skirts. It must be in Europe. They had grown accustomed to news of bombings and U-boats on that side of the world, it was inconceivable to think war had sprung up in the opposite direction, but as the afternoon passed and the same excited voices shouted the same incredible things, there could be no doubt.

Things were never the same again.

PART TWO

Despite Pearl Harbor, the winter of 1942 passed in its usual way. Children walked along the state road to school, swinging lunch boxes and throwing snowballs. The Martins skated on Webster's Pond, their darting forms dotting the ice like water-bugs. Virgil and Oscar milked thirty cows twice a day and hauled milk cans to the station in Clinton. It was cold. Howard had croup, and Dorothy sat up all night listening to his harsh breathing while he slept restlessly beside a steam kettle under a tent of old sheets.

As spring melted into summer there was talk of gas rationing, and those who remembered the first war bought flour in quantity. The draft board in Mumfert listed all the boys over eighteen in Havenhill and the surrounding villages, and a good many of them didn't wait to be drafted. Ration books gave people points for sugar and butter and cigarettes; even Howard had a book of coupons.

By the time fall flamed across the hills the Smiths were sure that Brewster was one of the ones taken at Corregidor. No one spoke of Bataan to them, but when Grace Baker (who was now divorced and never saw Harold anymore), heard about it she cried. She would never forget Brewster's eighth-grade essay, the one in which he said, "We must all work together to make it a better world," and her friend Franz Zimmerman, who had left Vienna a mere seven days before Hitler marched into Austria, couldn't think of anything to say to make it easier for her.

That April when Ruth came home for Easter the bus was crowded with men in uniform. She was accustomed to seeing them on the streets of Boston, but they looked out of place in the country, and she didn't like it. She didn't like anything about the war. The windows in the house on Marlborough Street where she lived were blacked out at night with heavy lined drapes. There were air raid drills at school twice a week, always on freezing days, and she would think crossly, *Who is going to bomb Boston?* They were miles from Germany and Japan was on the other side of the world.

She was aware that across the aisle from her a boy in uniform was staring at her legs, and she reached down and smoothed her skirt carefully over her knees.

"Going far?" he asked.

She shook her head. "Only as far as Mumfert."

"What do you know," he said, "so am I."

"Did you go to Mumfert High?"

He nodded. "How about you?"

"I graduated in 'forty."

"That's it then. I've been out since 'thirty-seven."

She opened the *Reader's Digest* she had brought with her and began to read, but he kept talking, telling her where he'd been since he graduated from high school. For a while he was in Colorado with the CCC and after that he worked on a farm in Iowa. He'd come home to enlist last fall and was stationed at Fort Devens.

"What are you in?" she asked.

"The infantry."

"Oh," she said, adding inanely, "that's nice." She knew from everything John had told her that the infantry was the last place anybody wanted to be, but she didn't know what else to say, so she turned the page and pretended to be engrossed in what she was reading.

"How about you?" the boy asked. "You got a boyfriend? How does he stand?"

"He likes the Air Corps."

"He's got the right idea. He won't be in the mud, and everybody's got to be somewhere."

Ruth didn't like thinking about it. She and John didn't look at it the same way, and they'd had a fight the night before. Not really a fight, she supposed. Her mother would call it a disagreement.

"Have you got a girlfriend?" she asked.

"That's what I'm coming home to find out."

"I'm sure everything will be fine," she said.

In Havenhill things were always fine, she thought grimly. Nobody seemed to realize what it was like to be in love. She couldn't imagine that anybody at home had ever been in love, not the way she was in love with John. At home the only things that mattered were the apples on the trees and who was going to be around to pick them this year. It had come to that. *Oh Lord,* she thought, *things are so fantastically normal at home.* Apples and cows and Howard knocking over his milk and Grandmother Howard consulting the calendar and remarking that it was time to think about marmalade.

If one of them, any one of them, ever came down to Boston, someone might understand what it was like in the real world. If they could just once hear the newsboys calling out "extra" and see the headlines, and hear the traffic, or see the men in uniform milling around everywhere, standing in line at the movies, crowding in everywhere, then they'd know there was a war and that apples and cows had nothing to do with the real world.

Frequently she and John met for supper in one of the steamy cafés in Harvard Square and more often than not he spoiled things by telling her the latest rumors.

"Look," she said, "I don't want to talk about it, John. It doesn't do any good. If they draft you, they draft you."

"The point is," he said, and he covered his hamburger with

catsup and pressed the top of the roll down on it, "the point is to get in a reserve. I'm going to try for the Air Corps. They're coming to campus next week."

"I don't want to talk about it," she said stubbornly, pushing away her half-eaten hamburger, which suddenly made her feel sick. "I don't want you to sign up for anything. I don't want you to enlist. I don't want you to go."

He shrugged. "Be realistic," he said, "either I sit on my can and let them call me up, or I volunteer. In another couple of months I'll graduate and they'll take me just like that. Do you want me to be drafted and march my way through this goddam war?"

"I don't want you to go."

"Christ," he said helplessly.

"You don't need to swear."

"Well, dammit," said John, "what do you expect me to do?"

"I didn't think things happened so fast," she said, "without time to even think about it."

"Well, they do."

"What about Virgil, he'll be eighteen next month. He doesn't talk about it."

"He better think about it," said John. "If he doesn't get into something, they'll draft him." He paused and reached for her hand. "Can't we talk about it, Ruth, without getting mad?"

"I want to get married," she said. "I don't want to be in Boston and have you miles away. I don't want to end up like Vera. I thought you wanted me."

He groaned. "I do," he said, "you know I do," and his hand tightened on hers, "but it takes a long time, Ruth, and a cadet's life is hell. When I get my commission we'll be married."

"Once you're commissioned, they'll send you overseas."

"I'm not going to argue with you, Ruth," he said. "I'm just telling you how it is. We're all going before it's done and all I'm thinking about is how I'm going. Am I going on a ship or in a plane or on my goddam feet?"

She didn't reply.

"I'll give you a ring," he said, "we'll be engaged and when I'm commissioned we'll be married."

"Is that a proposal?"

"Yes."

"Thank you," she said. "I accept."

He reached for both her hands and looked helplessly across at her, and she began to cry.

Virgil graduated from high school the following June, in 1943, and by then he couldn't think about anything but the war. He'd been restless all spring, working as if his mind were miles away, and the day after graduation he came in for milking in a state of wild excitement.

"Joe Martin enlisted in the navy."

"Is that so," said Ed.

"Just like that. He's all signed up."

"I can believe it," said Ed grimly. He turned toward the feed floor then glancing back said, "Go easy, Son. That's Rose. She's got a bad teat."

"I know it," said Virgil, pulling up his milk stool and settling down. He only half heard Ed when he said, "Come up to the office when you're done, Virgil. I want to show you something."

Ed's office wasn't much, just a space partitioned off with a desk and a light bulb hanging on a cord. Along the wall were racks for the publications he got from Mass State and the Dairyman's Association. What he wanted to show Virgil was an article on milking machines, and when Virgil had glanced at it Ed said, "We could double the herd and do the milking in half the time."

"How about that," said Virgil.

"I thought if you wanted to reconsider Mass State . . . we could manage here with something like this."

"I don't want to go to college, Dad. I've told you that all along. You and mother both know all I want is what's right here."

"That's the point," said Ed. "If all you want is what's here, then the more I can get for here the better it will be for you later on."

"I wouldn't mind going to Mass State sometime . . . but it would have to be later on."

"Fine," said Ed. "I just thought you might have other ideas. When I was your age I was all set for engineering."

Virgil laughed. "That'd be better than being a preacher like your own father, but I'll make you a bet and I bet I'm right. If you'd had a chance at a farm back then you would have taken it."

"I didn't have the chance," said Ed shortly, and added, "well, think about it, Son. Now's the time for college, it seems to me. If you want the farm, that suits me too, but I came to it late. Every day something comes up makes me wish I'd had even a couple years at some good agricultural school. What I get, I get the hard way."

"Joe Martin joined the navy."

"So you said."

"I been thinking a lot about it, Dad. Everybody's in."

"Not everybody, Virgil."

"I been thinking about it a lot."

"You think long and hard, Son. You're only nineteen. The war's not going to last forever. If there's any place civilians are needed it's on the farm, Virgil. Think about it."

That night Joe Martin and Virgil drove to Clinton and got drunk. If they'd gone to Mumfert or even Tipton it might have been different, but in Clinton nobody knew them and for three hours they sat in a booth at the Blue Lite Cafe, drinking beer and talking about people they knew who were in the army and overseas. The more they talked and the more they drank the more reasonable it seemed to Virgil to join up. Suddenly even poor Brewster Smith, tottering along in the dust of Bataan, became a heroic and enviable figure, which indicates well enough how far gone they were.

173

From the Blue Lite they drove down to the river for a swim. Leaving their clothes in the car, they stumbled naked down the bank and into the water.

"Now, Virgil," Joe said slowly, "don't you go and drowned yourself."

Virgil laughed. The idea of a future naval man cautioning him about the muddy Connecticut River struck him funny.

They splashed around for a while, taking the edge off their pleasant euphoria, and then they lay there in the mud and talked about girls. Joe had had experience and talked knowingly about the parts of girls Virgil hardly dared think about. By the time Joe stopped, Virgil's manhood was in a state of wild alert and his need to prove his virility so strong he thought he'd die right there in the mud if he couldn't do something about it.

He went back into the water. It was already getting light. Jee-sus, he thought, his mother would be going wild if she'd missed him, and he kicked Joe and said, "Get up, you bastard. Time to go home."

The next afternoon he told his father he was going to enlist.

"Did you hear me?" he shouted over the rump of the cow he was stripping.

"Yes, I heard you," said Ed. "I'm thinking about it."

"I thought maybe you'd tell Mother," said Virgil.

"What are your plans?"

"The marines. I thought I'd sign up once the hay's in."

Ed nodded. He could feel his head going up and down like a pump handle as he tried to think of the right thing to say. "You know," he said, "they deferred farm workers in the last war. Somebody's got to feed the troops."

"There's plenty besides me," said Virgil. "The boys in town feel the same. I thought Mother'd take it better from you than from me."

That night when they were getting ready for bed Ed said, "Virgil's thinking about signing up, Dorothy."

"No," she said.

"If he doesn't they'll draft him."

"They can't," she said, "you need him here. They defer farm workers. They did last time. They can't draft him."

"They can do anything they want to."

"Did you talk to him, Ed? Did you tell him you'd go to the draft board and try to get him deferred?"

"More or less, but it doesn't matter, Dorothy. He's going to do what he wants to do."

"How does he know what he wants," she cried, "he's only a boy," and she put down her hairbrush. "The ones who enlist are the ones who go first," she said desolately. "Why does he have to enlist?"

"If he's drafted, Dorothy, he'll be in camp before you can turn around and be shipped out and over there in the mud. If he enlists there's always a chance he'll get picked for officers' training and that would keep him on this side a while longer."

"They go in the front," said Dorothy, "the officers are 'over the top' first, Ed. That's the way it was."

"It's a different war, Dorothy," he said patiently. " 'Over the top' is a thing of the past. 'Up the line' is a thing of the past. Everywhere is 'up the line.' Planes fly hundreds of miles and drop bombs on people in their own houses. There's no 'over the top.' That's the kind of war it is this time."

When Virgil left for Parris Island in July the war came to Havenhill for Ed and Dorothy. It didn't matter anymore that they were using molasses instead of sugar or that gas was rationed and nobody could get new tires. All that mattered was Virgil and a war that had marched into their living room through the radio, a war that wouldn't end no matter how many bombs were dropped or how many little islands were invaded.

When Virgil left for boot camp, Dorothy put ten self-addressed penny postcards in his bag, and it was a good thing she did because they came back bent and scribbled on. She wondered if they would have heard at all if Virgil had had to go out and find a stamp somewhere.

In rained continually in South Carolina, wrote Virgil, and they pitched their tents in the mud. The food was terrible. He'd got his marksman's badge. They were getting leave at Christmas, he wrote, and Dorothy's spirits soared.

And then one day when Dorothy was making dressing for the Thanksgiving turkey, Mr. Godwin came up the lane with a letter from Virgil. This time he had written a letter, not a postcard, and she rinsed and dried her hands and tore open the letter. She had already given up the hope that he might get off for Thanksgiving, but she was counting on Christmas.

"News from Virgil?" asked Vera, who came into the kitchen with an armful of washing that had frozen dry, and as she paused for Dorothy to reply she saw that Dorothy was so absorbed she hadn't even heard the question.

Dorothy was reading rapidly, turning a page quickly as though she were looking for a real message, not the usual remarks about the weather and the food, and drill and inspection. She was searching for something more vital. Something that would tell them when he was coming home.

After a minute she folded the paper and put it back in the envelope. Standing at the table with her hands at her sides and her gaze fixed on the window, Dorothy seemed like someone in a dream, and Vera knew better than to speak. She began to fold the laundry, towels so stiff that to fold them was like folding paper. She hung them on the rack near the stove.

"He's not coming for Christmas," said Dorothy. "He's not coming, Vera. Why would they keep him there over Christmas? They aren't expecting an invasion down there, or are they? Does it make sense?"

"It's the army," said Vera, "and the war. Nothing makes sense," and she hung the last towel on the rack and filled the tea kettle. "Let's have a cup of tea," she said.

"Tea?" said Dorothy. "It's eleven in the morning. We'll be putting lunch on in another hour or so. Where's Ruby? What are we having for lunch?"

"Leftovers," said Vera, "and sit down. It's nice out here at the moment. I always like a cup of tea."

"Yes," said Dorothy.

"They may change their minds yet. Wait and see."

Dorothy didn't think they would and she spooned a little precious sugar into her tea and added milk and suddenly, feeling like tears, she said fiercely, "I suppose I ought to be grateful Uncle Sam is keeping them on post where they'll be safe, but I'm not. If I had the money I'd get on a train and go down there and see him anyway."

"Money," said Vera softly, "it was always money with me too."

"If I had the money I would . . ."

"What," said Vera, "what would you do?"

Dorothy shrugged. "When you don't have it," she said, "you think of all the magic it makes possible, but what good is it when the things you want aren't for sale?"

"Remember the Christmas Ed was in Concord and couldn't come home?"

"I'll never forget it," said Dorothy. "It seemed terrible then, but not like this. This is different."

Dorothy and Vera packed a big box at Christmas to send to Virgil. Cake and cookies and books and shaving lotion. Howard drew him a picture of a snowman. Granny Beane knit him a pair of red wool socks, and when she was told Virgil wouldn't be allowed to wear them she said, "I guess he can sleep in them if he wants to and from all I hear it's cold in the army."

Grandmother Howard sent him a ten-dollar bill in a Christmas card. Ruby brought a jar of her own watermelon pickle to go in the package that Ed wrapped and tied with twine. He took it to the post office, and when the postmaster noticed that Virgil was now stationed at Camp LeJeune in North Carolina he said, "I hear it's pretty warm down there this time of year."

Ed didn't know about that. All he knew was that North Carolina was too far away, warm or cold, and he didn't feel like talking about it. He nodded and mumbled something and drove slowly home in the dark, remembering for some unknown reason the time he and Virgil had taken that load of trees down to Boston. Trouble enough then, but nothing compared to now, he thought sadly.

Ruthie came home for Christmas but went back to Boston on the twenty-seventh of December when she had to be back for work. Dorothy hated to see her go, but Ruth didn't seem to mind. John hadn't been able to get leave for Christmas either. He called her up on the telephone and after they had shouted Merry Christmas couldn't seem to think of anything else to say.

Ruth said, "I miss you darling," and then she began to cry and John, who was furious and frustrated with the Air Corps and all its restrictions, said, "You couldn't guess what we had for Christmas dinner, Ruth!"

She sighed. She didn't want to talk about dinner. She wanted him to say he missed her, he loved her, he was going AWOL for her . . .

"Hot dogs," said John. "Honest to God, hot dogs and beans and some sort of glue pudding for dessert."

"Hot dogs? Really hot dogs?"

"I'm not lying."

"I think that's terrible," she said. "I think it's horrible. There's plenty of potatoes and chickens if there aren't any turkeys and cranberry sauce. It's terrible."

After that they talked about loving each other, and when the pain of that was used up they said good-bye, each waiting to see who would have the courage to hang up. Finally she said, "Good-bye, darling, you hang up and when I hear it I will too."

When she heard the click of the receiver she ran up the stairs to her own room and fell onto the bed and cried. *He will never come back,* she thought. *I will never see him again.*

Neither Dorothy nor Vera went up to see what the matter was because they knew and there was nothing they could do to change things. In four days it would be another year—1944— another year of war. "When will it end?" Dorothy asked Ed and he replied, "When they run out of ammunition, Dorothy. When one or the other's had enough."

"Enough," she said, "it's already been enough."

On New Year's Day they took down the tree, leaving on the strings of popcorn and cranberries, and Howard and Mr. Godwin dragged it out to the backyard and set it up for the birds. The sky was leaden that day and the wind died down. By teatime they could see the first snow falling.

Early in January a call came from the Red Cross for blood and the Red Cross in Clinton sent out a letter asking people to donate—Monday, Wednesday or Friday from nine to eleven in the morning. When Dorothy saw the notice in the *Clinton Gazette* she said to Ed, "I want to go to Clinton tomorrow."

"What for?"

"Just something I want to do."

"You're not thinking of going by the Red Cross, are you?"

Ed had seen the notice and already planned to go, but he didn't like the idea of Dorothy going. She was too thin and tired all the time. There wasn't any sense in it, he said.

"I am going, Ed. You can't stop me. I'm going as often as they'll let me."

"You'll do no such damnfool thing," he replied. "You're run down and you sound like you're getting another cold."

"I am not and if you won't take me Homer will."

"Virgil's here. Wait until he's overseas."

"I'll give then too. If they say they need blood, they need it. Maybe my blood will help some other boy and if the time ever comes when Virgil . . ." She stopped and reached in her apron pocket for a handkerchief and blew her nose furiously and mopped her eyes. "Well, anyway," she said, "are you going to take me or aren't you?"

Ed took her that Monday and she never had to ask again. They both went every eight weeks thereafter. When her blood flowed into the vessel she watched and tried to make herself feel she was doing something to save lives. But it wasn't easy. The sight of that stream of blood said just one thing to her—death—and she turned away in the end.

Virgil's letters came in almost regularly. One would say they were due for furlough and the next would consign that to the scrap heap. Rumors were always rife in wartime, said Ed, trying

179

to calm Dorothy. She couldn't believe they would ship out a whole division at the end of training without furlough.

Ed didn't believe any of it, and then one day they had a note that was more specific. Virgil wrote that his company was coming through Springfield on the twentieth of March. They were being shipped to Chicago, which in all likelihood meant the Pacific next, and were supposed to stop in Springfield to take on a squadron of officers from Fort Devens.

Dorothy's heart began to pound, and the thought raced through her head that if they were there in Springfield he could see them on his way through.

Dorothy read this twice and then ran out to the barn, waving the letter as she splashed through puddles toward Ed.

"Look," she cried, "it's from Virgil. He's coming through Springfield on the twentieth."

Suddenly it struck her that the twentieth was the next day and she gasped, "That's tomorrow, Ed. If we can be there in the station he says that maybe we'll see him."

It seemed unlikely to Ed that Virgil would know what the shipping orders were for his unit or any other. Besides that, he was familiar with the Springfield station, a maze of tracks lying at the bottom of a long flight of black iron steps, and he could imagine troop trains shuttled off on sidings, sealed and unapproachable. He and Dorothy could spend all day milling around in the wrong place trying to find him.

To satisfy Dorothy he came into the house and took up the telephone. He hadn't any real hope of getting the stationmaster in Springfield, and he already had a good idea what he'd say— troop trains passed through day and night, mostly they never opened up. All the same, Ed held on to the receiver for ten minutes until he was sure he'd been cut off and then he put it down.

"Never mind," said Dorothy, "we'll just go. We'll be there waiting, Ed. Whatever train it is, we'll be there and he'll find us."

They set out at five in the morning, tiptoeing up and down the dark hall and meeting Vera in the kitchen, where she had the coffee on and perking. "Don't worry about Howard," she said, "I'll be here when he wakes up."

Dorothy had packed a picnic basket because she was sure Virgil would be hungry. He was always hungry. There had been enough sugar for a cake, and Ruby baked a chicken. There were jars of pickles and raspberries, things he liked, and by the time Dorothy got into the car her spirits were so high she could barely keep still. It was going to be a good day. The air was sharp and the wind snapped through the tops of the trees. As they drove down the valley in the pale light of early morning all she could think about was Virgil.

In Holyoke the streets were deserted although here and there people in bathrobes appeared, coming out of their houses and down their walks to pick up newspapers and take in bottles of milk. Ed caught a glimpse of the tap and die and saw smoke rising from the chimney stack. As the car passed along he could see there was a new wing on the plant and two flags flying, which meant they were getting government contracts now. He wouldn't be surprised to find out he could have his old job back if he wanted it. He'd heard men like him were making eighty-five dollars a week working the line, all up and down the East Coast, and he said to Dorothy, "What would you think about getting my old job back?"

"Not much," she replied. She hadn't seen the plant or noticed the expansion because she was looking for Elm Street and suddenly there it was. She leaned forward and looked hard. "Oh," she said, "I do wish we had time to stop in and see Edith."

At the station in Springfield people were sleeping on benches in the waiting room and in the rest room Dorothy found young mothers sitting on their suitcases, nursing their babies. They sagged with weariness. Old women huddled among the bags and boxes that surrounded them, and children, twisted in their clothes like wrung-out washing, slept with their heads in their mother's laps.

Ed scanned the boards looking for anything that could be a train from the South destined for Chicago, but he couldn't tell much from the numbers. Chalk numbers had been erased and rewritten so many times the lines were crooked and the numbers smudged. He took Dorothy's arm and propelled her along to the stairs and down to the tracks where there was an empty baggage cart. He set the basket on it and boosted Dorothy up beside it.

"Not a bad seat," he said, sprinting up.

"It's dirty, Ed."

"Won't hurt. It's just dirt."

When they'd been there an hour he went upstairs to the lunch counter and came back with coffee and doughnuts. "Fifty cents," he said, but she didn't seem to hear him. Ordinarily she would have said, "Oh, Ed, what a price!" but today she wasn't hearing or seeing anything but trains. Every time the whistle screamed and the flag shot up, she stiffened. Bells rang and steam hissed up in white clouds as ordinary passengers boarded or disembarked.

From his perch on the wagon Ed could scan the tracks, but there wasn't much to see. Virgil could have been looking out of the window of any of a dozen trains that nudged one another in and out of the yard, coming and going in the smoke and steam without touching the platform or opening up.

At three in the afternoon Ed said, "Don't you think we'd better go on home, Dorothy?"

"No," she said.

Then for the tenth time Ed went back into the station and took his turn in line. There had to be somebody there who knew what was going on but after a while he gave up and went down the steps again. "It's after five," he said to Dorothy, "there's nothing posted and nobody seems to know anything. We might as well head home."

"No," she said.

"You can't sit here all night, Dorothy."

But Ed was wrong. She could sit there all night and all the next day and forever after that if there was any chance of seeing Virgil.

"Please Ed," she said, "just a little longer."

At six he helped her down and they went slowly up the steep flight that they had descended ten hours earlier. It was already dark, the early dark of a rainy night. They drove without speaking, crossing the river and heading up the valley toward Northampton. In houses and barns lights had begun to come on. The wind whistling around the car made a thin, sad sound. The rain, now a fine drizzle, was trying to turn to sleet, and the windshield wipers, going slap, slap against it, seemed to be sweeping away shiny particles of glass.

When they turned for Clinton Ed reached over and put his hand on Dorothy's knee. "I'm sorry," he said, as though it were her grief and her disappointment, not his own, and in a way it was because he hadn't actually expected to see Virgil. She had.

At that moment she was too crushed to say anything. She could hardly swallow or keep back tears, and when she felt Ed's hand all she could do was put her own on top of his.

And then she had an odd thought, remembering that Virgil used to have terrible earaches. Especially in weather like this. The raw cold of late winter invited them, she thought. *Oh dear God*, she thought, *why didn't they make him deaf. If only he were deaf. Nobody would have taken him if he were deaf.*

It was almost ten when they drove into the yard and saw lights all over the house. Light flooded through the windows like precious gold, as though nobody ever gave a thought to the cost of electricity, and Dorothy started up. Something had happened.

She jerked open the car door and dashed up the steps and through the back entry and into the kitchen where, as if he'd never left home, Virgil sat eating what was left of Vera's pie.

"Thank goodness you're home," cried Vera, "we thought you'd never come. We tried to get word, but . . . ."

Dorothy didn't hear any of it. All she knew was that Virgil was there, and she put her hands over her eyes and began to cry, and then laugh, and then, for the first time in months, things were all right again.

The morning Virgil left, Ed drove him to the bus station in Mumfert. Dorothy didn't go. She knew she'd cry and "wouldn't that be terrible," she said to Ed.

He thought it would be the most natural thing in the world, but he said, "You stay home. I'll see him off."

When it was time for them to leave, all the family came out on the back porch to watch him go. It was damp and chilly and they stood there shivering as they smiled and waved. Grandmother Howard raised her hand in a small salute and Virgil lifted his hand in return. He kissed female relatives these days, if it was required, but he liked his grandmother's reserve. It steadied him.

Beside her, Granny, wrapped in a purple shawl, leaned against the porch rail, her mouth opening and closing as she told him to behave himself. He couldn't hear her voice, but he knew what she was saying and he grinned and waved. Next to Granny, Vera stood with her hands wrapped up in her apron. The sun flashed on her glasses so that he couldn't see Vera's face, but it didn't matter. He knew what she looked like.

On the steps stood his mother with Howard beside her. The tears running down her face glimmered in the sun, but she kept nodding and smiling anyway and suddenly he turned and ran back across the yard and putting his arms around her he said, "It's all right, Mom. Don't cry. It's going to be all right."

And then, just as rapidly, he vaulted back and got in the car, swallowing rapidly and hard.

"Write when you can, Son," said Ed. "Your mother worries."

"I will," he replied.

As they drove out of the yard he thought of Ruth. He wished he'd been able to see her too.

Across the hard blue sky white clouds billowed and the sun burned down to sear the fields. It was as if the world had dried up when Virgil left, April cold, May gray, June stillborn. By mid-July Ed was hauling water from the river for the cattle. The corn was stunted, shriveled ears clung with withered hands to the dried stalks that rustled in the heat. Dorothy and Vera watered the garden in the evening when the sun was down. It was a summer like that one long ago when they had had to shoot Beau. Not a good time to remember, thought Ed, going from one burnt pasture to another.

Ruth came home in August, although she hadn't expected to because John was in Midland, Texas, and all through July they had written desperate letters back and forth about whether or not to get married. When it became more than she could bear, she wrote and said she was coming out to Texas whether he wanted her to or not, and then he phoned, getting her out of bed at midnight and subjecting her to the displeasure of her landlady. He sounded very far away and in the background she could hear music and voices.

"Where are you?" she asked.

"At the club. There's a line behind me, Ruth. We only have a couple of phones here."

"Why did you call? Didn't you get my letter? I'm coming out there."

"That's why I called."

"I don't care what you say, John. You said when you were commissioned we'd be married, and you are, so I'm coming."

"It's not that I don't want you, Ruth."

"What is it then?"

"We're flying nonstop," he said. "I've been assigned another crew. They're changing our orders, and it's not a good time. If you came I might not be able to see you."

"I'll sit in my hotel room and wait for you."

"There aren't any hotels."

"There are hotels everywhere," she said. "There's got to be a hotel. Midland is a city, I looked at it on the map."

"You should see it. It's as flat as a tabletop. There are people everywhere. People sit up all night in hotel lobbies because they can't get rooms. Service wives with children are living in single rooms with nothing but kitchen privileges."

"Oh God," she moaned, "what are we going to do?"

"Wait," he said. "I'm bound to get leave after this."

"I don't believe it," she said.

"Look, Ruth. Go ahead home. Take your vacation. When the time comes, if the bank won't let you off, you can quit."

There was nothing to do at home, and when she wasn't helping, she was in her room, writing long letters to John that didn't get mailed. The thing was, she realized now, if she had saved her money from the time she started at the bank she might have enough now to go to Texas whether he wanted her to or not. She'd spent too much on clothes. She'd never had so many pairs of shoes in her life. What good were they to her with John a thousand miles away?

One day she cleaned her closet and found a shoe box full of treasures. *My first diary,* she thought, *the one Vera gave me when I was fourteen.* She flipped it open and began to read, "John was here today. He is SO handsome. He ate six cookies and said the only thing he likes about school is sports. He said a boy got hit in the head with a hockey puck and got a concussion right through his helmet. I think he likes me because he looks at me, if you know what I mean."

This entry used up a week of days.

Lord, how simple things were then, she thought. She couldn't remember worrying about anything, not even money because there wasn't any money and money didn't matter then the way it did now. If she had the money, she'd buy a ticket to Midland.

She'd get a room somewhere. Other people did and once she was there, he'd want to see her.

Crossing to the window, she noticed a car coming along the state road. As she watched, it turned in and came slowly up the lane. *Callers,* she thought, and turned away. There was no one in Havenhill she wanted to see.

From the hall, Vera could see an unfamiliar car in the yard, and through the screen she recognized Mr. Harris from Mumfert. What did he want, she wondered, unhooking the screen, but when she saw the Western Union emblem on his cap and the yellow envelope in his hand, and the gray blank expression on his lined face, she knew. She began to tremble and when she tried to breathe there was a terrible, hard pain in her chest. He held out the telegram and she shook her head.

"I'll get Dorothy," she gasped, turning quickly down the hall.

Time had stopped. The house was utterly silent, yet thoughts beat rapidly through her head and she wondered desperately where Ed was. *Had I better get Aunt Alice,* she thought, but she had no idea where Ed was or what good Dorothy's mother could do, and as she went blindly down the hall, refusing to feel anything, she prayed she would say the right words when the time came.

Dorothy was at the sink washing dishes. She had been chopping onions for piccalilli and she looked up with streaming eyes. "Heavens, those onions are strong," she said wiping her hands with a towel, and then, suddenly, she grew still, the towel dangling in her hand, and she said, "What's wrong?"

"It's Mr. Harris," said Vera, "come over from Mumfert. He asked for you or Ed."

As the significance of this struck Dorothy, Vera stepped forward, for Dorothy, who had known, but forgotten, that Edgar Harris worked at Western Union, now began to sway, her face losing its color as the shock penetrated.

She scarcely felt Vera's hand on her arm, or the hard wood of the kitchen chair beneath her, or heard Vera's voice sounding faint and distant as Vera told her to put her head between her knees. There was a terrible rushing sound in her ears as she lowered her head, waiting in vain for the mercy of oblivion.

Virgil had been killed in a place called New Georgia on the fifteenth of August. Vera folded the telegram and put it back in the envelope. Her hands had begun to shake, but she took Dorothy's hands anyway and held them tightly and didn't say anything. She wondered when Dorothy would cry, but Dorothy only said in a small, tired voice, "It couldn't have been the fifteenth, Vera. We had a letter from him on the fifteenth. He wrote to us on the fifteenth."

"He wrote it before the fifteenth. It came on the fifteenth."

Dorothy nodded. She had now begun to cry, without a sound, almost without tears, a crying that went inward, too dreadful to show. After a while she turned back to Vera. "It's not true, is it?" she said. "It's not true."

But of course it was.

Ed saw the car in the lane and saw it leave shortly afterward. Not much of a call, he thought. He hadn't had time to make one full sweep of the field. In the brightness of the day with the sun hot on his back and the hayfield shimmering in the heat it began to seem to him that he was driving in the rippling current of a golden sea. With the whine of the mower in his ears and the sun in his eyes he almost felt possessed, as though he were battling an undertow that wanted to suck him right down and into the parched earth.

Sweat poured down his body, running from his matted hair into his eyes, and he shook his head to clear his vision, and then suddenly he thought he could see Virgil's face, like a vision, and lifting his head he caught a glimpse of Virgil's broad back as it disappeared into the blinding brilliance of the sun and fused with the radiance of the day.

He turned abruptly and headed for the barn.

At five that afternoon Ruby stood at the kitchen table cracking eggs. She and Vera moved silently around the room as they worked, aware of the ticking clock, the distant sound of dogs and cows, and the soft smack of breaking eggshells. Ed was in the barn and Dorothy was upstairs with Howard. The house seemed vacant, as though its breath had been sucked away, silencing them all. Ruby lifted her arm and wiped her face on her sleeve. "Land, it's hot," she said, and Vera didn't bother to reply.

When they heard Mrs. Howard's cane they looked up expectantly, but even she appeared to float indecisively about the room. "Have we enough fruit for a compote, Vera?" she asked. Once it was settled that there was plenty of fruit, she said to Ruby, "Use the omelet pan and warm the platter, Ruby. We'll sit down at the usual time."

As Mrs. Howard went through the dining room, she saw that Vera had set the table with a bouquet of zinnias in the center, stiff bright flowers of no significance. Nothing discouraged zinnias, she thought. For a moment, as she paused, she could see the table when all the family had been seated around it. Her glance moved to Virgil's place and lingered and her eyes filled with tears. How cruel life was and how bitter to be old. Why should she live on, what good was life to her, or she to life for that matter, and she stood with her hands tightly clasped and her head bowed. Then she went along into the sitting room, looked at the clock and saw that it was after five. Moving slowly, she started up the stairs.

In her room at the head of the stairs, Granny Beane sat in the Poole rocker. She sat perfectly still with her face to the window. Her eyes were closed, and her arms hung limp at her sides with her open hands, swinging gently like the useless paddles of a drifting boat. Her white face with its closed eyes was as still as death, and when Mrs. Howard rapped and got no response, she opened the door.

"Mrs. Beane?" she said, coming around the chair, "are you all right?"

Granny opened her eyes. Her thin eyelids, lifting like shades, revealed the deep and terrible sorrow she was feeling, despite the white film of cataracts. Her mouth worked helplessly, but she didn't say anything.

"We'll sit down at six," said Mrs. Howard.

Granny stirred then. She nodded with resignation and she accepted Mrs. Howard's offered hand as she struggled to rise.

"Thank you, Mrs. Howard," said Granny quietly, "I'll just do my hair and then I'll be down."

Ruth's door was closed and her grandmother tapped gently. When she entered she could see that Ruth had been crying. Ruth was sitting on her bed staring out the window, but she turned as the door opened, and when she saw who it was she began to cry again. Tears ran down her face and a small tired sobbing shook her.

"There, there," said Grandmother Howard, coming across the room and patting her gently, smoothing her hair away from her hot forehead. "It's all right, dear. We all cry." She took out her handkerchief and put it in Ruth's hand.

"I thought I'd finished crying," gasped Ruth.

Grandmother Howard didn't reply. Did anyone ever finish crying, she wondered. She said, "We'll sit down at six, dear, so you'd better wash your face and freshen up."

"I'm not hungry, Gran."

"That doesn't matter. You can try to eat something."

"I'd rather stay up here."

"You must come down, Ruth."

"I don't want to, Grandmother. Oh, please . . ."

"Ruby's making an omelet," said her grandmother. "You mustn't be late."

Dorothy's door was open and as her mother came along the hall she could hear Dorothy's voice. She was reading to Howard, holding him on her lap with the book open and light from the window streaming over the page. In a high, bright voice Dorothy said, "See, Howard, that's a beanstalk. Just like the beans in the garden only this one grew way, way up into the sky. And there's Jack climbing on it. See, he's climbing higher and higher . . .''

She talked as though Howard were three instead of almost five, her voice rising with each laborious pull up the beanstalk until suddenly her voice broke. The vision of Jack disappearing into the clouds was too much for her. As he reached the top, mist swirled around him as though to sweep him straight up to heaven and her voice shook as she swallowed rapidly and said with a gasp, ''and then he came to the castle. See, Howard, a beautiful castle . . .''

Dorothy turned to her mother, saw her through a blur of tears and said breathlessly, ''We're reading a story.''

''I see you are,'' said her mother quietly. ''Supper will be ready at six.''

''Oh,'' said Dorothy as she struggled to adjust to this new thought. Supper at six. ''I ought to be doing something,'' she said, ''but Howard was so restless.'' Her arms tightened around him and she began to rock back and forth. ''What time is it now?'' she asked.

''Five-thirty.''

''We'd better hurry,'' said Dorothy, but she didn't move.

Grandmother Howard stretched out her hand and said, ''Come, Howard, we'll go to the bathroom and wash your hands for supper and your mother will go out to the barn and find your father.''

Dorothy looked up quickly. Ed wouldn't want to come in. Her glance went beseechingly to her mother and she said, ''He won't come.''

''Tell him Ruby is making an omelet,'' said Mrs. Howard. ''Omelets can't wait,'' and she went down the hall to the bathroom with Howard.

Dorothy stood up. Howard was so hot he had left a damp place in her lap and she brushed at it feebly. She smoothed her hair and then she went down the back stairs and through the entry into the yard where the sun streaming from the fields sifted through the leaves to lie in the long thin fingers of gold across the grass. She could see the cows moving languidly toward the pasture and supposed the milking was done. How strange that on a day like this the cows would be milked as usual, that Ruby would be in the kitchen getting supper and her mother down the hall washing Howard's hands. Why hadn't everything stopped?

Dust rose as she crossed the yard, and as she entered the barn swallows nesting there rose with a great rushing of wings that made her heart begin to pound. In the silence that followed, Waxpaw, the barn cat, trotted out to meet her, arched his back and rubbed, purring, against her ankles.

"Ed," she called, "where are you?"

He was not in the grain room or the main part of the barn, and her gaze traveled up the ladder into the hay mow where dust motes danced in a shaft of sunlight that streamed down from a window at the top of the barn. She knew he was here somewhere, and she wanted to scream "Ed, where are you" because she felt lost and helpless and she couldn't bear what she had to bear alone.

She found him in the tack room sitting on a sawhorse and holding a bridle in his hands. In the dark he looked like a wooden man holding the reins of a wooden horse and, touching his shoulder, she said, "Please come in, Ed."

He nodded but he didn't move.

"Ed," she said urgently, her hand tightening on his arm. "Please, Ed."

He looked up then and said in a strained voice, "I'm glad he had a horse. I'm glad of that. I wish . . ." He stopped because he couldn't go on. What he wished was that he had bought another horse the day after they shot Beau. He wished he'd had the money, and then he remembered that they had had money in the bank. Money in the bank, he thought bitterly. Money they could have spent right then, not waiting until he had the Bruce money because by then Virgil didn't want a horse, not the way he'd wanted Beau.

"I know," said Dorothy. "I know."

"He was never the same after that," Ed said, and she knew

that he meant that Virgil was never the same after they'd shot Beau.

Ed raised his arm to his face and his shoulders shook and Dorothy said, "I'm sorry. I'm so sorry," repeating it in a strangled voice. "I didn't want him to have a horse and it was my fault. I didn't know. I didn't understand about boys and horses. I didn't . . ." and she began to cry. "Oh, Beau, Beau," she wept, "you were such a beautiful horse. You ran so fast. I should have understood how it was, but I didn't. It was always the money," and she began to sob, her face in her hands as she cried like a child until Ed pulled her shaking body against his own and then they wept together.

Ed didn't come in for supper. He stayed where he was until the line of old harness hanging on pegs against the wall changed from reins and bridles to long, gray bones; to limp, black leather; to the tattered remnants of dingy garments, and finally to indistinct lengths of line that became the veins and sinews of other lives.

He lay on his back on a pile of burlap bags, aware of the cat that roamed restlessly through the upper part of the barn, aware of the soft, fluttering sounds of the roosting pigeons, aware of the heat and the comfortable smell of old leather and the sweetness of new hay. Aware of the silence.

For a long time he didn't think at all, but gradually, as it grew darker and eventually cooler, he began to think about being a father. He had never taken time to think about being a father. What does a father do to be more of a father, he wondered, remembering his own father in the pulpit, his black suit buttoned to his chin, his manner austere as he uttered warnings and threats. Ed had never listened to his father's sermons or prayers, but there ought to be something positive he could remember about him, he thought, letting his mind wander until, as darkness settled over the fields, he fell asleep, tossing and moaning and waking suddenly to realize where he was and remember the terrible thing that had happened.

In the distance he heard dogs barking and he let his mind drift, willing it to take him away, out of this room, up through the rafters and into the blackness of the night. Then, as he rose, floating toward the stars, it seemed to him that he was dying, that he would never be whole and alive again, and he knew that if this was dying he would soon be in the presence of God and that he would not trust himself to meet his Maker with such pain and anger in his heart.

And then suddenly, out of nowhere, he could hear his father's voice saying things that he must have said from the pulpit, words coming at him, familiar passages that he could only have heard when he was sitting beside his mother and sister on the hard pews of the First Congregational Church in Millbrook. Words so familiar he could say them himself . . . God so loved the world that He gave His only begotten Son . . . This is my beloved Son, with whom I am well pleased . . . When I was a child I thought as a child and I spake as a child, but now I am a man . . . In my Father's house are many mansions . . . Father, forgive them for they know not . . . Though I walk through the valley of the shadow of death, I will fear no evil, for Thou art with me . . . For unto us a child is born . . . unto us a son is given . . . .

And suddenly he pushed himself up from the floor and ran his hands through his hair, tearing at it helplessly, shaking, choked with sobs, and staggering out of the barn he headed for the river where it would be cool, where his whole body could weep and all his tears would vanish in the river. Then, as he went down through the fields to the flats, moving farther and farther away from the barns, he thought in despair that all of it was for Virgil. *I wanted the farm,* he thought, *I wanted it, but from the beginning he did too. It was going to be his. It was all for him,* and he stumbled down to the river and into the muddy water that lapped its banks.

Toward morning it began to rain. Dorothy heard the rain and wondered if it was raining on Virgil somewhere in a place she would probably never see. Where was he buried, she wondered. Would she ever know? In the cemetery at Oak Knoll there were markers for Howards and Curries, and while she had never thought much about it she had assumed they would all be buried there together eventually.

Dr. Adams and Mrs. Gibbs already had stones there, with their names chiseled in the granite and under their names, their birth dates. Their death dates were, of course, a mystery, being the ending of their story. Virgil and Ruthie used to whisper and giggle about those stones and she could remember saying to them, "It's not funny at all. Shame on you. Those stones are there because they don't have any families left to take care of things like that."

Wasn't it ironic, she thought, Virgil had lots of family to do these things, but would it be a comfort, she wondered, to stand before a stone engraved with his name—Virgil Beane, born 1924, died 1944, age 20, in the service of his country. She wasn't sure.

Turning on the light she saw that it was after midnight. *Oh, Ed,* she thought, *please come in. You can't stay out there forever.*

But she had known him long enough to know that he could stay out there for as long as he wanted to and that he would come in when he was ready.

For a while after the rain, it was cooler. Ed stopped hauling water from the river, no one needed Cousin Gertrude's fans, people came and went, Howard played with his Lincoln Logs and the days of Ruth's vacation passed into oblivion. She did not want to go back to Boston and became almost hysterical trying to explain this to her mother, until Dorothy said, "It's all right, Ruth. You can stay here as long as you want to. Just tell me why you don't want to go back."

"I've told you," said Ruth. "I don't like it. It's stupid work. I want to get married. I don't want to be there in Boston, with

John in Texas. All I do is wait for something to happen. Every day that goes by I know he's just one day closer to being sent over and then I'll never see him again . . .''

"You mustn't think that, Ruth," said her mother. "He *will* come back and you *will* be married and someday you'll have a family and all of this will seem like a bad dream."

"It's never going to end," said Ruth. "It's going to go on and on until they're all killed. John will be killed, just like his father. Vera's William was killed. Virgil's been killed," and she began to cry.

In the end Ruth went back to Boston because there was nothing else to do, and John wrote and told her he was being transferred to a place called Twentynine Palms in California. He wrote that they'd be married when he finished there; he expected two weeks of leave then, he said.

Two weeks, thought Ruth, two weeks of married life because that's all there'd be. They had let Montgomery go, and Union City and Midland, and they were going to let Twentynine Palms go too because John said it was the jumping-off place. *There's nothing in Twentynine Palms,* he wrote, *go back to Boston, Ruth,* so she packed her things and Mr. Godwin drove her and her mother and Vera and Howard to Mumfert to get the bus back to Boston.

Vera sat in the front seat beside Mr. Godwin, clutching her purse and silent as they drove the six miles to the Greyhound station. She had come to keep Dorothy company on the way back, she said, although it was Ruth who troubled her, and now and then she would turn and smile sympathetically at her. Occasionally Vera reached up nervously to straighten her hat.

Dorothy held Howard on her lap, and whenever she saw something that she thought would interest him she said, "Look, Howard, there's a dump truck." Or, "Look, Howard, see the cows in the river." Her mind wandered uneasily. There ought to be something to say to Ruth to make things easier, and she said, "I know you aren't happy to be going back, Ruth, but I think in the long run you will be glad."

Ruth nodded.

They bought her ticket and as they stood in the heat, waiting for the bus, even Ruth wished she could think of something to say to make it easier. She had never noticed before, but suddenly her mother looked old and tired. She had never really looked at her mother before, not in that way, and she wished she could say something comforting about Virgil, but she couldn't. She couldn't even think about Virgil.

Poor Vera, she thought, noticing how thin Vera was. This probably made her think about William, and she wondered why Vera hadn't married him before he was sent across. Vera's hair was turning gray and she squinted as the sun flashed on her glasses. It was hard to think of Vera as ever having been in love, *but,* thought Ruth, *maybe people weren't in love in those days the way they are now.*

Howard tugged at Dorothy's hand and Ruth snapped, "Stop that, Howard. You're going to pull Mother's arm off."

She was glad when the bus pulled in and she kissed them all in relief and climbed aboard, going down the aisle until she found a window seat, where through a cloudy window, she continued to smile and wave. The smoky window glass obscured the dark circles under her mother's eyes and the tight line of Vera's mouth, and Ruth smiled until her face ached.

Then, all at once, she saw Vera break away and move to the front of the bus and suddenly there she was, pushing her way between the people who were boarding, as she came rapidly up the aisle toward her. For an instant Ruth thought that Vera was flying apart. Her dress seemed to flutter like ragged feathers, her breath escaped her open mouth in quick little gasps and her hat, toppled sideways on her small head, fell off as she fumbled frantically in her purse until her trembling fingers found what they searched for. Vera reached out and pushed an envelope into Ruth's hands.

"Oh, Ruth," she cried, "I shouldn't do this, but I can't help it. All I can think about is you and John."

What Vera meant was that all she could think about was William, but she couldn't say that. She had been thinking all night about him and what it would have meant to them to have had enough money to get married before he left for France. And it wasn't only money they needed. They had needed courage and support. She said desperately, "Here, take it. You can buy a ticket to California or wherever he is. If you saw him it might help. You could be married there or come back if you change you mind. It's for whatever you want to do, Ruth," and she crushed Ruth's hands in her own thin ones and cried, "I've got to get off. I've got to get off."

"I can't, Vera," said Ruth. "If it's money, I just can't."

"Yes, you can," said Vera. "Take it."

"What will they say?"

"It doesn't matter what they say."

Ruth's arms went around Vera and she half sobbed and half laughed, "Granny said you don't miss what you've never had, but it's not true, is it?"

"No," said Vera loudly because the motor was roaring and she felt it strongly, although she'd never put it into words before. "No, it's not true." She pulled away and went quickly down the aisle, pushing through the doors just as they were closing.

Dorothy waved until the bus was out of sight. Long after Ruth could have been expected to see even the color of her dress, Dorothy continued to smile her fixed smile. Howard tugged at her hand and as she bent to accommodate the force of his body in its persistent demand to go home she became a question mark, her body a curve above the small solid period of her son.

It was heartbreaking somehow to think of Ruth riding along alone, going somewhere she didn't want to go, to do something she didn't want to do. Why was life so filled with sorrow? Why wasn't there some other way? There ought to be a way to hold

198

the good times, but they slipped away; the more radiant the joys, the more quickly they seemed to escape as the inevitable sadness of parting came.

There were always endings. They were the shriveled bodies of life's bright promises, and to alleviate the pain of this, people dulled their senses by plodding along day after day, doing what was expected of them, accepting without question what they felt could not be changed.

She knew that they would move into the haze of September as they had in the past, picking apples, waiting for frost. In another year Howard would be old enough to go to school. Months would become years and her dear family would melt away. She would lose them all in the end. First the grandmothers, taking their departures one by one so that their hands would seem to slip from hers as they disappeared up flights of stairs to take their beds in rooms for which there were no doors. Virgil was gone. Virgil, Virgil, her heart cried silently. And she wondered when she would say good-bye as Ruthie made her way into that other life for which she yearned so desperately. What could they have done this time to make things easier? Wasn't there something they could have done for Ruth, something other than just clinging to the chosen path?

She moved toward the car, saying wearily, "Please, Howard, Mummie's tired," and she got in and settled him down between them, hoping he might fall asleep. It was hot in the car. A fly buzzed somewhere in the front, hitting the windshield with a small pinging sound. The doors closed and Mr. Godwin turned on the ignition.

As the fields flashed past, she felt as though she were being borne along on a great wave, up, up until she could see all of the countryside, the houses and barns and pastures of her neighbors shrinking to the farms and villages of Virgil's old electric train layout. *What tiny beings we are,* she thought, *we are as helpless as that fly beating itself to death against the glass.* She could remember when she had thought that all they needed was for Ed to find a job. A hundred jobs wouldn't have changed things now.

Beside her Vera was clasping and unclasping her hands. Why was Vera nervous, Dorothy wondered, and she pitied Vera, whose barren life rendered her vulnerable to triviality. She couldn't imagine what Vera might have to be upset about. It was true, what Granny said, you didn't miss what you'd never had. It must be true, but if it were true, why was Vera so agitated? *Poor thing,* she thought, *what does she know,* and reaching over, Dorothy touched Vera's hand and said gently, "What's wrong, Vera?"

"Oh, Dorothy," cried Vera, clutching Dorothy's hand in her own cold ones, "I've done a terrible thing. I don't know if you and Ed will ever be able to forgive me."

What could Vera have done, Dorothy wondered. What terrible thing had she done?

"It's Ruthie," gasped Vera. "I've given Ruth the money to go to California. I shouldn't have. I ought to have asked you, but I was thinking . . ." She spread her hands helplessly. What was there to say? Did she want to tell Dorothy how she longed for William after all these years? Would it sound ridiculous that she still regretted . . . that she was still haunted . . . . She said weakly, "I am so sorry."

What was Vera saying, wondered Dorothy as she tried to quiet Howard. Apparently Vera had given Ruth some money. *Why is that so terrible?* thought Dorothy. *Isn't Vera generous. She can't have much money,* and Dorothy reached out to take Vera's hand, thinking, *Why didn't we give Ruth some money? We could have given her enough to go to see John. Suppose it had been Ed, and I was here and he was there. Oh,* she thought sadly, *we could have bought her a ticket to California,* and suddenly she remembered Vera, who sat beside her with a stricken face, waiting to be absolved, repeating again in a voice that shook, "Can you ever forgive me?"

"Of course I forgive you," said Dorothy. "There's nothing to forgive."

"What about Ed? How will he feel about it?"

"The same as I do," said Dorothy.

With Vera's money Ruth bought a train ticket from Boston to
Los Angeles. She packed her trunk and called Railway Express to pick it up and ship it out to Havenhill. Everything
else in her rented room on Marlborough Street went into a
suitcase and a Filene's shopping bag. She called the family
and she didn't ask them if she could go. She just said, "I'm
going," and then had a funny lost feeling when her mother
replied, "Darling, I'm glad you're going," and her father
said, "You're going to have to stay with Evelyn, Ruth. Your
mother and I have talked with her and told her you're coming,
and it can't be any other way."

The next time Ruth called home she was in Evelyn's apartment in Hollywood. It was midnight and she had just sat down
at the kitchen table to write them a letter when Evelyn came in
from work and said, "Ye gods, Ruth, it's midnight. Who are
you writing?"

"The family."

"Can't it wait? You'll be dead tomorrow."

"We're getting married," said Ruth. "We decided tonight.
We're getting married on Saturday. I thought I ought to tell
them."

Evelyn kicked off her shoes and sat down. "For heaven's
sake, Hon," she said, "pick up the phone and call them. You
don't get married every day."

"Wouldn't it be terribly expensive?"

"Forget it. This one's on me. Go ahead, Ruth, dial the op-
erator. They'd want to know."

Evelyn overlooked the fact that in the east it was three o'clock
in the morning.

The telephone was in the hall near Vera's room. She stumbled
up and pulled on her bathrobe and reached it just as Dorothy
appeared at the top of the stairs.

"Hello," said Vera in her high, anxious voice. Calls before dawn could only mean death or disaster.

"Vera," cried Ruthie, "is that you, Vera?"

"Ruth! Yes, dear, it's me. What's wrong?"

"Nothing," gasped Ruth, "it's just that John and I are getting married this Saturday. I want you all to know, especially you, Vera."

"I'm so glad," said Vera, and began to cry, scalding salty tears that choked her, and she handed the phone to Dorothy, gasping, "It's all right." Then she took a hankie out of her pocket and dabbed at her eyes as she thought about William and what might have been.

"Ruth?" said Dorothy sharply. "It's not even daylight, dear. You've scared us to death. Are you all right?"

"I'm fine. John and I are getting married day after tomorrow. I wanted you to know. I want you to call his grandfather and tell him too. Evelyn said I should call. I was writing a letter, but she insisted. She's paying for it."

"That's lovely," said Dorothy, "but, Ruth, wouldn't it be better to wait? Until you can be married at home. Surely John will have some leave, and—"

"No," said Ruth.

"Your father—"

"No, Mother. We're getting married on Saturday."

"What about a dress, dear?" asked Dorothy, whose vision of a real wedding for her only daughter included a white dress and flowers in the church.

"Aunt Evelyn says she can get a dress from the studio. I don't care. I'd be married in a gunny sack if I had to. That's just the way it is, Mother."

Ruth put down the phone and then she began to cry. Everything seemed to make her cry these days. She could see her mother climbing the stairs, opening Howard's door to make sure he was all right, soothing Granny if Granny had happened to hear and come into the hall in her nightgown with her thin white hair in a skimpy braid hanging like a bit of frayed rope over her humped back. Probably her father hadn't woken up,

202

but if he had she knew her mother would say, "Go back to sleep, Ed. We'll talk about it in the morning."

But she was wrong. Ed had woken up and come out into the hall where he had heard most of what Dorothy said. He started down the stairs, ready to grab the phone and order Ruth to come home, but he could feel himself shaking inside and didn't trust his voice, so he stood and waited.

"What is it?" he asked as Dorothy came up the stairs. "She's getting married, isn't she? Goddam, I knew it," he said, clenching his fists helplessly.

"Yes," said Dorothy.

"What did you tell her? Why didn't you tell her to come home?"

"I did, but she won't. They're engaged, Ed. Why shouldn't they get married?"

He didn't have an answer for that. All he had was a gut feeling that things were moving too fast. The family was breaking up. He was losing another child. He muttered angrily, "It's a damnfool thing to do on the spur of the moment."

"It's not the spur of the moment, Ed. It's been coming for years. It's just that I wanted . . . I had hoped," and she began to cry.

"There now," he said, putting his arm around her, "no use to cry, Dorothy. John's a good boy."

"She doesn't even have a dress, Ed, or a nightgown," and Dorothy remembered that the nightgown had been more important to her than the wedding dress. How she looked when she gave herself to Ed was the thing that mattered most to her, and she reached for the sheet and began to mop her face with it.

"It's all right," said Ed gruffly, "go ahead and cry."

"I don't want to cry," she choked. "I want to be there. I don't want her to be all alone when she gets married."

"Go," he said, "we've got the money. What else is it good for? We can get you on a train tomorrow. Money's the least of it."

"It won't be soon enough, Ed," she said, "they're being married in two days, there won't be time."

Besides that she was thinking about the bills, and the next payment on the milking machines, and the way Ed sounded, hard and defeated, as if nothing much mattered anymore, as if the farm and all he'd worked for had lost its meaning now that Virgil was gone.

"I'm sorry," he said and he put his arm around her. "All we can do is the best we can. She got herself out there, I guess she can get herself married if that's what she wants."

When the wedding pictures came in the mail Dorothy spread them out on the dining room table and all of them walked around and around, picking up first one and then another. Ruthie looked like a princess in a fairy tale, which wasn't surprising because Evelyn had borrowed a dress from studio wardrobe and that's what it was—a costume for a princess in an MGM fairy tale.

Vera looked at them slowly and thoughtfully, and, although she knew she was being foolish, it seemed to her that in some of the snapshots Ruthie looked just a little like her, the way she looked when William . . .

Grandmother Howard handed one to Dorothy. "There," she said, "she's the image of you when you and Ed were married. I'll never forget it."

Granny, with her glasses on and holding a magnifying glass as well, looked at them by the window, holding them up in the sunlight and muttering, "My, my," until suddenly she recognized Evelyn in a dark dress with a white collar and then she said, "Why, that's Evelyn. My stars, she looks better than she did in the last picture she sent."

One bright afternoon in October, Dorothy took the snapshots up the hill to show John's grandfather. Cornstalk wigwams dotted the fields, and orange pumpkins lay among dry vines. She followed the old path, and as she went up the hill under the trees she was aware that the breeze was rising, whipping through the bare branches of small trees, sighing and rushing among the last leaves of the giants. The sound gave her a terrible sense of the passage of time and she hurried on.

Eventually she came to the fence that marked the line beyond which the Currie fields stretched away, and as she stood there in the late afternoon sun she thought about Richard and his un-claimed inheritance. She wondered if his father had felt the way Ed felt now, that it was all in vain, or if the years had already healed the wound. Time helped, she supposed, but how many small deaths of caring and feeling died in the passage of that time? At least Ed had something John Currie hadn't had. Ed had Howard. All he had to do was reach out and there was Howard, but Howard was not Virgil and Howard was still a baby.

John's grandfather saw her coming across the field and rec-ognized her instantly. He had always had a special feeling for Dorothy, although he had learned long ago not to dwell on the what-might-have-been. He left the creamery and crossed the yard, knocked the dirt off his boots in the back entry and pulled on his house shoes. As he came into the kitchen he smelled something baking and saw that Mrs. Hobbs was setting the tea cart.

"She's in there," said Mrs. Hobbs, "now don't you upset her."

He grunted in acknowledgment. Meddlesome woman, Mrs. Hobbs. Why would he want to upset Dorothy?

He stepped to the sink to wash his hands and then he went into the parlor. "Well, Dorothy," he said, taking her hands, "well now, how are you?"

"Fine," she said, "the fire feels good. It's getting cold."

"Bound to."

They heard the rattle of the tea cart and then Mrs. Hobbs appeared with biscuits and teapot. She handed round the cups as though it were a daily occurrence.

"I've brought some snapshots," said Dorothy, "I thought you'd like to see them."

He took them to the light and went through them slowly. As he studied them he nodded, murmuring, "ah yes, ah yes," as though it were a benediction and as much as he was capable of at the moment, then he handed them to Mrs. Hobbs.

"Oh, my," she said, "just look at that dress. They make a real handsome couple, don't they?"

"When's she coming home?" he asked.

"She doesn't say. I think they're hoping John will get leave."

He set down his cup and took a deep breath. "That would be fine," he said.

Before Thanksgiving they knew there wouldn't be any leave after all. John had his orders, and by the time Ruth's letter reached them he had shipped out. They could only imagine the anguish she was feeling because her letter was so short, as though she had thought that compressing the news might lessen its impact.

"I'm going to stay here with Evelyn," Ruth wrote. "It's not that I don't want to come home, it's just that we were married here, and . . . well, you know. Evelyn says I can pay board so I won't be sponging, and I've already got a job at the place where she works."

Dorothy put the letter down and Ed picked it up. "She's waiting table," he said abruptly.

"There are worse jobs, Ed."

"She ought to be at home."

"It's the same everywhere," said Dorothy, "girls every-where are doing it," and as she thought about it it seemed to her that all over the country the war was gobbling up sons and daughters and spitting them out in strange places to do new things as they tried to grab at life as it flashed past them.

While the snow fell and the wind howled, Dorothy imagined Ruth in the California sunshine. She had a letter from Edith Callahan, who wrote that Mary Catherine had joined the WACs and was now in Alabama. It was probably warm there too. Edith also wrote that Mick's brother Kevin and his family had finally moved out and were now in New London where he had a job as a welder and was making more money than he'd ever made in his life before.

One day in January they heard that Shirley Maddern was at home for a visit, and when Dorothy wrote to Ruth she mentioned it. She even went so far as to say that if Ruth were at home it might be nice to get together with Shirley, but later on she was glad this hadn't worked out. Shirley was married to a sergeant in the Quartermaster Corps who was stationed at Langley Field in Virginia. They lived in an apartment in Newport News and Shirley shopped at the PX. Shirley's mother told people all the things Shirley could get in the PX, things that other people stood in line for or never got at all. Somehow Dorothy thought it wouldn't have been much pleasure for Ruth, whose husband was flying missions over the South China Sea, to hear about Shirley in Virginia with her husband and all the things they could get at the PX.

In February word came that Joe Martin was reported missing in action, which was just another way of saying he was presumed dead. The destroyer on which he served was sunk by a mine in the North Sea and there was no hope of survivors. When the news got around to Dorothy, she and Vera went down to the Martins with a cake and an African violet, which was the only thing they had that was in bloom.

It was a raw day, and as Vera and Dorothy walked down the hill past Webster's Pond to the Martins they said very little. They were thinking about Joe. It was hard to believe he had drowned in the North Sea. As they passed the pond they saw the older children scampering about on the frozen surface that lay like a silver coin on the breast of the snow, the same bright surface over which Virgil and Joe had darted on their skates playing hockey after school.

She couldn't believe they were both gone, leaving nothing

but their shadows to taunt her. It was hard to believe that Brewster Smith had died in the Philippines four years ago. It was almost impossible to believe the things Grace, who had married her refugee, told them about the Jews in Germany, but even that must be true, she thought, because people said he became almost incoherent with rage if anybody mentioned Hitler.

She and Vera marched silently along beside the road at the edge of the snowbank. Birds wheeled and cried overhead, and around the Martin house evergreens, burdened with snow, seemed to droop in sorrow. Drifting snow covered a litter of broken machinery in the yard, but here and there a rusty appendage broke through the white crust. They went up the rickety steps and onto the porch, stepping around milk bottles and wood boxes of kindling, circling broken chairs and tools to reach the front door. Dorothy knocked and stepped back, and suddenly the door swung open and LaVerne, one of the older girls, appeared.

"We've come to see your mother," said Dorothy.

Inside the youngest Martins peeped from behind dark curtains that hung in the opening between the living room and the back bedrooms. Their faces appeared, small and rodentlike, as they scuffled among themselves, peering furtively through the crack to see who had come into the room.

Joe's mother sat in a rocker with her back to the door and LaVerne, who had left her own children with her husband's mother in Vermont and come home to see what she could do to help, ushered Vera and Dorothy into the room.

Sweaters, cats, dirty dishes, old magazines, baskets of mending and in the middle of it all Mrs. Martin, wearing a print housedress and a green sweater, sat rocking and staring out the window as her chair creaked back and forth.

"Look who's here, Ma," said LaVerne, raising her voice as though her mother were deaf. "They brung you a flower and a cake, Ma."

Mrs. Martin turned to look. Her eyes, dull with pain, gleamed in the fleshy pockets of her ruined face. She recognized Dorothy and nodded.

"Nice you could come," she said. "Take a seat."

Dorothy and Vera sat down on straight chairs. "I'm so sorry," said Dorothy. "Is there anything we can do?"

Mrs. Martin shook her head. What could anyone do? Her eyes glistened and she closed them. For a while they all sat there silently, waiting.

Finally Dorothy said, "Virgil always thought so much of Joe."

It was evident she paid dearly for this because her voice trembled and she began to swallow rapidly. Vera's hand reached for hers, but Vera couldn't think of anything to say either.

Then, once more, Mrs. Martin looked at them. "I know," she said, "and I thank you."

Was she thanking them for coming, for the cake and plant, or was she thanking them for Virgil, who had been her son's friend? What did it matter, thought Dorothy, as she rose to leave, and she was glad Ruth wasn't here to know about this too.

At the end of February a letter came from Evelyn. Usually Evelyn's letters were addressed to Ed Beane and family, but this was addressed to Mr. and Mrs. Ed Beane. Evelyn didn't write very long letters, but this one was shorter than most. "I think it would be a good idea for you to get Ruth to come home, Ed," she wrote. "Considering how things are I think she ought to be at home."

"What does she mean by that?" said Ed.

"I don't know," said Dorothy, but she didn't like the sound of it. In the beginning she had wondered if there was any chance. . . . She hadn't wanted to ask, and as time went on she just assumed. . . . No one kept that kind of news to themselves these days and it was about six months.

"I don't see how it could be," she said, "she would have told me."

"Told you what?" said Ed desperately.

"She could be pregnant," said Dorothy.

As soon as the night rates came on they phoned Evelyn, who answered almost immediately. "What's wrong?" she said. A long-distance call from Ed could only mean one thing—something had happened to her mother—but Ed said, "Nothing's wrong here, but we got your letter, Evelyn. How are things there?"

"All right, Ed. Ruth's not here. She's on today. I would of been gone, but I twisted my ankle real bad so I'm home for a change."

"What's the matter with Ruth?"

"Nothing's the matter with Ruth, but she's six months now. She can't work much longer, she'll be showing too much, and I thought you'd want her to come home."

Ed turned to Dorothy. "She's pregnant," he said. "She's still working."

Dorothy took the phone. "We didn't know, Evelyn," she said. "Ruth hasn't told us."

"She swore she had. I wondered, though . . . I didn't see how you'd want her to be out here with me when she could be at home. I don't know how I could manage when the baby comes, Dorothy. This is a small place, and . . ."

Ed had the phone again and he said roughly, "She didn't tell us, Sis. I wish you'd let us know sooner, but we'll see she comes home now."

"It's not going to be easy, Ed."

"We'll send her the money. You tell her it's going in the mail in the morning. Just tell her that."

"It's not the money, Ed. She's saved enough for her ticket. I think she's scared to come home, Ed."

"What's she scared of? She's married, isn't she? There's nothing wrong is there, Sis?"

"Let me speak to Dorothy."

"It's me," said Dorothy.

"There's no use trying to tell Ed," said his sister, "and this is costing you money. She won't come, at least she won't come alone, Dorothy. She's scared. You know how it is. She thinks she has to stay here because of John. She thinks if she goes home it will be like giving up on him. I've talked to a lot of wives out here. They dig in and wait, Dorothy. To them going home looks like giving up.''

"I'll come," said Dorothy. "Don't even tell her I'm coming, but I'll get there as soon as I can, Evelyn.''

"I can't understand why she wouldn't want to come home,'' said Ed.

"She does want to come home. She just doesn't want to leave John.''

"He's not there.''

"But they were married there, Ed. She feels closer to him out there.''

He nodded. Dorothy seemed to understand it. If she could, so could he.

"I take it Evelyn thinks you ought to come out there and bring her home?''

"What do you think, Ed?''

The truth was she had already made up her mind that she would leave as soon as she could pack her bag, and could now see herself sitting on the train, her hands fastened tightly to both straps of her purse. Suddenly she realized how much it would cost and she said, "It will cost a fortune, Ed. I'll have to have enough money with me for food and other things and you just wrote that check for feed and fixing the tractor.''

"We'll find the money,'' he said.

"I'll ask Mother.''

She turned back the bedspread and began to fold it. She would ask her mother in the morning and then they would drive on to Clinton to the bank and then see about her ticket.

"Not this time, Dorothy,'' he said.

"Not this time what?''

"You've done enough asking. This time I'll ask.''

Ed confronted his mother-in-law before breakfast, but before he had half stated his case she had her checkbook out and in five minutes he was up the stairs and down the hall to Dorothy, who stood at the mirror fixing her hair.

She knew instantly something was wrong.

"What's the matter?" she asked.

He held out the check. "It's not a loan," he said, "it's a gift."

"A gift?" She reached for it, saw the amount and gasped, "Good heavens, will it cost that much?"

"That's what I asked for."

"It's a terrible amount of money," she said.

He nodded and said abruptly, "Well, take it. That ought to do it."

"What's wrong?"

"Nothing . . . I'll eat in the kitchen and get on back to the barn."

"What's the matter?"

"Nothing's the matter."

"Something is the matter, Ed. I can tell."

"I asked for a loan, Dorothy. Plain and simple. A loan. I wanted a loan."

"I should think you'd be glad, Ed. For heaven's sakes. Why shouldn't she if she wants to? It's her money. What else has she got to do with it?"

"You're right, Dorothy," he said. "Just let it lie."

"But you're upset. Why on earth are you upset, Ed? Why does it bother you?"

"I can take care of my own family, Dorothy. It may take a little juggling, but I can do it."

"Of course you can do it. You do it all the time. Mother's just being generous."

"You always stand out against me, don't you, Dorothy?" he said.

"No . . . you know I don't. I always support you, Ed. I always have, but this is different, it's for Ruth, and . . . something Mother wants to do. That's all."

"Fine," he said, "have it your way. Don't think I'm not grateful. I only wish to God I could sit down and write a check like that. That's all. You just have a good trip out there, Dorothy, and then bring her home where she belongs."

"I will, Ed, but I wish you could come too."

"No need for that," he said shortly.

Her ticket cost $150 round-trip. She was going out coach, but coming back Ed reserved two berths in the Pullman. Ruthie's ticket one way was almost $90. Under different circumstances it might have seemed foolish to spend the extra for berths, but Ruthie was pregnant, and after Dorothy had ridden coach all night for three nights, she was thankful Ed had had the sense to make reservations.

She was almost too tired to enjoy being in California, and when Evelyn took them to the train a week after she'd arrived, it all began to seem like a dream, something she had read in a book or seen in a movie.

Evelyn's ankle was still sore, and she limped along as they pushed through the station looking for their car.

"You shouldn't have come, Evelyn," said Dorothy. "It will make your ankle worse."

"I can put my feet up later," said Evelyn, "but I can't see you off later. Here we are. Now, don't worry," she said, putting her arms around Dorothy, "she'll be all right. It will take a little time, but she's OK."

She handed Dorothy a bag of sandwiches. "You can't count on a diner and even if there is one there's no guarantee you'll get in. I put in some oranges. You'd never hear the end of it if you got back without some oranges. I know how *she* is." *She* being Granny, of course.

She kissed Dorothy and turning to Ruth said in a husky voice,

"Now don't you forget you've got berths in Ogden. Ask the conductor, he'll tell you when to switch cars. Have you got your ticket, Hon?"

"Mother has it."

"Then all you have to do is take care of that little fellow in there."

Ruth nodded. Tears ran down her cheeks and she sobbed as Evelyn put her arms around her.

"It's going to be OK," Evelyn said. "I've seen hundreds of them leave for overseas, but they all come back. A year or so later there are their ugly mugs all over again," she lied, "you know, at the canteen."

Ruth blew her nose and dried her eyes.

"You better get on," said Evelyn. "Take the first seats you come to, Dorothy. Be good, Honey. Give my love to the family."

"Thanks for everything," gasped Ruth. "I couldn't have come if it hadn't been for you."

"Forget it," said her aunt, "that's what families are for."

As they went up the steps Evelyn called out, "Hey, Ruthie, you want to know what I do when I'm scared? I pretend I'm playing a part in a movie. I pretend I'm somebody else," Evelyn shouted, running and limping along beside the car as it started to move. "That way it's nothing but a movie."

They stumbled through the coaches, pushing through groups of servicemen and civilians, stepping over bags until they spotted two seats together. During all of this Ruth had been pretending she was somebody named Celia, a young Englishwoman traveling to a girls' school in Scotland where she would teach French to the daughters of titled parents and fall in love with a man, recently wounded and released from the service, who walked with a crutch and smoked a pipe.

Meanwhile Dorothy glanced around looking for a place to put Evelyn's sandwiches and then, giving up, she sat holding them on her lap. She wasn't pretending anything. She knew exactly who she was. She was Dorothy Beane, bringing her daughter home, with only five days and four nights separating them from the family and everything else she cared about. She didn't have any doubt that Ruth would feel better about it as soon as they got home.

In a way she worried more about Ed than she did about Ruth. It was hard for a man to feel helpless, and she wished he could have seen the mobs of people milling around in the train stations she'd passed through. If he could see the drawn faces and the families and lovers standing together in tense little knots, waiting for trains they wished would never come, clinging to one another, kissing, waving, crying. Who among them didn't feel helpless as they struggled in the web of a war they hadn't made and couldn't escape?

When the train reached Ogden, Utah, it took on two Pullmans, and gathering their things they pushed up the aisle. The doors between the cars were almost too heavy for Dorothy to open, but she managed to hold them back for Ruth and hung on until Ruth had hopped over the coupling that joined the cars. The connection jerked and scraped and, from the road bed below, cinders and gravel flew up like popcorn as the train rocked along with a terrible grinding sound.

They made their way through coaches jammed with soldiers, with old women holding bags and staring with glassy eyes at nothing at all. Young women, no older than Ruth, jiggled fussy babies on their laps. Lights burned brightly overhead and would burn all night, Dorothy supposed, and the people sitting in the glare of those unshaded bulbs looked white, hollow-eyed, exhausted and sad. People lighted cigarettes, flicking ashes everywhere, and choking clouds of smoke filled the cars. Servicemen in the aisles stood aside to let them pass, some giving her a hand with the bigger bag and others whistling softly as Ruth brushed past. The heat was stifling and the dark smell of coal seemed to enter her nostrils and pass down and through her lungs to lodge inside of her in that place where anxiety and dread and fear had taken hold so that now she wasn't thinking about anything except Ed. She wished he could have come with her. It would have been better if both of them could be seeing this part of the war. It might have helped them all.

Suddenly they were in the Pullman and it was cool. The porter took their bags. "Evening, ladies," he said, checking their tickets, "right this way. Looks to me like you got an upper and a lower," and he led them down the aisle.

Ruth undressed lying on her back, wriggling out of her dress and rolling it into a ball that she put in the hammock next to her shoes and her pocketbook. She didn't try to put on her pajamas; they were too tight anyway. She'd sleep in her slip, and that would make it easier in the morning. Sliding between the sheets, she reached to turn off the light and twist the air valve. The rushing sound of cool air was wonderful; it smelled clean, and she lay there feeling sorry for the people in the coaches. She could hear the sound of the wheels on the tracks, a steady clickety-clack beneath her. Her hand reached to touch Mary Catherine's cross, which she had worn since John left. And then gradually her breathing grew regular as she surrendered to the pulse and throb of the train.

The train seemed to be racing and she imagined it, a black force hurtling through the darkness, streaking over the barren stretches of the West, slowing occasionally for a crossing to whistle its long, thin wail of warning.

Isn't it funny, she thought as the train roared into the night, leaving Hollywood behind and beginning its slow gallop toward Boston, *that for as long as I can remember Evelyn has been the odd one in the family, like an outcast, and now suddenly Evelyn is the most real person in my life.*

Evelyn was probably the only one who could understand how she felt right now. The others might want to, but they wouldn't know how, but Evelyn knew because she had seen what the army did to people's lives, and because Evelyn knew and cared she had given them her privacy, and her ration book, and her bed. Evelyn had hugged her and said, "Chin up, kid," just like in the movies, but she wasn't playing a part because that's what life had suddenly become for Ruth.

And I didn't do a thing for her, thought Ruth sadly, *I didn't even buy her anything and she did so much for me.*

During the day as Wyoming and Nebraska flowed past the cloudy window of the train, white and barren, flat as a calm sea, Ruth sat with her face turned toward the world, watching for a house or a town, a barn, a herd of cattle, anything to keep her from thinking about airplanes. Sometimes her eyes began to close and all the trees and fences and houses would blur and then she'd start up with a jerk. Where were the hills and rivers and valleys, she wondered.

Once her mother said, "Wouldn't you like to play twenty questions?"

Ruth shook her head.

"Oh, come on," said Dorothy, "I'm thinking of an animal."

"Is it human?" Ruth asked, knowing that of course it would be. Her mother always put people first.

"Yes."

"Is it a male animal?"

It was male, she had known it would be. Her mother was absolutely predictable. She would want to play a game as the world came to an end. Ruth sighed and said, "Is he living?"

"Yes."

"Is he a movie star?"

"You're going to run out of questions, Ruth."

"I don't want to play, Mother."

"You've still got sixteen."

"Is he under fifty?"

"No."

"You didn't say if he was a movie star or not."

"He's not."

"Then he's famous and over fifty and an American and he's living. Is he the president?"

"Yes," said Dorothy, "but you shouldn't guess one person

that way. It might not have been him and then you would have wasted a question."

"But I got it," said Ruth. "I did get it, Mother."

"You did, and now it's your turn."

"I don't want to play, Mother."

"Later then," said Dorothy.

When they crossed from Nebraska into Iowa, the porter began to make up the berths again and Ruth climbed up the ladder, zipped the curtains and shut out the world. Below her Dorothy undressed slowly. They would be in Chicago in the morning and change trains for the last time. Coming out she had changed in Chicago, and a sailor, who was going from Norfolk to Omaha, carried her bag.

"I'm on my way to Los Angeles to see my daughter," she said. "Where are you going?"

"Just to Omaha, ma'm. That's my home. My folks live there, and my girl. I'm going to see her."

Dorothy had never really thought about Omaha before, but suddenly she thought of a mother and father in Omaha waiting to see this boy, and his girl counting the minutes until he arrived. It occurred to her that she knew the names of most of the big cities in the country, but she had never given them much thought. Now suddenly they were pushing into her consciousness—Terre Haute, Lincoln, Nashville, Cedar Rapids, Cheyenne, Boise. People lived there, families of servicemen, wives, children, grandparents, people who had lost sons too. The whole country was alive with people moving helplessly back and forth. If only Ed could have seen the things she'd seen, then he might not feel shut out and helpless. His grief, which he bore so silently, would have become less solitary. Not lessened—perhaps even magnified—but shared. It might have helped.

She was worn out with the excesses and deprivations of travel. The noise and dirt, the blowing soot, the grit and cinders, the clouds of escaping steam that hissed like a kettle boiling over beneath the train. The screaming whistles and ringing bells. As the hours dragged on, Dorothy wondered if they would ever get home, but on that last morning, as they were approaching Springfield, the strain eased, and as they moved slowly into the station she gazed out the window looking for Ed.

He had to be there. She had wired him from Chicago and she scanned the crowd hopefully, her eyes sweeping over the scene, taking in once more the nameless strangers she had seen everywhere, the colorless faces, weary with acceptance. Resignation and anxiety looked up at her as the train slid slowly along, and she could almost hear the combined scream of all the tightly closed mouths sunk in those lined gray faces as they inched along.

And then suddenly she saw Ed, turning slowly as he looked anxiously up and down the tracks. She didn't notice the lines in his face or see the way his coat hung on his stooped shoulders; all she saw was the way his face lit up when he caught sight of Ruth, and relief poured through her. They were home. The minute they turned up the lane and saw the house, Ruth would feel it too.

Oh, she thought, people are suffering everywhere, not just us, but every family, and she knew as surely as she had ever known anything that there was no defense as strong, no comfort as sure, no strength as enduring as the strength and comfort of family.

Brushing past the porter who stood at the bottom of the steps, she pushed through the mob toward Ed, and as she saw his arms go out to Ruth she heard him say, "Welcome home, Mrs. Currie."

When Ruth came home Granny decided Ruth was on vacation. No matter how many times she was told that Ruth was married and expecting a baby, Granny would forget it.

"Is that so," she would say for the tenth time, looking up slowly, comprehension stirring as she rallied to remark, "looks to me like somebody would of told me before this. Where's she going to live?"

Once more it was explained to Granny. John was in China. When he came home he and Ruth and the baby would probably live at Berry Bay until they decided what to do.

Granny could understand all of this except the problem of deciding what to do. Married men worked and married women tended to the house and children, and at this point she would usually interrupt to reach out, groping for Ruth's hand, or Vera's or Dorothy's, as she said, "Now, dear, there's no use to worry about things like that. It all works out in the end. John's a smart boy, he'll find a good job and everything will turn out fine."

For a while this bothered Ruth, who would sit patiently beside Granny and explain once more that she had been to California and that she and John were married there.

"Evelyn's in California."

"Yes, Granny. We were married at Evelyn's. In the garden out back. There was a minister and Evelyn made punch. We had a wedding cake."

"My, my," murmured Granny, "wedding cake. You don't remember my wedding cake, do you, dear?"

"I wasn't born then, Granny."

"That's so," said Granny. "Well, now, it was a raisin cake. Mercy, but it was heavy. Three layers with white frosting and rosebuds. Bessie McCullough made it. She was a great one for cakes. When I married your father she said, 'Now, Minerva, I want to give you something special so I'm going to make your wedding cake' . . ."

"You married my grandfather, Granny."

"That's what I said."

"Don't let it bother you, dear," said Dorothy, who, with the others, had grown used to Granny's ramblings. "If she could see you clearly she'd know you were pregnant and she'd know who she was talking to. She's over eighty and she doesn't remember things. Don't let it bother you."

But it did bother Ruth. It was evidence of decay. It was the passage of time, the decline of self, the diminishing of life, the ever present threat. It began to seem to her that at some time in the past year she had come to a corner and in turning it had plunged from day to night. From the bright sun of childhood she had stepped into the dark night of adulthood. Nothing was the same anymore. Virgil was dead. Her father, silent and morose, disappeared through the barn door every morning, and her mother, determinedly busy, appeared with cups of cocoa and glasses of milk at all hours, saying as she presented them that pregnancy was the happiest time of a woman's life. Besides that, Granny was losing her mind; the others didn't see it the way she did, they were so used to her. And Howard. Howard ran raucously through the house making truck and train noises, stamping on the stairs and doing all the things she and Virgil had never been allowed to do.

And then one day early in April Granny didn't come down for breakfast.

"I spoke to her as I came through the hall," said Dorothy.

"Perhaps she didn't hear you," replied her mother.

"I know she heard me."

"She's been looking awfully white," said Vera. "Shall I go up and see if she's all right?"

Ruth moved her chair back. "I'll go," she said.

But Dorothy jumped up. "I'll go," she said.

As she went up the stairs she paused on the landing. It was going to be a beautiful day. There were still patches of snow along the north side of the house where the sun never shone, but Ed had been ploughing all week and the earth looked as black as chocolate. In the distance she could see the willows turning yellow, and she wouldn't be surprised, she thought, to discover her mother's crocuses emerging beside the steps at the front porch.

She went briskly up the stairs and along the hall. Granny's door was ajar, and as she pushed it open she said, "Granny, are you all right?"

Granny stood at the window gazing down the lane toward the state road where, in the distance, an occasional car passed. As Dorothy entered, Granny turned slowly and smiled. "My," she said, "everybody's going someplace."

Dorothy crossed to the window and looked out. She saw the bread truck from Mumfert and wondered if Granny could really see it, or anything else that far away. Perhaps there was a special brightness in the spring sunshine that illuminated things so sharply their images penetrated even cataracts. Everything was in focus, the clouds bleached, the sky brilliant, bare trees stark, and as she turned to look at Granny she was taken by something different, a softening of expression, an unlikely resignation, almost as if Granny were, before her eyes, becoming blurred, and Dorothy reached out quickly and said, "It's time for breakfast."

"Coming and going," murmured Granny, "all this coming and going."

And then she straightened up with a little shudder, her eyes opened wide and she gasped, "Oh, my."

Putting her hand behind her she touched the edge of the bed and giving a little sigh she sat down. She looked up at Dorothy and took a sudden, deep breath and then fell backward.

It was almost a minute before Dorothy realized that Granny was dead. A long, long minute during which she stood there, paralyzed and dumb, ready to do something, to hear Granny snap, "Mercy!", ready to take Granny's arm and help her down the stairs to breakfast and the start of another ordinary day.

Mrs. Howard offered Ed space in the Howard plot for the burial.

"I thought a good deal of your mother, Ed. She wasn't the

easiest person in the world to get along with, but neither am I, and I'll miss her."

"Thank you."

"Well," she said, "you and Evelyn do whatever you think is best, but we have a whole section in the cemetery here. Your mother has been a faithful member of this congregation for almost ten years. I just wanted you to know that she'd be welcome here."

"Evelyn won't be coming," he said.

What Evelyn had said was that she couldn't afford to come east. Then she'd started to cry and said, "Oh God, Ed, I thought she'd live forever. I wish I'd come for her birthday. I really wanted to."

"I know you did, Sis."

"What can I do? I can pay my share. There's no problem there, but I really haven't got it for the ticket."

"It's all right," he had said, "we can take care of things at this end. I'd send you enough for your fare, but things are a little tight here." Things would always be tight, he'd thought bitterly. He'd never known it any other way.

"I wouldn't let you do it, Ed," she'd said. "Besides, I can't be off that long. You do whatever you think is right, Ed, and send me my part of the bill. I'd feel better if you did."

He glanced up, saw that Dorothy's mother was still there and mumbled something about appreciating her offer.

"Would you like me to call Reverend White?"

"I guess not," he said. "She wanted to go to Millbrook."

"That's quite a drive."

"I know it, but the stone's there. It's where she wanted to be."

Mrs. Howard nodded. "I can understand that," she said.

They loaded the casket on the truck and tied a tarpaulin over it. A hearse would have cost over thirty dollars, and although it seemed to Ed that he could almost see his mother, perched there on top of the load, shaking her head and saying to anybody who would listen that she never thought she'd be going home in a box tied to the back of a truck under a piece of canvas, even so it seemed the only thing to do.

He parked the truck in the yard where the light from the barn shone on it, and Mr. Godwin said he'd sit there in the barn door and keep watch. From the bedroom window he could see a shadow that he assumed was Homer, sitting in an old wicker rocker, a dark shadow, probably dozing, thought Ed. He turned abruptly to Dorothy. "It's a long drive," he said. "You don't have to come."

"I want to come, Ed," she said. "You know I wouldn't not go."

"Suit yourself."

She reached for his hand. "It suits me," she said. "Everything will be all right here, and I loved your mother."

But it was a long ride to Millbrook. It would be a long day. Down the river to Northampton, Holyoke, Springfield, Hartford and then, finally, Millbrook. She hoped it would be a nice day. It would be a hard drive in the rain, and a cemetery in the rain . . . She had never been to Millbrook, but she could visualize the cemetery at the back of a small, white church, dismal under dripping pines, the ground spongy, stones leaning and fringed with dead grass, and in the Beane plot a dark hole surrounded by the dirt and stones and roots of the black soil that would seal Granny's casket away forever.

Who would be left in Millbrook to come to a Beane funeral? It had been years since Ed's father had died. Whoever remained of his congregation would be dead or infirm and they would remember Granny as a youngish woman standing with her tall, dark-haired son and her saucy red-haired daughter who used lipstick and wore high heels.

Even so, Dorothy said hopefully, "Maybe the ladies of the church will have something after the service. Coffee or something."

"Don't count on it."

"How did the minister sound?"

"All right."

She sighed. "We'll go right through Holyoke, Ed. Coming back it will be just about supper time. We could spend the night with Edith and Mick. What would you think of that?"

At the thought her spirits began to rise and she could see herself at the Callahans' front porch ringing the bell and waiting for Edith to open the door. The house would be warm. There would be lights on, and while they were there they could look across at their own house and see how it looked and if the people living there now were keeping it up as well as they had.

"Do you think we could, Ed? I'd love to see Edith."

"I don't see why not," he said. "Do what you like."

"I'll call her," said Dorothy. "I'll go down and call her right now. It's not too late." And she got up and turned on the light and pulled on her bathrobe, and the minute she heard Edith's voice she knew she had done the right thing.

"You're here," cried Edith, opening the door and almost pulling them into the house. Her arms went around Dorothy. "Oh, I am so glad to see you," she said. "How have we let all this time go by?"

And then she broke away and turned to Ed. "I am sorry about your mother, Ed. I can remember her so plain. I s'pose she'd failed a good deal. I wish we'd got up to her party, but Kevin and his family were still here then, and things were at sixes and sevens. . . . Well, come in," and she led them along the hall to the downstairs bedroom.

"We're putting you out of your room, Edith."

"Our room! We moved upstairs when Kevin and Mary came. It's our guest room now."

"It must have been hard on you to have them here, Edith."

"It was," said Edith, "but it was family. You can put up with a lot when it's family."

"I can smell supper," said Dorothy. "You've made a boiled dinner."

Edith laughed. "For old times' sake."

225

"I haven't had a boiled dinner as good as yours since the last time we were here."

"Well, settle in," said Edith. "Bath's down the hall, and then come to the living room. I want to show you the pictures of Mary Catherine's wedding."

"She's married!"

"Last month. Down there, and I couldn't go. It nearly broke my heart, but I suppose you felt the same about Ruth. The towels on the back of the door are for you and Ed."

Dorothy stood at the bathroom window and gazed across the yard to their old house. In the shadows of late afternoon she could imagine Ruth and Virgil coming up the back steps and into the kitchen. A lump rose in her throat. Granny's window upstairs was dark, and it seemed fitting. There had hardly been time to miss her, but they would.

Standing alone in Edith's bathroom Dorothy began to cry. It had been such a miserable day. Granny's casket had gone right down in the mud, the earth still frozen in places so they'd had to chop it away with pickaxes, and when they began to fill in the grave she had almost screamed in protest. It wasn't just Granny, it was Virgil too, and she put her fist against her mouth and thought, *Virgil, Virgil, it's time to come home. It's getting dark,* and then with a sob she turned the water on full, washed her face and hands, and went up the hall to the living room.

No one spoke of Virgil, but in the kitchen when they were taking up supper, Edith turned to Dorothy and said, "I can't say anything about Virgil, but you know how I feel," and then she turned quickly away and Dorothy could see that she was crying.

"It's all right, Edith," she said, reaching out to her, "I know." And, turning quickly, Edith wiped her eyes on the corner of her apron, and taking a deep breath she said, "If you'd just put the dressing on the slaw, Dorothy. I know a boiled dinner means cabbage, but I've been hungry for something green lately. It's been a terrible winter."

In the living room Mick and Ed were talking. As soon as he came through the door, Mick had said he was sorry about Ed's mother, and when Edith and Dorothy disappeared in the kitchen he said gruffly that he was sorry about Virgil.

Ed, who sat by the fire, only nodded. He didn't trust himself to speak.

Then Mick said, "I saw an old friend of yours today, Ed."

"That so?"

"I wouldn't of thought to tell him you was coming, but he brought it up himself."

"Who you talking about?"

"Ned Carter . . . down at the tap and die."

"Is that right?"

"There's been big changes down there, Ed."

"I know. We drove through going to Springfield . . . last year about this time. . . . Looks like they added a wing and were going full blast."

"They're hiring, Ed."

Ed shook his head. "I spent long enough on that line, Mick. They'd have to offer me more than they've got to get me back."

"They probably would," said Mick, "and it wouldn't be on the line. You'd go in as foreman now. They're desperate for trained men. Matter of fact that's what Carter was saying. You're like to find a letter in your mailbox when you get home making you an offer. If you was to go round there in the morning before you left I guarantee you he'd make you an offer you'd have a hard time turning down."

In the kitchen Dorothy was saying, "I looked over at our house and it's all dark, Edith. Isn't anybody living there?"

"Family named Beamis. Sounds like Beane, doesn't it? He's in the navy. She works in the mill."

"What about children?"

"There's a boy about fourteen. He's down at the Y most afternoons, and the girl's eleven. I think she stays across town with her aunt after school. We haven't seen much of them, Dorothy, what with Kevin and all."

"I saw a FOR SALE sign on the Turner house," said Dorothy.

It was a house she had always admired, a large white house on the corner with a beautiful lawn and a double garage in the back.

"That's a good buy," said Edith. "He got transferred to Philadelphia and a big raise, I hear. They're in a hurry to sell. Somebody says they've bought a real mansion out there."

"I suppose it costs a fortune. Do you remember that curved staircase, Edith? I always thought it would be a lovely place to have a wedding if you had somebody married at home."

"Their Sally was married at home, but Mick and I weren't invited."

"You should have been."

"I thought so at the time," said Edith, "but we didn't know his family and they're Presbyterians."

She began to drop dumplings into the boiling broth and steam rose in a cloud around her. Steam made Edith's hair curl, and she looked glowing and healthy in the steamy warmth of the kitchen. Dorothy could almost imagine that it was 1937 again and they were all eight years younger.

"What are they asking for it?" asked Dorothy.

"Seventy-five hundred," said Edith.

"That's a lot."

"It is, but it's a beautiful house, Dorothy. Someone said the bank would give a two percent mortgage. Payments wouldn't be much more than rent on a house that size. I wanted Mick to look at it, but he won't budge. You know how he is."

The next morning when they left the Callahans, Dorothy waved until the house was out of sight, but Ed didn't look back. He was thinking about the plant and wondering what Dorothy would say if he told her what Mick had said about Mr. Carter. He started to speak when she cried out, "Oh, Ed, slow down. I want to look at that house."

He pulled over to the curb. They'd come to the intersection of Elm and Hamilton. He didn't see anything remarkable about any of the houses, except for the FOR SALE sign on one of them and then he said, "Isn't that the Turner house?"

"Edith says it's for sale."

"It appears to be."

"She said it was seventy-five hundred, but that the bank would make a two percent mortgage and then the payments wouldn't be much more than rent."

"I always liked that house," he said.

"I didn't know that."

"I passed it every day coming from the bus stop. I can remember when they put out those birches, spindly little things. Look at them now."

"I used to go there sometimes for literary. There's a curving staircase, Ed. It comes right down into the front entry, and there's a bedroom on the first floor that would be just right for . . ."

"For what?"

She had been going to say Granny. She had even been imagining how nice the remaining Poole furniture would look in that room, and she realized with a little pang that they hadn't even begun to miss Granny yet. It made her sad.

"For a guest room," she said, "for Ruth and John and the baby when they come to visit."

"Would you like that house, Dorothy?"

"Oh," she said lightly, "I don't suppose so, really. It's just that it always looked like the perfect house to me. I liked our house, but it was narrow compared to this one and I used to think about all that room for Ruth's friends. You remember when Virgil had a chemistry set, and . . ."

Ed nodded.

"What would I do with a house that big now?"

"There's Howard," said Ed. "He's already got more stuff than Virgil ever had."

"I know, but . . ."

"Mick told me Mr. Carter'd been asking about me."

"What did he want?"

"He's looking for trained men. Mick says he'd take me on as a foreman. From what he says I'd be making enough to buy two houses like that one, and send Howard to college besides."

"Oh, Ed," she said, turning and grabbing his arm. "Think of it, Ed, after all this time, the things we've wanted . . ."

He nodded. "It's something to think about."

"Yes," she said.

"Well . . ."—he turned the ignition and put in the clutch—"I could go around there now and see what the story is, or we could talk about it going home. What do you think, Dorothy?"

For an instant she wanted to say, "Go. Drive straight down there and talk to him," but she couldn't seem to get the words out. "I don't know," she said at last, "what do you think, Ed?"

"I don't know," he replied, and shifting into low he eased away from the curb and headed north.

How many times had they driven up the valley, following the river with the hills ahead of them, passing brown tobacco barns and red cow barns clustered around white farmhouses where herds of cattle stood in dumb submission waiting to be milked.

As they went through Northampton Dorothy noticed a sign for the Wiggin Tavern. She had always wanted to eat at the Wiggin, but it was too early for lunch and Edith had given them a big breakfast. Why don't we do things like that, she thought; we're missing things that are just down the road, and she glanced at Ed to see if he might have noticed too. She used to know just to look at him what Ed was thinking, but not anymore. He drove without looking away from the road. For all she knew he was sitting there regretting that he hadn't stopped to talk to Mr. Carter.

Suppose he did get rehired, she thought, and his salary was as much as Mick thought it would be. Couldn't they buy the Turner house? After all, there it was, as if it were waiting for them, like a letter that had been lost in the mail for eight years and had now suddenly tumbled out of the mail bag and been delivered to their mailbox. Hadn't she always wanted a house like that? And just to see Edith made her realize how much she had missed her. Why, she thought, there aren't even any women in Havenhill that I can enjoy the way I enjoyed those women in the literary.

As the car roared along she began to imagine herself going through wallpaper books, and yet, as they approached Mumfert her thoughts took a sudden turn, as if she were waking up from a dream. What about Ruth? Suppose Ruth and John did settle at Berry Bay, how often would they see her and the baby if they were in Holyoke? And what would it be like for Vera and her mother to have to turn back the years, the way you might turn back the pages in a book to find a favorite passage only to discover when they reached that comfortable place where there had been just the two of them that they were, now, really alone in the house, without even Angus for company. *Besides,* she thought, *literary only meets once a month. What were once-a-month friends compared to the companionship and support of Vera and her own mother,* and glancing up she saw that they had come to the lane. *Home,* she thought wearily. *I'm glad to be home.*

Ed drove past the sign for the Wiggin Tavern without giving it a glance. The idea of going back to the plant danced in and out of his head, but when he saw himself in Holyoke he saw a different man from the man he'd become. It was the idea of a paycheck and a house Dorothy really liked that kept coming around in his mind, but somehow it didn't set right. You can't turn back the clock, he thought.

They were coming into Havenhill, past the post office, Dr. Adams's, Sunnyside School. Around Webster's Pond the Martin children were playing with sticks and throwing stones at the water. He took it all in without seeing it any more than he saw the first Berry Bay fields. And then suddenly as the car headed up Webster's Hill and came to Howard property he noticed the line of fence he and Oscar had strung in the fall. It was as neat a job as he'd ever seen, corners reinforced, wire tight, no slack, he noted with satisfaction. One day before he died he'd like to see all the pastures fenced, and his glance swept to the other side, where the earth was already turned for planting. He didn't think there was any place in the valley with better soil.

As he turned up the lane he saw that Oscar was loading milk cans in the pickup, moving deliberately although it was getting late, and Ed thought tolerantly, *Oscar's slow, but he's steady.* He could be counted on. He'd be as old as Homer when Howard was in his prime and he'd be more help to Howard then than Homer'd ever been to him.

"Here we are," he said, and springing down he came around the truck to Dorothy's side, put up his hand and clasped hers and then, for just a moment, they clung to each other, hands locked, faces close.

"Well," he said, "how do you feel?"

"Glad to be home," she said.